Burke p[barcode D0974883]**her waist**

Leaning ove[...]e whispered in Laura's ear. "Elena has told everyone that I'm your boyfriend, so I think we should make it look convincing. If it helps you to get the right look in your eyes, you could try picturing me naked."

A vivid image of Burke that day she'd caught him just out of the shower suddenly popped into her mind—but her imagination kicked in and she saw him dropping the towel he'd wrapped around him. Her mouth went dry and her heart began to pound.

Burke gave her an utterly charming smile. "Ah, I see it worked. Your cheeks are flushed."

"They are not," she protested quickly, then, looking around, saw they were being watched by a couple dancing past. Laura forced herself to smile.

"That's better. Keep smiling and let's dance. That'll help," Burke said.

"No, it won't. I'm an awful dancer. I'll step on you."

Burke grabbed her hand and led her out onto the dance floor. "I'll risk it."

Dear Harlequin Intrigue Reader,

The suspenseful tales we offer you this month are much scarier than Halloween's ghouls and ghosts! So bring out your trick-or-treating bag and gather up all four exciting stories.

And do we have a *treat* for you—a brand-new 3-in-1 compilation featuring authors Rebecca York, Ann Voss Peterson and Patricia Rosemoor. Ten years ago, three men were cursed by a Gypsy woman bent on vengeance. Now they must race to find a killer—and true love's kiss may just break the evil spell they're under in *Gypsy Magic*.

Next, Aimée Thurlo concludes her two-book miniseries SIGN OF THE GRAY WOLF, with *Navajo Justice*. And Susan Kearney starts a new trilogy, THE CROWN AFFAIR, in which royalty of the country of Vashmira must battle palace danger and treachery, while finding true love along the way. Look for *Royal Target* this month.

When Jennifer Ballard dreamed of her wedding day, it never included murder! But no one would harm the beautiful bride, not if Colby Agency investigator Ethan Delaney had anything to say about it. Pick up *Contract Bride* for yet another nail-biter from Debra Webb.

Happy reading!

Denise O'Sullivan
Associate Senior Editor
Harlequin Intrigue

NAVAJO JUSTICE
AIMÉE THURLO

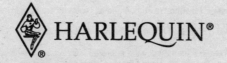

HARLEQUIN®

TORONTO • NEW YORK • LONDON
AMSTERDAM • PARIS • SYDNEY • HAMBURG
STOCKHOLM • ATHENS • TOKYO • MILAN • MADRID
PRAGUE • WARSAW • BUDAPEST • AUCKLAND

ISBN 0-373-22681-0

NAVAJO JUSTICE

Printed in U.S.A.

ABOUT THE AUTHOR

Aimée Thurlo is a nationally known bestselling author. She's written forty-one novels and is published in at least twenty countries worldwide. She has been nominated for the Reviewer's Choice Award and the Career Achievement Award by *Romantic Times* magazine.

She also cowrites the Ella Clah mainstream mystery series, which debuted with a starred review in *Publishers Weekly* and has been optioned by CBS.

Aimée was born in Havana, Cuba, and lives with her husband of thirty years in Corrales, New Mexico. Her husband, David, was raised on the Navajo Indian Reservation.

Books by Aimée Thurlo

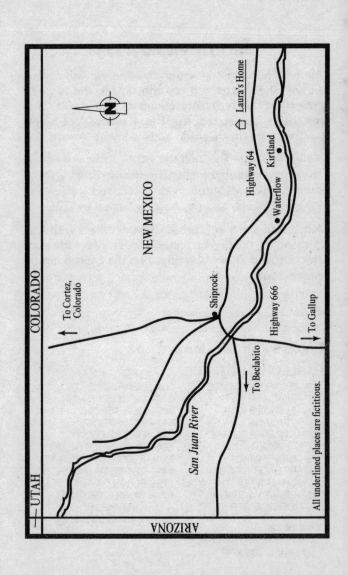

All underlined places are fictitious.

CAST OF CHARACTERS

Handler—Just who was the faceless owner of Gray Wolf Investigations and why did he have so many friends in high places?

Burke Silentman—He had a debt to pay, and in that price lay his redemption.

Laura Santos—The men she wrote about were only fantasies until Burke Silentman rode up on his motorcycle.

Doug Begay—Though he was far away, his actions could exact the highest price on them all.

Karl Maurer—The Center was his life, but how much would he risk to keep it?

Nicole Maurer—Her husband knew the kind of company she was keeping—or did he?

Michael Enesco—He was an outsider and that made him the object of suspicion. But was some of it deserved?

To Pat and Jack Kelly—
the best neighbors anyone could ever want.

Chapter One

It was a beautiful morning in late March. The sky was a clear, almost brilliant blue, the air clean and crisp—the kind of day where the breeze whispered of dreams that were still in the making, and songbirds celebrated the coming of spring.

Laura Santos drove home from the post office slowly, taking back streets off the main highway that, although graveled and bumpy, gave a great glimpse into the true character of the small New Mexico town. One-story houses stood like sentinels between fields of sandy soil dotted with tall clumps of blue-green sage and eager green-and-yellow native grasses. Horses wandered lazily, seeking the fresh green fare. Their slowly shedding, thick winter coats were now the only reminder of the long, cold months behind them.

Today, she could afford to take her time and enjoy the day. She'd finally finished her latest novel, *Dawn of Desire*. It was the story of a wounded ex-soldier who'd come home to find the love he'd left behind. Laura sighed. It had been a beautiful love story with a delicious hero. Best of all, the book had flowed easily, as did most tales told from the heart.

Restless now, she wondered how to celebrate the completion of the book. There was no special man in her life.

The relationships she'd had in the past hadn't worked out for one reason or another, and she wasn't the kind of woman who'd settle for a man who was "good enough."

Of course, her life was simpler this way. Her work was very time consuming, and she also had her *madrina,* her godmother, to take care of, so her days were full. Although she dated occasionally, and had all the usual healthy urges, no one had ever really come close to touching her heart.

As she entered the more densely populated neighborhood where she lived, the pavement began and the dust level dropped noticeably. Turning onto the street that led to her home, Laura looked down the block and caught a glimpse of her new neighbor, Burke, sitting astride his motorcycle, adjusting something on the engine. The tall, black-haired Navajo man had the palest brown eyes she'd ever seen and a smile that, although rare, could undoubtedly coax a pulse out of a stone.

As she slowed to make the turn into her driveway, her gaze strayed over him. Looking up just then, Burke waved. She smiled back at him, feeling her heart start to beat a little faster.

Aware suddenly that she hadn't been watching where she was going, she focused back on the turn, hoping she wasn't about to hit the mailbox—again. She'd been checking him out last week, daydreaming, when she'd brushed against it with the front bumper. The pole that supported the box had broken off at the ground, and the custom-designed mailbox, shaped like a house, had ended up looking like something used in a television commercial to advertise tornado insurance. At least Burke had been stepping inside as she'd knocked it down, so she hadn't had to make a lame excuse.

The man had moved in about a week ago, and had already doubled the machismo level on their street, as every woman on their block would have happily attested. There was something powerfully and wonderfully masculine about him. Laura had no doubt that it was partly due to the arrogant confidence with which he did virtually everything. His long-legged stride, so filled with purpose and a hint of aggression, gave something as mundane as "walking" an entirely new meaning.

She sighed and lowered her head, resting it on the steering wheel. Reality-check time. The romantic in her was taking her very good-looking neighbor and rewriting him into a fantasy hero. Burke was probably a businessman or some form of engineer, like many of the men in her new, upper-middle-class neighborhood. His masculine walk was probably due to a sore spot left after taking a corner too fast on his motorcycle down one of the graveled back roads.

She'd have to make a point to talk to Burke and find out more about him next time he came up to the cedar fence that bordered their properties. So far only her *madrina*, Elena, had actually spoken to him. With luck, Laura's fantasies would come to a screeching halt once she met him and found out he was a salesman with a high-pitched voice and the tendency to try and sell life insurance policies to everyone he met.

Laura switched off the ignition, grabbed her purse and climbed out of her sporty but sensible Chevrolet sedan. Flipping through her Scooby-Doo key chain on the way up the sidewalk, she found the right key and unlocked the front door.

The second she stepped across the threshold, an invisible cloud of foul-smelling gas slammed into her like a massive wave. She staggered back, coughing and fighting to catch her breath.

She turned her head away from the house, trying to catch her breath so she could go back inside. All the oxygen inside the house had been replaced by natural gas, making her light-headed.

"Elena!" she called out frantically, but there was no response.

"Elena, where are you?" Laura yelled again, fighting the feeling of nausea from the noxious gas. She stepped back from the door, looking around for Burke, hoping she could ask him to call 911, but she couldn't see him now. Knowing there was no time to lose, she took two deep breaths of fresh air, then rushed into the house.

For a moment, her blood turned to ice and she couldn't move. The interior of her home was in shambles. Everything that had been on the bookshelves was now on the floor, swept into random piles. Cushions from the sofa and chairs had been slashed, then torn open and gutted. Stuffing lay scattered around the room like the aftermath of a bizarre snowstorm.

She tried to focus her thoughts quickly, feeling dizzy from lack of oxygen. Her godmother was here someplace and she had to locate her and get her outside, fast.

Laura's lungs felt as if they'd burst any second. Knowing that she had to take a breath, she rushed to the living room windows and threw open the first one she reached. She took a deep lungful of air, then plunged back into the nightmare her home had become.

Laura quickly searched the bedrooms and the kitchen, resisting the urge to turn on the lights and risk a spark-initiated explosion. But Doña Elena wasn't there. Halfway back to the living room Laura was forced to take a breath. She tried to make it a shallow one, but the smell was overpowering. She ran into the bathroom, slid back the small window and breathed deeply, then dove back into the poisoned atmosphere.

The hall seemed endless as she ran along it, heading directly for the next closest window. But when she tried to lift the sash, it was stuck tight. Out of air now, she was forced to take a short breath, but that proved to be a mistake.

Suddenly very dizzy, she leaned against the wall. Elena was in here somewhere and Laura had to find her, but her eyes had lost the ability to focus. Vaguely, she remembered the garage and turned to head in that direction. As if someone were playing with a dimmer switch, the room grew darker and she slipped slowly to the floor.

Laura fought to stay conscious, but oddly shaped patterns exploded before her eyes. Asphyxiation—she didn't want to die this way. Yet even as the thought formed, it slipped away and darkness greeted her.

Laura wasn't sure when her thoughts began again, but she awoke to the feeling of being carried. A man's arms, strong and warm, were wrapped around her, pressing her securely against a rock-hard chest. His strength was comforting, but also deeply stirring on a primitive level.

Still groggy, she wondered if this was what happened to romance authors when they died—perhaps God had created a special heaven for them. She didn't struggle. If she'd gone to romance writers heaven, she would enjoy every single moment of it.

As a strong light hit her eyes, she buried her face against his chest. The Light. It was harsh. She'd expected more— or maybe less. And where was that tunnel she'd heard about, and those departed loved ones stepping up to offer encouragement?

Slowly, she realized that she was able to breathe now. Did the dead breathe?

"You're going to be okay," a deep, sure voice said.

She turned her head to look at her rescuer, but his face was lost in an iridescent haze. A soft glimmer in his eyes seemed to pierce it somewhat, and she found herself captivated by the light brown eyes that held hers. "Am I dead?"

"No, not hardly, though you'll probably have a killer headache later on."

The haze that clouded her vision began to give way and, like a slowly developing photograph, his face grew clearer. She knew this man. It was her next-door neighbor, Burke, and his eyes were shining with a vibrant inner fire. She allowed herself to bask in the warmth of his gaze, and in the knowledge that she was alive and safe.

Then suddenly another thought made a bolt of panic shoot through her. "Elena!"

"She's not at home. Relax," he said, his voice utterly compelling and reassuring.

Burke laid her down gently on the grass of her front lawn. "I heard you calling for her and coughing, then saw you rush inside the house with your hand over your mouth. I tried to stop you but I couldn't reach you in time."

Relief flooded through her, erasing her fear. "I thought—" Her voice broke and she buried her face against his shoulder again.

Burke held her tightly. "What you did was very brave, but completely unnecessary. Doña Elena—Mrs. Baca—left over a half hour ago in the senior center's van."

It felt wonderful to be held by him. He was all hard muscle and lean strength. "I don't know how to thank you."

"Let me show you." He leaned down and captured her mouth in a tender kiss.

He tasted of cinnamon and strong, dark coffee. Seconds stretched out as a sweet, slow fire coursed through her veins.

But it was over too soon, and he drew back.

"Now we're more than even. In fact—I may owe you, lovely lady."

Chapter Two

Laura took a long ragged breath. The taste of Burke still lingered in her mouth, teasing her. What she'd found in his arms was pure fire. He remained close to her now and she breathed in his incredibly masculine scent. It was a blend of the rugged outdoors and pure danger.

She sat up slowly, trying to get her bearings. She'd spent years writing about the devastating magic of a man and a woman's first kiss—but she'd never thought this would happen to her. Now, out of all the places in the world where she might have found that sweet fire, it had happened here on her own front lawn.

Laura shook her head. She was still daffy from the gas. She was confusing life with the *Wizard of Oz*.

"You're darned tootin' you owe me," she answered him at last. "And just to make it even, the day I collect, I'll take *you* by surprise."

His eyes grew dark and sparkled with the excitement of a challenge. "Anytime." His voice was like steel and velvet. "I'm a man of honor—most of the time."

She laughed. "I'll remember that." And everything else that had just happened, for as long as she lived.

Burke stood and, holding her firmly by the waist, brought her to her feet.

She gripped his shoulders, enjoying the hardness of his

body. For a second their eyes met and she experienced something else that had never happened to her before—she was at a loss for words.

She was suffering from oxygen deprivation. That was the only answer that made sense. "I need to call the gas company and have them fix that leak. I should also call the police." Hearing sirens, she looked down the street and added, "Or did you do that already?"

"I called 911 before I went after you." As the paramedics drove up, he waved them over.

It took fifteen minutes for Laura to be checked out and for her to convince the paramedics that she was okay. Fortunately, her vital signs were normal, and the medics didn't believe she was in any more danger. Laura agreed to see a doctor if any symptoms reappeared.

During that time the gas supply leading to the heater was turned off inside her home. After signing a release form the paramedics presented, she went to meet the gas company serviceman as he came out her door.

"I've opened every window I could find in there, ma'am, but you should still be careful inside. The connector leading to your furnace is damaged and will have to be replaced, and the furnace itself will need some work. You'll still smell the chemical added to the natural gas so you can detect a leak, but that will fade pretty soon. The rest..." He shrugged. "What happened in there?"

"Someone must have broken in and trashed the place. That's all I've figured out so far." As the man walked back to his truck, Laura looked up and down the block, trying to figure out if the police were coming or not. Giving up on them, she started to go back into the house.

Just then Burke came up to her. "Can I help?" he asked.

"I'm going to take a look inside, now that it's safe. If I remember right, my house was in a shambles. I must have had a burglar."

"Let me go with you. And by the way, as a precaution, *don't* turn on any of the lights just yet. The gas should have dissipated enough, but there's no sense in testing it with a spark."

As Laura walked into the living room she grasped the full extent of the damage clearly for the first time. All the things she'd loved, that had defined her home and herself, had been tossed onto the floor like trash. She saw her collection of music boxes there, chipped and cracked, some smashed beyond recognition. The small knickknacks that held little value but gave her so much pleasure, like the wind-up toy drummer bear and her collection of mice, had been stepped on, probably not even on purpose. There was so much clutter on the floor it was nearly impossible to pick a path.

"Why would anyone do this to me?" she asked, her voice trembling.

"Take it one step at a time. See if there's anything missing." In a gesture of support, Burke placed his hand on her shoulder.

The warmth of his touch melted the coldness that enveloped her. Yet even as it comforted, it stirred other unsettling emotions.

She moved away and picked up a brightly decorated clay pot that had somehow survived undamaged. The miniature rose that had been inside it lay next to it. Laura placed the plant back into the pot along with all the soil she could scoop up.

The small act of restoration made her feel better.

"Look, but don't touch anything else yet," Burke said, gazing around the room. "The police will want to work the scene and check for evidence. They'll search for fingerprints."

As she saw the debris in the hall, Laura felt a new wave of panic slam into her. Her office. She had to check her computer. The book was finished, but she had other important files on her hard drive—the beginning of a future book, for one.

She rushed down the hall, but although the room was in shambles, her computer appeared untouched. She counted that as a major blessing, and tried to ignore the way her chest tightened as she looked at the chaos surrounding her. Files lay all over the floor, papers everywhere. Reference books had been tossed around, and some of the older ones had lost pages and had their spines broken. Taking a deep, unsteady breath, she stepped back out into the hall.

As she went into the bedrooms, she saw they had not fared well, either. Everything had been rifled through. In her room, the contents of every drawer had been dumped onto the floor. Her small jewelry box had been upended, but as she sorted through the jumble of pieces, she saw that nothing was missing, not even her most expensive watch, earrings or matching pendant.

Laura went through the rest of the house numbly. She checked for the obvious things burglars usually took, like the TV set and VCR, but both were there, intact, and none of the simple tools in the garage had even been touched.

"I just don't understand this," she muttered. "What on earth were they after?"

Hearing a loud knock, she returned to the living room. A police officer in a blue uniform had come in the open door and was looking around. She introduced herself and took him from room to room.

"Any idea who did this?" he asked her. Seeing her shake her head, he added, "Smells like you had a gas leak, too."

She gave him a quick rundown of what had happened, including what the gas company serviceman had said.

"I'm going to check for the point of entry and dust that area for fingerprints, but I've got to tell you, we generally don't have a lot of luck finding the perps in these cases. Our best chance is if we catch them in the act somewhere else, or fencing the stolen property. Of course, we'll ask your neighbors if they saw or heard anyone or noticed an unfamiliar vehicle. We'll cover all the usual bases, but after that…''

Laura felt her stomach plummet. In her books the cops always had sufficient resources and the determination to solve every crime. But this was real life, and too often victims were just that—victims. The label made her angry. Someone had broken into her home and turned her life into chaos, and she was supposed to just shrug it off?

Burke came to stand beside her. It was a small gesture, but one she appreciated. He had a commanding presence about him that she found oddly reassuring.

''What you can do is figure out how to get your life back to normal—fast,'' Burke advised. ''For starters, you'll need to have dead bolts installed and a good, solid back door. I think the burglar was able to kick it in because it wasn't constructed to stand up to punishment. Learn from this and you can keep it from ever happening again.''

''And who knows?'' the officer agreed. ''We may get lucky and catch the perp and recover whatever he stole from you.''

''For now, let's finish going through the house and see what that could be,'' Burke said. ''You'll need to make a list.''

It was like walking through a nightmare. Laura went down the hall with the men and, as they passed the closet containing the gas furnace, Burke stopped and crouched down beside it. The metal panel had been ripped off the heater.

''From the marks I see, it looks like they were trying to search the space between the furnace and wall,'' Burke said. ''Of course, in doing that, the intruder moved the furnace enough to extinguish the pilot light and break the gas connection. It looks like he damaged the furnace as well."

As they entered Elena's room, Laura saw a tiny silver pendant Elena cherished on the floor, along with other items from the top of her dresser. She picked the pendant up, grateful that it hadn't been stepped on. It had been the last gift Elena had received from her husband before he died. Laura placed it inside her jacket pocket in an attempt to protect this one special thing.

As her thoughts turned to her godmother, Laura began to worry. Elena was in her late sixties and had a weak heart. The last thing she needed was to come home to a disaster like this, and then be forced to spend the night in an unheated house. Lately, the nighttime temperatures had been in the low forties here in the desert. They'd have to find a motel.

"I've got to start cleaning up and making arrangements for a place to spend the night," Laura said.

"I'm going to need a list and description of what's missing first," the officer said.

"I haven't found anything missing yet," she answered.

With obvious reluctance, Laura headed back to her office. It was here, where she created her stories, that the chaos the intruder had left behind bit into her heart the most. In this room, alone with the ghosts who peopled a writer's imagination, she'd found peace. But now all there was in here was confusion. The sense that the dearest part of herself had been violated almost brought her to tears.

It would take days to get everything back in order. Thank goodness she'd just ended a project rather than being in the middle of one.

"Was this someone's idea of a sick joke? They must have looked through every page in here," Laura murmured, her spirits sagging.

"It appears that they were searching for something in particular, perhaps a letter or document," Burke said. "Can you think of what that might have been?"

Hearing a familiar but frightened voice calling out from the front of the house, Laura spun around. "Oh, no! Elena's back early."

Laura rushed to intercept her godmother. She'd hoped to find a way to soften the blow before Elena returned. As Laura reached the front door, she saw her frozen there, terror and shock on her face.

"It's all right," Laura said gently. "No one's been hurt. We can always replace *things*."

Elena was a petite, well-rounded woman with an affable manner and an easy smile that made friends almost anywhere. Now she looked as if she'd just witnessed the death of a loved one.

"Someone broke into the house. In the process, they created this mess and even managed to break off the valve on the furnace," Laura said calmly. "But the gas is turned off now, so it's just a matter of cleaning up and repairing or replacing the furnace. And believe it or not, I haven't discovered anything missing."

"That's a blessing. But without heat, how will we stay warm tonight?" Elena asked. "And just look at what they did to our beautiful home!"

"We'll be fine. We can stay at a motel until everything is back to normal again. It'll work out."

"We'll need someplace close, Laura. We'll have to be here daily. We can't just leave everything in the hands of repairmen," she countered.

"The motels along the main highway aren't too far away. We'll make do."

"I have an idea, ladies," Burke interjected. "You know I bought the large three-bedroom next door, and it's much too big for just me and my dog. Why don't you both come stay with me until your house is repaired?''

Laura felt a prickle of excitement as she heard his offer. But, of course, it was out of the question. Sharing the home of a drop-dead-gorgeous guy was not her idea of a safe haven. Before she could say anything, however, Elena spoke.

''Such a nice offer! We accept,'' she said, looking up at him with a smile. ''Okay, Laura?''

Laura nearly choked. ''Wait a sec.''

Seeing the police officer coming toward them, Burke turned to him. ''Why don't I go speak with the officer while you two talk things over?''

As soon as he'd moved out of earshot, Laura glowered at Elena, but the older woman beamed a wide smile.

''God always makes something good come out of even the worst of times,'' she said. ''That young man is single and very attractive. And with me there, he *will* behave. In the meantime, you two can get to know each other. Before long, you might find out that he's perfect for you.''

''How can you say that? We don't know a thing about him! I haven't even figured out if Burke is his first or last name!''

''That's one of the things you can ask him,'' Elena replied, undaunted. ''And we do know quite a bit about him. We know that he always dresses like a gentleman and that he pays attention to details. He heard Mr. Romero call me *Doña* Elena once, and ever since then he's addressed me the same way. On a practical side, his offer means we can be close by to let repairmen in and out. I think we should take advantage of his hospitality.''

Seeing that Laura was still hesitant, she played her trump card. ''And my heart…well, this has all been quite a shock. I'd like to stay close to home, because here is where I feel the most comfortable.''

Laura's eyes narrowed. "Do you realize that you *never* mention your heart unless you want me to do something?" Seeing the crestfallen look on her godmother's face, she laughed. "All right. You win. We'll accept his offer."

"Laura!" A male voice suddenly boomed out from near the front door.

Laura looked up and expelled her breath in a whoosh. "Not *him* again," she said softly. "Ken Springer is the last person I want to see here now."

The police officer who was packing away his fingerprint kit looked up and, seeing Laura's expression, went to head off the new arrival.

As he approached, Ken flipped open his badge. "County arson investigator, Officer."

"There's no arson here, Ken," Laura said, impatience tainting her tone. The tall, lanky lieutenant from the fire department wasn't bad looking, but his cocky, self-absorbed attitude put Laura off. They had a brief history, one she never wanted to repeat.

"I just heard the report. Do you have any idea what that gas leak might have done to you if you'd flipped on the light? This is attempted arson as far as I'm concerned."

"No. The gas leak was an accident. The break-in..." She shrugged.

Seeing Burke, Ken placed his arm over Laura's shoulder.

Biting back her annoyance, Laura shrugged it off. "I'm very tired, Lieutenant Springer. If you have business here, then get on with it. Otherwise, please leave."

Burke's gaze locked with Ken's. The fireman reached into his back pocket and once again flashed his ID. "And your business here is...?"

"Mine," Laura said firmly.

Anger sharpened Ken's features as he glanced at Laura. "You don't need help from a civilian, Laura. I'll handle this."

"I *want* him here," she said firmly. "Remember that you're in my home."

Ken held her gaze, a muscle in his jaw twitching. "I'm going to take a look around."

As he strode off, Burke glanced at her. "Old boyfriend?"

"I went out with him twice—and that was two times too many."

"But he's never given up trying to make himself part of her life." Elena shook her head sadly.

Burke nodded, but before he could comment, the police officer came up to Laura. "I just wanted to tell you that I'm leaving now. We'll be increasing our patrols in this area, but stay alert and call us if you have any problems." He reached into his pocket and handed her a card.

After the man left, Laura saw that Ken was still walking around the house, looking through her things. Annoyed, she strode up to him. "It's not arson, Ken. Not even a match was lit in here. Perhaps you should go work on one of your cases."

"How do you explain what's happened?" he countered harshly.

Elena came up and joined them. "I didn't mention this to the officer because it's just speculation, but the break-in is more than likely the work of my brother-in-law," she stated. "He's been hoping to get his hands on the deed to a piece of property my husband left me, or the original will. He filed a lawsuit, but no hearing has been scheduled yet."

Laura looked at Elena with dawning understanding. "You're right. This would be something he'd do."

"You shouldn't have to put up with this from anyone," Ken said. "Tell me where I can find him and I'll go over and take care of this for you."

"No, Ken, you won't," Laura said firmly. "I'll handle this myself. I appreciate you coming by, but as you can see, this has nothing to do with the type of case you handle for the county."

Ken looked at Burke, his expression venomous. "Then it looks like it's time for us to go."

"Burke, if you don't mind, I'd like you to stay for a while. You can help us get things organized here," Laura said, more to make a point than anything else.

"If you want—" Ken said.

"Ken, go," she interrupted. "You're working now. He's not."

"Unemployed?" Ken sneered.

The cold, level look that passed between the men made a shiver course up Laura's spine.

"Call if you need me. This is my new cell number," Ken said, handing Laura his card.

She took it, then set it down on a coffee table. "Goodbye, Ken."

The tall fireman left wordlessly.

Laura exhaled softly as soon as Ken had gone. "Ken Springer is harmless, but he's such a pain. I've tried to tell him I'm just not interested, but he keeps finding a reason to come around."

"Nothing but a solid hit with a two-by-four deters a man of that kind," Elena said.

Burke laughed. "Listen to your godmother," he said, looking at Laura. "I think she's right on target."

His generous lips curved sensually when he smiled, and Laura felt a sudden jolt of awareness—the earthy kind that reminded her that he was all-male, and she a woman who enjoyed her femininity. She took a breath, trying to tone down her reaction to him for the sake of her own peace of mind.

A man as confident as Burke surely knew the effect he had on women. He'd undoubtedly grown to accept it as natural—something that was as much a part of him as his broad shoulders and six-foot frame. The last thing she intended to do was feed his ego by letting him sense her reaction to him.

"Why don't you both go through the house one last time and make a list of all the repairs that'll have to be done? We'll need it when we file the insurance claim," Elena said.

"Good idea," Laura answered.

"You should look at the back door," Burke said to Laura. "That's one of the first things you'll need to get fixed."

Laura went into the kitchen and studied the damage. The door frame had been splintered and the lock damaged by a vicious kick. A partial boot print was still on the door. This had clearly been the point of entry. "I never thought of that door as flimsy, but I'll make sure I get a solid-core one now."

They methodically checked out each room in the house, Laura adding to the list of things to do. As they worked, she was acutely aware of everything about the man beside her. She stole fleeting, furtive glances at him, taking in his square-cut jaw and his absolutely delicious mouth.

A guy like this is used to leaving a trail of brokenhearted women behind him. Be careful. Don't add to the number.

The sun had sunk well below the horizon by the time they rejoined Elena in the living room. They'd been able to close the doors and windows and turn on the lights, but the house had grown decidedly chilly.

"It's going to take awhile to get things back to normal," Laura said with a sigh.

"Don't be so pessimistic," Elena chided. "Once we clear up the mess, everything will look one hundred percent better. We'll have a claims adjuster come over tomorrow, then the repairmen can come to fix the heater, replace the door and put in better locks. The damaged furniture can go out to be repaired, or we can go shopping for some new pieces. Before you know it, we'll be back at home and it'll be like nothing happened.'' Elena stood, wavered, then sat down heavily.

Seeing it, Laura felt her stomach fall. ''Are you all right?'' She should have expected this. The whole thing had been a total shock for Elena.

''I'm fine. It's nothing. I just took my pills a little late today and I'm a little woozy.''

''Let's just sit here for a bit then,'' Laura said, watching her for signs of a serious problem with her heart.

Burke sat on an easy chair that had been slashed but not completely depleted of stuffing. He leaned back, projecting an ease that helped Elena relax. For several minutes he made small talk, discussing the neighborhood and the upcoming growing season. Elena bragged about Laura's rose garden, promising to show him around in full daylight to point out the buds and new season's growth.

Burke seemed interested in everything about them, though Laura couldn't tell if it was genuine or if he was simply being charming and polite.

Finally, after the tension washed out of Elena and she had relaxed again, Burke turned the conversation back to business.

''Tell me about this brother-in-law of yours, Doña Elena,'' he said, his voice calm but authoritative.

''He's a difficult man,'' she answered. ''If he thought I kept that land deed here, or the will, that would explain all this,'' she said, waving a hand around the room. ''My brother-in-law has claimed that the tract of land I inherited should have gone to him because, originally, he was half owner. But he sold his share to my husband several years ago when he needed cash. My attorney, Ernest Martinez, says that Al has no further claim on the land. But Al has accused me of tampering with Diego's will, saying that his brother had left the property to him.''

''After we received word that he'd filed a lawsuit, Elena started getting nasty calls at all hours of the night,'' Laura added. ''We finally got caller ID and started disconnecting the phone when we went to bed.''

Laura watched her godmother as she filled Burke in on a few more details. Burke had worked his magic on her and she was answering all his questions without becoming upset or excited.

Laura suppressed a sigh. There was no denying that Burke was attractive and charming. But something was warning her to be cautious, and she always trusted her intuition. Theirs was not a neighborhood that had known many break-ins, but he'd only been around a week, and now this. It was possible that he was totally innocent, but it was all working out too perfectly. He'd been there to help her; now he was offering two strangers his home. If this was all completely coincidental, she'd eat her shoe.

She had to start thinking in nonfiction terms, concentrating on facts only. If she didn't do that, she had a feeling she'd end up with some major-league trouble—trouble that would no doubt answer to the name of Burke.

Chapter Three

Laura watched him carefully, trying to freeze out her hormones with a dose of logic, but it wasn't quite working. It was hard to even think when he trained his pale brown eyes on her. Contrasting sharply with his dark copper skin, they were nothing short of mesmerizing.

Irritated with herself, Laura brought her thoughts back to what her *madrina* was saying. "My brother-in-law, Al, has always been a problem for my husband's family. He never amounted to anything, because he's lazy and always searching for the easy way out. Diego wouldn't even allow him into our home for a long time because Al had started drinking heavily. After Diego passed away Al thought he'd get a windfall. Reality hit him hard. The man has never learned that the only thing that pays off with any certainty in this world is hard work and dedication."

As a cold draft came in from the kitchen, where the damaged back door couldn't be properly closed, Elena shivered and wrapped her shawl tighter around herself.

Noticing the gesture, Laura went to the closet and got her godmother's winter coat. "We have to get going," she told Burke. "Now that the sun has set, it's going to get cold in here pretty fast.

"*Madrina*," she continued, looking at Elena, "I wondered if you would enjoy a bed-and-breakfast. We really shouldn't impose on our new neighbor.''

"It's no imposition," Burke assured them quickly. "It'll be a pleasure." Taking off his leather jacket, he placed it around Laura's shoulders. "Let's go to my house so Doña Elena can get settled in, then we can come back and get some of the things you'll both need.''

Feeling the warmth of his jacket around her was like being embraced by this man, whose scent spoke of the wildness and freedom of the night. But it was all too distracting.

"You don't have to give me your jacket," she said, trying to pass it back to him. "You'll freeze." She felt like an idiot for not having taken out her own coat when she went to the closet for Elena's.

"I'm fine. I'm bigger and tougher," Burke answered playfully, placing it back over her shoulders.

He led the way to his home, a modern structure constructed in a classic Southwestern style known as Territorial. When he stepped around them to open the heavy wooden door, Laura noticed that he hadn't bothered to lock it.

"Don't you lock your doors?" she asked, aghast. "I know we don't have many incidents—"

She stopped suddenly when a huge, shaggy beast came shooting across the brick foyer, plopping down at Burke's feet when he called, "Sit!" The black-and-silver animal looked a lot like a cross between a giant German shepherd and a wolf.

"Holy saints!" Elena whispered. "I thought you said you had a dog."

"That's not a dog. That's a bear," Laura managed to gasp. "No wonder you're not concerned about leaving your house unlocked."

"He's really friendly." Burke took her hand in his own

and held it out in front of the beast. Laura stopped breathing.

"Friend, Wolf."

Wolf sniffed her hand. "See? Now he knows you," Burke said.

The warmth of Burke's hand intertwined with hers made a tingle spread all through her body. As his gaze fastened on hers, she saw that his eyes had darkened slightly, awareness and desire touching their depths. Everything feminine in her came suddenly and vibrantly alive.

Laura pulled her hand away and tore her eyes from his. Even casual contact between them held danger. Needing to distract herself, she crouched down and petted the dog.

"Shake hands with the lady," Burke said.

Wolf held out his paw, then yawned as if the whole business was beneath him.

Laura laughed and took his paw. "Pleasure to meet you, Wolf."

Elena crouched down and scratched him behind the ears until Wolf's eyes closed and he made a contented sound.

"What a wonderful companion you have," Elena said.

"My godmother adores dogs," Laura said. "Her mastiff, Bruno, died last year right before she moved in with me. She's been wanting to get another one, but she hasn't convinced me yet."

Once he knew they were at ease around Wolf, Burke showed them to a room down the hall. It was simply furnished, with a four-poster bed and a chest of drawers, yet the furniture, constructed of dark woods, suggested a discerning taste.

Exquisitely crafted antique Navajo rugs, woven in earth tones, adorned the walls. "Those are beautiful," Elena said. "The one on the left in particular."

He nodded, pleased she'd complimented it. "It's what my people call a *Yei* rug. The tall slender figures are the

Holy People and, in this case, they're shown carrying yucca strips. That rug is made up of elements our medicine men depict in sandpaintings used for healing. We believe that the Holy People are said to restore health when properly appealed to.''

"So it's a religious artifact?''

"No, it's not, but a sandpainting made to look like that, and done according to our ways, would be a religious object. This is just a wool rug, deliberately woven with a flaw—a thin line made from the center to the edge. That's done as a tribute to Spider Woman, who taught our people the art of weaving.''

Elena studied everything in the room, from the beautiful handcrafted quilt on the bed to the small woven basket, made from grass coils and dyed yucca, that rested on the nightstand. "This is such a lovely room.''

"I thought you'd feel that way, so this one is for you,'' Burke said. Then he glanced at Laura. "I think you'll prefer the room across the hall.''

Laura followed him and saw another Southwest style room, in harmony with the rest of the house. This one had high ceilings composed of hand finished, stained logs, or vigas, and more modern milled lumber. The large bed in the middle had a hand carved headboard that was really an elaborate bookcase. She looked up at Burke quickly, wondering if he'd guessed what she did for a living.

"I met your godmother at the fence several times and she mentioned you loved books,'' he said. "I thought you might appreciate this room, since there's a light on the headboard for easy reading at night.'' He demonstrated how to work the small, adjustable brass lamp.

"I do love books, that's true,'' she admitted, not quite willing to say anything more about her work at the moment. "I'm really amazed at what you've done here in such a short time. I expected to find a lot of unpacked boxes.''

"I hired people to help me move in and put things away so I wouldn't miss any work. I don't have a lot of possessions, and it didn't take long." Burke glanced at his watch. "And now, I'm going to have to get moving. I'm late for work."

"What kind of work do you do?" Thinking about the way he'd seemed to know what to do in the aftermath of the break-in, she added, "Are you a cop?" If so, that would put a new slant on things...."

"Something like that," he answered, then whistled for Wolf. "You stay here with the ladies." The dog sat, panting, but it looked for all the world as if he were grinning. "And try not to look so happy about it. You're a guard dog, remember?"

"Is he trained for that kind of work?" Laura asked, suddenly apprehensive.

"Yes," Burke said, then with a twinkle in his eye, quickly added, "He's a danger to any crook who'd trip over him."

Wolf made a low grumbling sound in protest.

"Sorry, Wolf. I should have told the ladies you were absolutely ferocious."

The dog barked once and Laura laughed. "It's as if he understands you."

"With this dog, I truly never know," Burke answered honestly. "The keys to my castle, madam." He took her hand and placed the keys in her palm, but he didn't let go right away.

Laura held her breath. The warmth of his touch seemed to travel through her, slipping around barriers she'd learned to put up between herself and the world.

"I'll be back before you know it. You're safe here," he said, then released her.

As the words still resonated through her, Burke opened the front door.

"Your jacket," she said quickly, and started to slip it off.

"Keep it on until you warm up. I have a good windbreaker in one of the saddlebags of my bike," he said, then disappeared out the door.

A moment later, Laura heard him gunning the engine of his motorcycle. She went to the window to catch a final glimpse of him, and at that moment he glanced up, saw her and waved.

Cursing herself for letting him see that she'd been looking at him, she moved back into the center of the room.

"You see? He's as charming as I told you he'd be," Elena said softly.

"We still don't know a thing about him, Elena. We have to be careful."

"I'm very seldom wrong about people, *hijita,* you know that."

Laura shook her head. "Yes, I do, but there's something about him that makes me uneasy."

"That's only because he reminds you of things you're missing from your life. Back in the days when you believed in love and were open to the possibilities, a man like Burke would have sparked your imagination, and your heart would have beat a little faster every time you saw him. But now…"

"I've had relationships before, but they didn't work out. Once we mature, our hearts toughen up. We learn the hard way to avoid pain."

"Life comes with joy and pain. You can't avoid either, even if you try." Elena paused, gathering her thoughts. "But these days, your work has become enough to make you happy, and that just shouldn't be."

"I'm very lucky to be able to make my living doing something that I love. If I don't socialize much it's because writing is very time-consuming. People think you get an idea for a book, then just sit down and type it out. But the truth is that the idea is just the beginning. The real work comes when you do draft after draft, until you practically know the book by heart.''

''You create fantasies and cater to illusions woman have held dear since they first heard of Prince Charming. But you're not willing to take the same risks your heroines take. These days you want safety and guarantees before you give any man the time of day.''

''You make it sound as if I'm turning away truckloads of eligible men. But let's face it, in my work, I seldom meet people at all. Creativity and solitude are companions. And when I do meet a new guy, they turn out to be like Ken.'' She shuddered. ''I'd rather be alone than with him.''

Elena smiled. ''I don't blame you there, but there've been others. Now this wonderful man steps into your life and you're already busy finding fault—anything to keep from getting too close.''

''I'm not *finding* fault, Elena. I'm just pointing out that he could be a serial killer, for all we know.''

''He's not.''

''And just how do you know that?''

''Because I keep my eyes and ears open. First, I've heard talk about him. He's in some kind of law enforcement work. Mrs. Patrick told me that her son worked with him once.''

''The attorney?''

Elena nodded. ''She wouldn't give me the details. She said it was all confidential, but she spoke of our new neighbor with respect.''

Laura looked across the room pensively. Something still didn't add up, but she just couldn't put her finger on it.

''And look at what this house tells us about him. He's a man who cares about the place he calls home and his heritage. Did you see the fetish in the *nicho* in the wall in the living room?''

Laura remembered seeing the recessed niche in the wall, but she hadn't taken a closer look at what it contained. "No, I didn't. What animal does the fetish depict?''

"The mountain lion. It's on a special earthenware dish sprinkled with cornmeal, which is supposed to keep the fetish's powers strong. The mountain lion is his animal medicine and that tells you about the man he is.''

"What's it represent? Do you know?''

"Yes, I learned about animal fetishes and their medicine years ago because they fascinated me. The mountain lion is the hunter god. Think of the spiritual attributes of the animal—courage, faithful to his purpose and committed. That's the animal medicine he draws upon.''

"Okay, Sherlock,'' Laura teased. She took off Burke's jacket, feeling warm now in a properly heated home. "But, for my sake, don't be so quick to think the best of him. People in law enforcement, no matter what their background, aren't always nice and stable.''

Elena shook her head. "I wouldn't worry so much about you if you were at least curious about him and trying to learn more, but as it is…''

Wolf came up beside Laura and pressed his muzzle into her hand, asking to be petted. She scratched his head, enjoying the soft feel of his thick fur.

"You've never had a love that lasted,'' Elena continued, "but now when you look at Burke, I see it flickering to life. Hold on to that. If your fears and doubts win over every time the opportunity comes, you'll end up letting life slip right through your fingers.''

Laura started to make excuses, but decided to be honest instead. "I like my life the way it is. I don't depend on anyone for my happiness, and that gives me a sense of security and accomplishment.''

"But there's so much *more* to life. You've got to go out and meet new people and give yourself a chance."

"There's more to Burke than meets the eye, Elena. There's a hard edge to that guy that doesn't quite fit in with the charming man who graciously offered us his home."

Elena sighed. "I'm going to bed. I can see that you're determined to find a reason to back away. Will you at least think about what I've told you?"

Laura kissed her good-night. "I always do."

After Elena had gone to bed, Laura wandered around the house, with Wolf padding along beside her. She stopped by the *nicho* in the wall where the animal fetish was kept, and studied the mountain lion. The four-inch figure, hand carved out of petrified wood, was exquisitely made. She started to touch it, but drew her hand back. It seemed too personal to disturb.

Laura continued to the den. The leather furniture looked comfortable and held that touch of masculinity that so defined Burke. This was a man's room through and through. There was a no-nonsense, no-frills style of decor here that fitted in with what she'd learned about him so far, but nothing here really cast a light on his personal life.

In her own den there were photos of her mother, and a rare one of her father. He'd died when she was three. There were shots of picnics with Elena and Christmases with friends and family, a chronicle of good times past. But there was nothing of that sort here.

She looked at his bookcase, wondering what she'd be able to learn about him from his choice of reading material. She recognized several titles from her college days, such as *The Prince* by Niccolò Machiavelli. If memory served her right, the author's philosophy was simply that theological and moral arguments had no place in the political game. It was a gruesome, practical book that modern day military people were required to study. There was *The Art of War* by Tzu Sun, which ran along the same vein, *A Book of Five Rings,* which had been written by a famous samurai master. Then on a lighter vein—if one could call them that—were books by Ludlum, Clancy and Trevanian.

Missing were the kind of books she treasured—ones by Tolkien, or David Eddings, or Danielle Steele—books that mingled fantasy with romantic adventure. Of course, generally speaking, she didn't share the reading tastes of most men, something she attributed to yet another instance of the left brain–right brain dichotomy.

Wondering which of the books on the shelf was his favorite, she leafed through several. It was clear from the wear and tear on the Clancy books that he'd reread all of them.

Well, at least he favored fiction.

Not in the least bit sleepy, Laura sat down on the leather sofa and looked around the room, wondering why there was nothing in the house, with the exception of the fetish and the books, capable of giving her a glimpse into Burke's personal life. The more she mused about it, the more uneasy it made her. The place was beautiful, but more like a model home than an actual residence.

Finally, too restless to continue sitting, she stood. She had things to do. Wasting time was not her style. She'd go over to her own house and start putting things away and cleaning up. When Elena went to bed she rarely woke up until morning and, in the meantime, Wolf would keep her safe. No one in his right mind would risk getting an animal that large ticked off. Besides, Burke had said he wouldn't be gone long.

As Laura put on Burke's jacket and headed to the front door, Wolf came trotting up and sat directly in front of her, so close she could feel his breath on her leg. It was a little disconcerting, but as she looked down at him and saw him wag his tail, she knew it was okay.

Laura crouched down beside him and sank her fingers into the rough fur around his powerful neck. "I'm going to leave for a little while. You can watch Elena and make sure she's safe."

Laura tried to slip out the door, but the dog forced his way beside her.

"Wolf, no. You have to stay here."

She pushed him back, hoping she wouldn't get him angry, then slipped out the door quickly. Standing outside for a second, she heard him scratching at the door, but there was no howling or barking. Figuring she'd won this round, she locked the door and headed to her home.

Laura unlocked the front door and went inside, turning on the lights. The chaos the brightness revealed depressed her considerably.

Deciding quickly, she started in her office, knowing it was the one room she needed to get organized first, for her own peace of mind. Was it just her imagination, or did the room really look worse than when she'd left it a few hours ago? A relatively intact folder she was sure she'd seen earlier on the desk was now on the floor among the scattered papers.

Suddenly she saw a shadow out of the corner of her eye. Before she could even turn her head, a hand clamped down hard over her mouth and her arm was twisted painfully behind her back. It hurt so badly tears formed in her eyes.

"If you make a sound or struggle, I'll rip off your arm," the man growled. "Now tell me where it is, or I'll just kill you right now," he said, moving his hand back slightly from her mouth.

"What? What are you looking for?"

"Don't play games," he ordered, his voice no more than a rumble.

Terror shot through her. The man was crazy. Remembering a self-defense move the heroine of one of her books had used, Laura moaned and collapsed as if fainting, forcing the man to shift his hold to keep her from slipping away from him.

As his grip loosened, she stiffened and brought her heel down hard on his instep, simultaneously elbowing his stomach.

Laura screamed and twisted free. Only a few seconds ahead of her assailant, she raced for the front door, knowing it was her only chance.

Chapter Four

Laura threw the door open, ran out and collided abruptly with Burke. He wrapped his arms around her, steadying her.

"Laura, what's wrong?"

Her heart was pounding so hard she could hear it beating. "Someone grabbed me from behind," she said. "He's inside!"

"Wolf, guard her!" he ordered the dog, anger flaring on his face.

As Burke went past her into the house, Laura caught a glimpse of a figure going through the living room into the kitchen.

Realizing the man intended to escape out the back door, Laura made a split-second decision. She'd go around the outside of the house and try to catch a glimpse of him when he came out to the street. She *needed* to know who her enemy was and, with Wolf beside her, the man wouldn't dare attack.

She was just approaching the driveway when the man leaped the fence that bordered her backyard, sprinting in her direction. She could hear Burke on the other side, closing in. Night shielded the stranger's face in shadows and, before she could get a clearer look, he scooped up a large metal trash can and threw it directly at her.

At that instant, Wolf leaped up and knocked her to the ground, and the trash barrel missed by at least a foot. As it bounced across the yard, the man jumped into the passenger side of a parked car, barely escaping Burke's leap over the fence and desperate lunge at the door. The vehicle roared away with squealing tires.

Burke ran a few more steps and, catching the vehicle tag number, wrote it down.

By the time Laura got to her knees, he was at her side. He helped her up, trying to gauge the extent of her injuries.

"Where do you hurt?" he asked brusquely, looking her up and down.

"I'm not hurt at all, I'm fine," she assured him. "I have a few scuffs and bruises, but I'll live."

Burke shook his head. "Why did you try to head him off like that? What did you think you were going to do if you caught up to him?"

"I just wanted to get a look at his face. He threatened me in my own home." Her voice trembled and she swallowed hard. "No one has a right to do that."

"Home should be a place of safety, and he violated that. I understand. But you reacted without thinking it through," he said, his tone somber. "And in situations like this, you can't afford to do that. It's dangerous to act impulsively, Laura. You have to be more careful."

"I know, but I figured that with you at his heels and Wolf by my side, his focus would have been on getting away, not attacking me. And believe it or not, I never even noticed the car until he got in."

Burke exhaled softly. "As you've seen, trouble can be anywhere. The intruder obviously had a partner. From now on, be more careful." He looked down at the dog. "Okay, furball, if Laura ever goes off like that when you're guarding her, subdue her. Knock her down and sit on her if you have to."

Laura laughed. "He can't possibly understand all of that."

"No, but he does understand 'Laura' and 'subdue.' I wouldn't try to run after a bad guy next time."

"You mean he'll bite?"

"Nah. He likes you. He'll just knock you to the ground and stand over you, drooling. He'll probably lick your face, too. Considering that he's got a tongue that feels like a meat loaf, I can guarantee it won't be a pleasant experience."

"Ugh. That's gross."

"But true." Burke cocked his head. "Come on. Let's get back to your house."

As they walked side by side, the warmth of his body so close to hers was unsettling. "I thought you worked at night," she said, trying to bring her thoughts back to the business at hand. "Why did you come back so soon?"

"I just had to go meet with a contact. Investigations don't depend on set hours."

"So you *are* a cop?"

"A detective. Now tell me why you went back to your house when you did."

"I couldn't sleep, so I decided to get a head start cleaning up and making whatever repairs I could."

They stepped inside her house a few moments later. The lights were still on and, as she looked around, she sighed. "I'm going back to my office," she said, leading the way. "It makes me crazy to see paperwork from a project that took me between six months to a year to complete, scattered all over the floor like trash."

"First, we need to call the police again. Don't touch anything, but check as best you can to determine if anything is missing," Burke advised.

Laura nodded. "I can tell it's going to be a long night."

LAURA STOOD WITH BURKE in the living room as the police car drove away. As before, there were no revelations, but at least the officers had the vague description Laura could give of the intruder.

"Now maybe I can pick up some of this mess," she sighed.

"You've had two break-ins back-to-back," he said, following her into her office. "Could they be related to something associated with your work?" Burke began helping her pick up the papers. Then, giving in to curiosity, he read the top paragraph of the page in his hand. "'His mouth closed gently over hers...' Whoa."

"I write romance novels, Detective."

He grinned widely.

It was the same condescending, amused look she got from men who'd never picked up a romance novel in their lives. The look she gave him in return made the temperature in the room drop by twenty degrees. "They're not Machiavelli, but they take thought, skill and a lot of work," she said in a hard voice. "And they're *not* just about sex."

"What did I say?"

"It was written all over your face." She'd spent years pointing out to critics of the genre that romance novels qualified as "real" books, and often wondered whether her readers went through the same nonsense.

"Do you write other stuff? Maybe I've read your work."

"I doubt it."

"How can you be so sure?"

"If you'd read my work, you would have remembered," she said, looking him straight in the eye.

He laughed. "Okay. Point taken." He looked around. "If the break-ins aren't the result of your work, then what's your theory? Who's doing this, and why?"

"I don't know," she said slowly. "That man was crazy, angry, or both. He twisted my arm behind my back and told me he'd tear it off if I screamed. I honestly thought he might. It hurt that much."

"So you *were* hurt." Without even thinking about it, Burke moved closer to her, and she felt his nearness with every fiber of her being. Ripples of uneasiness and excitement danced through her.

"I'm fine now," she stated, stepping back. She couldn't even breathe when he stood so near. "He just scared me, particularly when he said he'd kill me unless I told him what he wanted to know."

"And that was...?"

"He wanted me to tell him where 'it' was. I told him I didn't know what he was talking about. But I was terrified of what he was going to do next." Laura told Burke about her self-defense move, then shivered.

He placed his hands on her shoulders, then slid them upward in a slow caress until he cupped her face. Awareness shimmered between them as they stood facing each other for one breathless moment.

"You don't have to be afraid again," he said, his voice low and seductive. "I'm going to stick around to help you even out the odds."

Laura couldn't think; emotions swirled wildly inside her. His palms were rough, hard and very male, and his touch intoxicating.

Hearing a loud crash in the direction of the kitchen, Laura jumped. Burke reached beneath his jacket, and she saw that the same hand that had caressed her now held a gun.

"Stay here," he said.

He moved purposefully out of the room toward the sound. "It's clear," he called out a moment later.

She found him and Wolf next to the open door in the kitchen. A gust of wind blowing in had stirred a window curtain, which in turn had toppled a miniature carnival glass hurricane lamp from the counter.

Laura began picking up the broken pieces with a heavy heart. It was a keepsake from long ago—one of the few things she'd kept since high school. Some boy whose name she'd long ago forgotten had won the little lamp for her at the fair while on a double date. The trinket, which would have cost only a few dollars, represented a time in her life when she'd been open to the possibility of romance in her future. She'd later used the lamp in her first published novel to represent that same hope for her heroine.

"That lamp obviously meant something special to you. I'm sorry it's broken," Burke said.

Sadly, she gathered up the pieces, wondering if she could glue them back together. Then, with a sigh, she dropped them into a wastebasket.

"Maybe it'll help if you talk about it," he said softly.

She shook her head. "Like with most things, what made it special were the memories it held for me."

Before Burke could ask more, and she'd have to explain all about the lamp and what it meant to her writing career, she switched the topic of conversation. "I really want to try and secure my home from another break-in before we leave tonight. Any ideas?"

"Since the lock in the front still works, that should keep any street thugs temporarily at bay. We could use some boards to hold the back door shut. But it'll mean that the repairmen will have one more thing to do when they come."

"It's still a good trade-off as far as I'm concerned. But where am I going to get wood at this hour?" She glanced at her watch. It was nearly one in the morning.

"I think I've got a few pieces of plywood in my garage—mostly scraps the previous owner of the house left behind, but I think they'll work."

"I have a hammer, hand saw and a box of nails in the garage."

"So we're all set," Burke said, walking to the door.

"Let me give you a hand bringing the boards over," she said.

"No, don't worry about it. I'll be back in a minute." He paused, then quickly added, "But if you don't want to stay here alone right now—"

"I'm fine." He hadn't meant it as a challenge, but it was one nonetheless. Pride set Laura's course. "While you're taking care of that, I'll start cleaning up here."

"I'll leave Wolf with you. Just remember, he'll knock you down and drool all over you if you don't stay put," he added with a smile.

"Okay," Laura said. "But don't think I'm going to be taking orders from now on. Next time I'll wear a wet suit and do whatever I please, anyway."

"I think I'd enjoy seeing you in a wet suit." His slow, languorous grin made her tingle in all the wrong places.

She threw a pillow at him. "So far you've been gallant— a knight in leather armor. Don't ruin it for me."

He laughed. "I'm no romance hero."

"How would you know? Have you ever read a romance novel?" she countered smoothly.

"Nope. You busted me there," he said. "Well, I better go get what I need."

It took another half hour of work before the back door was secure. Laura helped, and nailed some of the pieces in place herself.

"For someone who works with fantasies and fiction, you're very helpful in the real world," Burke commented.

"I've had to be. My mother was sick most of my life and I had to take care of both of us. Money was scarce for us back then, so I learned to do a little bit of everything. Now that I own this house, that's come in handy. I'm starting to collect some tools, and I don't always have to call in a plumber or a handyman when I need something done.''

Finished, Burke looked through the rear window at the garden, a place he'd run through only a short time ago without paying much attention to anything except a fleeing criminal. Just beyond the glow of the porch light, moonlight spilled over multicolored tulips and other spring flowers. A stone walkway, bordered by white flowers, glittered with specks of silver and led to the central flower bed. It astounded him that anyone could create something that dazzling in a place where the soil was basically nothing more than sand. "I've never met a romance author," he said quietly, then glanced back at her. "But it actually suits my image of you."

Laura watched him carefully, trying to figure out what he'd meant. From his tone of voice, she was almost certain it was a compliment. But experience warned her that men often confused a romance author with a fluffette, and she wouldn't have taken kindly to being seen in that light.

Before she could ask him, he gestured to the wooden kitchen chairs that had survived intact, and sat across from her. "Laura, there's something I need to explain. I'm not associated with the police. I'm a private investigator. I work for Gray Wolf Investigations."

She'd heard of the firm. It was a prestigious one, often mentioned in the newspaper in association with VIP cases, or with crimes they'd solved that the police had been unable to close.

"With people breaking in and threatening you, you've obviously got a serious problem," Burke continued. "With your permission, I'd like to look into this situation for you. It won't require you hiring the agency. I'll do it on my own time."

"No, I can't accept that. I have my own financial resources. Let me hire you instead."

"I'll tell you what. Let me do some preliminary work. That's free of charge, and after that, we can talk."

Laura shook her head. "I know you're giving me a chance to keep it informal and just between us, but I'm not comfortable with that. It's a very generous offer, mind you, but the fact is I know absolutely nothing about you. I'm not even sure of your name—is Burke your surname, or, as my godmother would say, your given name?"

"My name is Burke Silentman."

"I understand from living next door to the reservation, so to speak, that the Navajo people don't like their proper names used. Do you have a nickname?"

He smiled, pleased that she'd extended him that courtesy. "Burke is an Anglo name. I got used to having people use it when I served in the military, so it doesn't bother me. But many of us, like me, also have secret names we never divulge. We believe that to know someone's secret name is to have power over that person."

"All right. Then Burke it is."

"I'm very good at what I do for a living, Laura, and, from what I can see, you need help, the kind the local police can't provide. Let me at least find out what you're up against."

"Okay," she said, blinking against the light through heavy-lidded eyes.

"But right now you're tired, and so am I. The house is secure. What do you say we go back to my home and call it a night?" He stood, and Wolf was instantly by his side.

She nodded. "That's a great idea. We'll talk more tomorrow."

As the three of them walked down the sidewalk to his place, Burke stayed close beside her on the street side. Although they weren't even touching, she was acutely aware of everything about him. Moonlight spilled over him, accentuating the sculpted angles of his face. He spoke of inconsequential things, but his voice held her captivated. It was a rich, deep baritone, tailor-made for dark, midnight promises.

Annoyed with the turn her thoughts had taken, she focused on the present. Burke was, simply put, a complication in her life—one she just didn't need. She'd use his professional expertise and pay him and, in that way, make it clear that although she'd accepted his hospitality, she wasn't interested in a personal relationship.

When they entered Burke's home, the place was silent. Careful not to wake Elena, Laura started down the hall, following Burke, who was going to get some extra blankets from the linen closet. As she reached her room, Laura crouched down to pet Wolf, who'd followed her. "Are you sleeping with me tonight?" she asked softly.

Burke actually choked when he heard the question. His head snapped around quickly, then he saw her speaking to the dog.

Laura saw the look on his face and realized what had happened, but before she could comment, he focused his attention on the dog.

"Wolf, come!" he ordered, and Wolf complied instantly.

"I wouldn't have minded if he'd slept at the foot of the bed," Laura said.

"No way. He'll sleep on his blanket in the hall and guard all of us."

"All right." Laura took the blankets Burke offered her, entered the room and shut the door behind her. This room—this entire house—was Burke's domain. She could feel him here in the furnishings he'd chosen, and in the dark, rich colors that contrasted with the light walls and ceiling. Even the very air she breathed held his unmistakable mark, making her senses come alive.

She sat down on the edge of the bed and gathered her thoughts. This just wouldn't do. The attraction between them was too strong and too dangerous to indulge, even a little bit.

Burke had walked into her life and, unless she was careful, would turn her entire world upside down.

She sighed softly. Fate had conspired against her, and instinct told her that nothing would ever be quite the same again.

USING THE PHONE in the den, Burke called in and made his report. Handler didn't like to be kept waiting. Burke had spoken to him when he'd gone to retrieve the wood for Laura's back door, and asked for a trace on the license number and vehicle the intruder had used to escape. At the time, he'd promised to call back within a half hour in case Handler had tracked it down. But Burke hadn't been able to do so until now.

"Handler" was the code name for the owner of the agency. His identity was shrouded in secrecy, and though Burke was the most senior operative and supervised the other investigators, he'd never learned who Handler was. For what he'd been told were security reasons, Handler's identity remained a secret, even from him.

"So she's with you now?" Handler asked, verifying what Burke had reported.

"Yes, Laura Santos is here and safe for now," he answered. Remembering the softness of her lips and the way her body had melted into his, *safe* was probably not the word he should have used.

"And she doesn't know that you've already been hired to protect her?"

"No, and I really don't think she has the remotest idea what's going on, or why she's a target."

"I know you'll stay on top of things."

The idle remark, in this instance, made a very graphic

and vivid image form in his mind. His body grew instantly hard.

"Keep me posted, Burke."

"Yes, sir."

"I've e-mailed you the information you asked for on the license plate of the suspect's vehicle. You'll find it next time you log on."

As he placed the receiver down, Burke leaned back in the chair. Handler's electronically altered voice had originally bothered him, but he was getting used to it now. As far as he was concerned, it was a small inconvenience that came with a job he loved. His years with Gray Wolf had been good ones, and once he'd become supervisor, he'd given up his code name to remain the only traceable operative at the firm.

He was the number one operative of an elite team, took on the most dangerous assignments himself, and, best of all, he'd avoided working a nine-to-five job—something that ranked close to getting a case of malaria on the Burke Silentman scale of really bad news.

The house was still and the hour late, but he wasn't ready to go to bed yet. As was his habit, he switched on the computer at his desk to check his e-mail, and while the program booted up, considered the events of the last few hours. This whole case was a strange one, and had been from the beginning. Since that day three weeks ago when Doug had sent him an e-mail from West Medias, a country in Europe known for its warring factions—an e-mail that had been mysteriously cut off midsentence—things had been far from normal.

Burke fished his wallet out of his back pocket, then reached for a photo of him and Doug. It had been taken shortly after they'd completed Intelligence training in the Special Forces.

He smiled, looking at the younger version of himself and

his friend. Throughout his entire life, after the death of his brother, Hoops, he'd only had one close buddy, Douglas Begay. Like him, Doug had seen hard times on the rez. They'd joined the Special Forces together as soon as they could to escape the poverty of the Navajo Nation.

Over the years, they'd managed to stay in close contact. But all Burke really knew of Doug's life now was that he officially worked in Europe for a legitimate publishing house—a job Burke had deduced was nevertheless a cover for what he really did. His buddy was heavily involved with Freedom International, a privately funded watchdog organization that championed human rights.

Then, out of the blue, he'd sent that e-mail letter hiring Gray Wolf to protect the writer, Laura Santos—someone Doug had never met, as far as Burke knew. Unfortunately, the e-mail hadn't only been incomplete—it had been impossibly vague. The only thing Burke knew for a fact was that Doug wouldn't have hired them to protect Laura unless it was imperative that they do so. Recent events seemed to bear that out.

Yet the only connection he could see between Doug and Laura was that Doug worked for a small publisher abroad—and Laura was a romance novelist. Laura's background hadn't revealed any link to West Medias.

He needed to contact Doug and find out more, but there wasn't any way for him to do that without heading overseas for a visit, and that just wasn't possible. He was afraid to try and send an e-mail or a letter, or attempt a phone call, in case Doug was in as much trouble as he suspected, and was being monitored.

Checking his e-mail, Burke found only a message from Handler informing him that the license tag was stolen, and probably the car as well. Finding nothing from Doug, Burke turned the computer off. It was time to call it a night. He walked down the hall silently, leaving Wolf to guard them, and went inside his room, closing the door behind him.

Burke stripped off his clothes, letting them fall on the floor. He preferred sleeping in the nude, but considering the events of today, he decided to wear a pair of jogging pants for pajamas in case of an emergency.

Setting his weapon on the nightstand, within easy reach, he crawled into bed. But sleep wouldn't come. The cool touch of the sheets against his chest reminded him of the silkiness of Laura's hair and the smoothness of her skin. He'd never forget her taste and the way she'd felt in his arms.

Annoyed with himself, he pushed her out of his mind. He had normal, healthy urges, just like any other man, but he'd never found it this difficult to keep anyone out of his thoughts, particularly a woman he'd just met.

Of course, he'd known from the moment he'd kissed her that things would be different with Laura. This case would test him, but the real danger would have little to do with the men that might come after them before it was all over.

With a groan, he shifted to his side and closed his eyes. No more thoughts. Not tonight.

As he drifted off to sleep, his mind filled with vivid images of spring blossoms, a dark-haired beauty and a passion that wouldn't be denied.

Chapter Five

Burke woke up slowly, opening his eyes and listening before he moved, as always. The house was quiet. The two women were undoubtedly still sleeping. Today, he'd make it a priority to try and find out if the relative Elena had mentioned was responsible for what had happened to Laura. Maybe the incident had nothing to do with Doug.

But even if that were the case, Burke knew he'd still be honor bound to help Laura. After all, Doug had never said what he was supposed to protect her from—he'd only hired Gray Wolf to keep her safe, and that, in Burke's estimation, meant from anything that threatened her. It didn't matter to him if it was a foreign conspiracy or merely a greedy relative.

He slipped out of bed slowly, cursing mornings in general. His brain still hadn't kicked in, but checking the clock on the nightstand, he saw it was time for him to get going. He shaved and took a quick shower, then, with nothing but a towel wrapped around his middle, and using another to dry his hair, stepped out into the room.

Hearing a sound, Burke stopped in midstride and looked up. Laura was about five feet from him, and looked as if she'd been ready to place a piece of paper on his bed.

"I—I was going to leave a thank-you note—" she stammered.

Her gaze seared over him. He was sure that she had no idea what she was doing to him with that look, but his body was growing hard, something that would be impossible to hide behind a towel. "Turn around. I need to get dressed," he growled.

Laura did, but he sensed her hesitation. Male instinct told him that she'd liked what she'd seen. A smile of wicked satisfaction curved his lips.

"Don't let me rush you," she said. "I just didn't want you to get up and find us gone. We're going next door to pick some of the clutter off the floor before the workmen arrive. With the sun shining, the house will warm up on its own."

"Give me a moment. I'll walk over with you. I need more information on Doña Elena's relative."

"Take your time. I can wait in the living room."

"No need. You can turn around now."

Burke had his jeans on, but he was still bare chested. He'd done it on purpose, wanting to see that luscious, hungry look on her face again.

He was rewarded when her eyes widened slightly and her lips parted. But then, in a flash, she was suddenly very interested in the ceiling, then the window. As he saw her struggling to discipline her thoughts, he wondered if she would have better luck than he'd had. There was definitely strong chemistry conspiring against both of them.

"Was that a tattoo?" she asked.

"Where?" He knew perfectly well that she'd seen the wolf tattoo on the inside of his forearm, a place normally concealed by the large black wristwatch all Gray Wolf operatives wore, but he couldn't resist baiting her. "You caught me just out of the shower and I want to make sure we're talking about the same thing."

"On your arm," she said, her cheeks turning red and her breathing a little unsteady.

Burke laughed. "Easy. I was just giving you a hard time." He slipped a sweater over his head. "All Gray Wolf operatives have this tattoo," he said, showing it to her. "It's to help us recognize each other in an emergency situation."

"Wouldn't you recognize each other as co-workers, anyway?"

He shook his head as he reached for his watch. "The identities of all the agency's operatives are closely guarded, and I'm the only one without a code name, being their supervisor. It insures our safety. We work solo, but if any of us was ever in an undercover situation where we had to request agency backup, the tattoo would help us recognize an ally instantly."

Unable to resist, she reached out to touch it before he could slip the watch over it. "It fits you…somehow," she said, her voice low.

Her fingertips brushed lightly over his skin. Her touch was like velvet, but it left a trail of fire in its wake. Seeing her here in his room was almost too much of a temptation. He drew his arm back and quickly slipped his wristwatch on.

"Okay, let's go." Burke pulled on a pair of boots, then walked to the door.

"But you haven't even had breakfast yet," Laura protested as they walked down the hall.

"That's okay. I generally don't eat breakfast," he said, knowing full well that he *always* did. He'd known hunger as a kid, and as an adult he seldom missed a meal. It was a matter of pride to him that he'd never gone hungry since leaving home.

Elena came out of the kitchen. "Good morning. I hope we didn't wake you up."

"No, not at all." Burke smiled.

"He's going to come over with us. He needs to ask you some more questions," Laura said.

"He can't go to work without eating first," Elena said firmly. "At least some eggs and toast," she added, immediately searching the kitchen for what she needed.

"You don't have to do that."

"Sit," Elena said firmly.

Both Wolf and Burke immediately sat down. Burke grinned, noting that Laura, too, had taken a seat.

"You might as well resign yourself to the fact that you're going to have breakfast," Laura said softly. "It'll be easier than trying to argue with her, and eventually losing, anyway," she added with a gentle smile.

It was a great breakfast. While Laura was making calls to arrange for the repairmen, Elena made a delicious omelette using some eggs, leftover potatoes and bits of cheese. There was also toast and fresh coffee. Although Elena wouldn't allow him to bring up "unpleasant" topics during the meal, Burke found it a small sacrifice to pay.

Wolf looked so hungry, despite the full dish of kibbles at the bottom of his automatic food dispenser, that Elena scrambled an egg for him and placed it in his dish. The women, who'd already eaten, drank a second cup of coffee, keeping Burke company while he ate.

"This was a wonderful breakfast, thank you," Burke said at last.

"Now you'll have the energy you need for a morning's work," Elena said, satisfied.

Cleaning up became a group effort. He had never been in a family situation like this. The whole atmosphere in his kitchen changed. There was laughter and companionship—the very things he'd seen with television families but had never experienced. All his life, especially after what had happened with Hoops, Burke had told himself that this warmth and sense of togetherness was not something he either wanted or needed. But seeing it firsthand tugged at his emotions.

Before he could analyze it further, Laura and Elena started scuffling over which of them would give Wolf the last piece of toast. Their playfulness with each other made him laugh, especially after watching Wolf cock his head, trying to figure out what the strange humans were doing.

When the phone rang, Burke picked it up, still laughing as Laura and Elena chased each other around the kitchen table.

Laughter was a stranger to Burke, and he wasn't aware of what he was doing until he heard Handler's electronically altered voice on the other end. Quickly, he shifted back to a business mind-set.

Cordless phone in hand, Burke walked into the hall, instantly serious again.

"Any news on Begay?" Handler asked.

"No, not as of last night." He continued down the hall to his office, and checked e-mail on his computer as they spoke.

"The subject, Laura Santos—will she be staying in your house long?"

"For another night, perhaps two. The repairs in her house will take some time, especially if the furnace needs to be replaced."

There was a pause. "I'm worried this arrangement might have a detrimental effect on our case. You seem...to enjoy her company."

Burke thought of denying it, but then realized it was probably a futile gesture. Handler picked up on nuances most people missed.

"It can be dangerous for both of you if you get too friendly with the woman you're assigned to protect," Handler added.

"I agree," Burke said. "But there's a matter of maintaining cover, too. Our client didn't specify if we were to tell the subject he hired us to protect, so, for now, I haven't said anything. I'm strictly undercover on this one.''

"All right. Follow your instincts. But until you know what you're fighting, stay on your guard.''

"That's what I intend to do.''

Burke hung up, staring at the computer monitor pensively. There was still no e-mail from Doug. With every passing day Burke became even more convinced that his old friend was in serious trouble. Fear for Doug's safety touched the edges of his mind, pressing in on him, but he pushed it back, keeping it at bay. Fear could paralyze or energize, depending on how he channeled it.

Years ago, when he'd lived day to day, never knowing if there'd be enough food for the next meal or a warm place for himself and his brother to sleep, fear and uncertainty had been his constant companions. Yet that shadow over his spirit had often compelled him to do more than he thought possible, and, eventually, he'd begun to realize that fear could be a friend and an ally.

As an adult, he'd learned that fear had another advantage. It gave life a delicious edge. These days he welcomed it, along with all the challenges and excitement of his work.

His lifestyle suited him perfectly. He was a free spirit, far removed from anything even remotely domestic, or the urge to settle down. Yet this morning he'd sat down to a family style breakfast and, instead of being bored into a coma, he'd actually *enjoyed* it. What the hell was happening to him?

Disgusted with himself, he went back down the hall to the kitchen to join the women, grabbing his jacket along with way.

"Are you ready?" Laura said, seeing him enter the room.

He nodded. "Let's go.''

Wolf accompanied the three of them as they walked next door.

As they went inside, Laura's expression turned grim. "Maybe we should have all this stuff hauled away and just start over again," she said, half-seriously.

"Absolutely not," Elena said firmly. "We'll get down to work and have everything back to normal as soon as possible."

Burke watched Laura as she showed the repairmen who began arriving what needed to be done. Her jeans and smooth-fitting cream sweater accentuated the gentle curves of her body. She was petite, barely five foot one, made to please a man who would know how to be gentle with her. Experience told him a large man would have to be careful not to hurt her in bed. The vivid image that formed in his mind had his brain reaching meltdown.

He cursed himself silently. He had a job to do. Laura was part of a case and that's all she'd ever be to him.

"Elena will be free in a minute," she told him, looking back toward the kitchen, where her godmother was busy using the phone. Elena wanted a carved, solid wood door for the back, and had to find a shop that would work to her specifications. "She'll answer your questions then."

Burke's thoughts centered on business. On this ground he was sure of himself and what he had to do. "I'd like to pay a visit to the man your godmother mentioned—I believe she said his name was Al."

"Yes, that's him," Laura answered with a nod. "But I should warn you, Al Baca is a strange bird."

Before she could say more, the contractor selected to work on the furnace problem arrived. Laura made sure he knew what was expected of him, then rejoined Burke.

Elena had finished in the kitchen by then, and was sitting at the breakfast bar, which divided the kitchen area from the living room. While Burke gathered the information he needed, Laura began picking up debris off the floor. Wolf remained with them, lying on the tile at the edge of the kitchen area, his ears up and his expression alert.

"I'm going to start by looking into why your home was targeted," Burke said. "I'd like to begin by questioning your brother-in-law, but first I'm going to need his address."

"He won't talk to you," Elena said flatly.

"But he might, if I go with him," Laura said. "Well, let me qualify that—I can get you in the door," she told Burke. "What happens after that is anyone's guess."

Burke considered it for a moment, then nodded. He had no legal jurisdiction, so having Laura there would be an asset. Though Baca might turn out to be trouble, Burke was more than capable of protecting her.

Doña Elena wrote down the address, and Burke paid close attention to the directions, because it was a rural area with few signs.

"All right," he said, standing up again. "Let me go have a talk with him. If he's responsible in any way for what happened here, I'll know. I'm good at finding the truth."

"I'd call ahead for you, but his phone service was switched off when he didn't pay his bills," Doña Elena said.

"It's just as well," he answered. "I don't like to give people advance warning."

Laura gave her godmother a kiss on the cheek. "I won't be gone long. Don't overdo any cleaning while I'm gone. I called a housekeeping service, and they can put away things while you supervise. You might want to start in your own bedroom."

Elena met Burke's gaze and held it. "Take care of my Laura. My brother-in-law is not the most pleasant of men."

"I will. You have my word on that, Doña Elena," Burke

said, signaling for Wolf to stay with Laura as they reached the door.

Laura smiled, thinking that Burke had humored Elena with his right-out-of-medieval-times style of chivalry. But as she glanced at his face, she realized he'd meant every word. More curious than ever about him, she found herself glad for the chance to be alone with him in a relatively safe situation.

"I need to make a call, then get my car," he said. "I'll be right back."

"You're not taking the motorcycle?"

He smiled. "When I'm working a case, I have to take Wolf with me, and that means using the agency car." Seeing the disappointment on her face, he added, "The chopper's fun. When I'm not working, I'll take you for a ride to one of my favorite haunts. I think you'll like it."

"Deal."

As he strode off, Burke wondered about his sanity. Just because she'd looked disappointed was no reason for him to throw common sense out the window and invite her for a ride. Sharing a seat on the bike with her would be pleasant, but hardly a good idea. He visualized her riding behind him, her body pressed against his, her hands around his waist—then suddenly cursed. If he kept this up, the heat would damage his brain.

Burke called Handler on the cell phone and filled him in as he pulled the agency car—a gray SUV—out of the garage and drove next door to Laura's.

"I'll be very curious to see what you find out," Handler said. "Just make sure the woman remains safe."

"Affirmative."

Burke's thoughts drifted back to the time he'd failed to protect someone in his charge—an innocent who hadn't had a chance. The blood spilled on that afternoon so long ago had left a permanent shadow on his soul. He'd never failed since then and he fully intended to keep that record intact.

As he pulled into her driveway, Laura and Wolf were waiting outside. Burke reached over and opened the passenger door, and Wolf immediately jumped in. The dog rode shotgun. It was his favorite spot.

Burke groaned, but Laura laughed. "Okay. I guess I'm supposed to sit in the back," she said, and opened the door.

"No, wait," Burke said. "Wolf, back seat!" Burke expected a protest, but Wolf looked at Laura, then, with a sigh, turned and leaped onto the back seat.

Laura shut the back door, then joined Burke in the front. "He was a pretty good sport about it," she said laughing.

"He's not always like that," Burke said.

"I guess he likes me." She smiled.

"Yes, I think he does."

As they got under way, Laura glanced over at him. "Do you like being a P.I.?"

"The job suits me. Police work would have had too many rules and requirements." He paused, then added, "Do you like your work?"

"Very much. In a way, you can say that I spend most of my day charting the road to places that have never been. My readers give me their time and, in return, I spin dreams for them."

"I've never been much of a dreamer," Burke said. He'd seen too much of life—the bleak side that most people never even knew existed—and all he'd ever had were bad dreams, the kind that usually sent Navajos to their medicine men for protection from bad influences or foretold events. He no longer had the power, or the inclination, to believe in dreams of happiness and the promise of a love that endured. Yet, as he glanced at Laura, he felt himself being drawn by her innocence. She was like a breath of fresh air to him.

"My imagination has always been my constant companion," Laura said. "When things got really rough after my mom got sick, I was often lost in daydreams, where I could be anyone and go anywhere."

And that same imagination would make it hard for any man to measure up to her standards, Burke thought to himself. How could anyone meet impossible ideals?

Laura shifted sideways so she could pet Wolf, who'd stuck his head between the seats. "I was really worried about Elena last night, but I think she's going to be fine. Getting things organized and making sure jobs are done is what she does best."

"You two seem really close."

"We are. She's always been there for me. Asking her to move in with me after her husband passed away was the most natural thing in the world."

"For someone used to working at home and living alone, the transition must have been difficult."

"Not at all. She's family," Laura said, her voice firm.

Burke nodded thoughtfully. Laura had the kind of courage that would always compel her to do what was right. He admired that. But what drew him to her went even deeper. It was the way her gentle heart reached out to others who needed her, and the loyalty she showed those she loved. Laura had an innocence of spirit that warmed him like a ray of sunshine, and it was all packaged up in a body that could tempt any man who was still breathing.

"You have a beautiful home," she said, interrupting his thoughts, "but I noticed that there aren't any photos of your friends or family around. Do you keep all that stuff in an album?" she asked.

"There are no photos because there's no one special in my life," he answered simply. Then, making a spur-of-the-moment decision, he decided to show her Doug's picture. "There is one photo I've kept. It dates back a ways, but it's of an old buddy of mine. It was taken right after we completed basic training. Douglas Begay and I have been friends since we were kids.'' He watched her reaction to the name, but there wasn't one.

Burke reached into his back pocket and, as he drove, pulled out his wallet and handed it to her.

She took out the photograph, treating it carefully, as if she sensed how special it was to him. ''And you've remained friends throughout the years?''

He nodded. ''Ours is the kind of friendship that stays the course.''

She nodded, then slipped the photo inside his wallet again and handed it back to him. ''I carry one of Elena,'' she answered.

He slipped the wallet into his jacket pocket for now. If she knew or recognized Doug, she'd hidden it well. There had been no trace of recognition on her features, only curiosity.

Silence stretched between them. Finally Laura spoke, her tone somber. ''I've been thinking a lot about everything that has been happening to me, Burke, and I want you to know that I intend to take an active part in finding out what's going on. It's me they're after, and I'm not going to sit idly by while some crazy person turns my life upside down.''

Burke studied her expression. This was going to be a problem, but it didn't need to be handled right now. ''We can talk about this later. Right now I'd like you to tell me whatever you can about the man we're going to see.''

''In all honesty, I don't know him very well. I usually do my best to avoid him.''

''Have you been to his house?''

''No. He doesn't like to have visitors.''

After traveling down the main highway, then along several graveled back roads between newly plowed fields, they arrived. Doña Elena's brother-in-law lived in an old, unfinished stucco farmhouse at one end of a dried-up field close to the river. A few gray, dead apple trees lined an irrigation ditch on the side closest to the river.

"I understand that he rents this place for a song and that's why he lives here," Laura said. "But, geez, it's pretty bleak to live on a run-down farm full of weeds and dead trees. You'd think he'd at least plant some alfalfa and cut down the trees for firewood."

As they walked from the end of the dirt driveway to the rickety-looking front porch, they noted that the front door was open about a foot and the tattered screen door was swinging back and forth in the breeze.

"His car's not here," Laura said. "I don't think he's home, but it's odd that someone who supposedly hates visitors would leave the door open like that."

"I'm going to take a look around." Burke glanced at the dog by his side. "Wolf, guard," he said, then looked up at Laura. "He'll take care of you."

"I'm not staying behind. If Al's around and sees you peering in a window, he'll go nuts. I'm staying with you."

"Okay. But stay behind me."

Burke stepped up onto the porch, Wolf by his side, and knocked on the door, while Laura tried to see through the thin curtains at the window. The door swung open a bit more from the force of Burke's knocking, but not far enough for him to see inside the darkened room. He gave the door another nudge, and when nothing happened, took a step forward. "Hello?"

"Stop!" Laura grabbed at his jacket and yanked him back.

"What's wrong?" Burke asked, looking over at her, and signaling Wolf to stay.

"I just saw what's inside through a gap in the curtain," she answered, then pushed the door open carefully. Light filtered into the darkened room, revealing a large, bow-shaped mechanism on the floor, right in the path of anyone coming through the front door.

Burke's blood ran cold as he saw the gleaming metallic teeth of a steel bear trap waiting for any unsuspecting intruder. It was cocked and ready, the jaws showing evidence of recent filing to sharpen the points. His leg would have been sliced all the way to the bone, and maybe broken, as well. He would have bled to death in minutes. "Good call, Laura, thanks."

"Teamwork," she answered, her voice wavering slightly as she stared down at the cruel device. "You see? You need me. I can always look at things from a slightly different angle," she said with a tiny smile.

"I'm not big on partnerships, except with the dog." This was the last thing he needed—an amateur sleuth who would tag along everywhere, telling him what to do. "Don't let one lucky call go to your head."

"I've already made up my mind. You're going to need me to give you information and help point your investigation in the right direction. I need your expertise and protection. It's a give and take situation."

Burke clenched his jaw. Handler would love this. All in all, this was turning out to be a very bad day—and it wasn't even lunchtime yet.

Chapter Six

Burke glanced down at Wolf and saw the dog had that panting grin that always made Burke suspect the animal knew far more than anyone realized. Though he couldn't be sure, gut instinct told him that Wolf's intelligence far surpassed what most people would have willingly conceded to an animal.

Burke looked at Laura, then around the front yard. "Stay here with Wolf. I'm going to get a piece of firewood and spring that trap. If a curious neighbor decided to go in, especially a child, they could sever their leg and die within minutes."

"I can't imagine anyone just wandering in around here. It's pretty isolated. The closest home is what, two miles away?" she asked, pointing. "And I'm not even sure that's a house. It could be a barn."

"Yeah, all that's true, but this is still an accident waiting to happen."

"You'll get no argument from me there."

Burke picked up a piece of firewood from the stack near the side of the house, then tossed it onto the bear trap. The deadly jaws of the metal monster snapped the four-inch piñon log in two like a matchstick.

"A man who leaves something like that lying around isn't playing with a full deck—either that, or he's made some deadly enemies,'' Burke said, joining Laura and Wolf once again.

"Both, possibly,'' Laura answered. "Al is so annoying he's bound to make enemies by the minute. I'm sure he's got plenty of people who'd love to punch his lights out.'' She paused, then added, "Me included.''

Laura stepped away from the house, looked around carefully, then decided it was safe to sit down on the trunk of a fallen tree. "So now what? Do we wait until he comes home?''

"If he doesn't show up in twenty minutes, we'll leave. But don't sit there.''

She stood up quickly and glanced down. "Why? Is something crawling on it? Is it another trap?''

He shook his head. "That tree looks like it was hit by lightning at one time. The *Dineh,* the Navajo People, believe it's bad luck to touch anything struck by lightning unless you're a medicine man and properly prepared.''

Laura moved away out of respect for his cultural beliefs, and he gave her a grateful nod. At least she hadn't argued with him, or just shrugged it off as superstition. It was funny how often people were willing to label someone else's religious beliefs as superstitious, while taking giant leaps of faith with their own.

Unwilling to dismiss the cold prickly feeling at the back of his neck, he studied everything around them carefully. "We're being watched. All I've got is a gut feeling, but I'm going to check it out. Walk back to the car. I'm going to take Wolf with me and check out the thicket beyond those pines.''

"If Al is the one out there, you'll need an extra set of eyes, and me to run interference. He won't hurt me, or even risk hurting me—not as long as he wants something from Elena.''

Burke was tempted to throw Laura over his shoulder,

carry her back to the car and lock her inside, but he was nearly certain Handler wouldn't approve of him treating a person he was assigned to protect in that manner. Still, the idea was tempting. "If you're coming, let's go," he snapped.

He moved quietly, and to her credit, so did Laura. Burke remained focused on the dog, knowing Wolf's senses were sharper than a human's. If the dog sensed something, he'd signal Burke. Minutes passed slowly, but Wolf gave no sign that anyone was about. Still, the feeling that they were being watched persisted, and Burke had learned a long time ago never to ignore his instincts.

"Let's go back. It's time to leave," he said firmly.

"Did you spot someone?" she asked, her voice a whisper.

"No, but there are too many places for him to hide out there. That puts us at a disadvantage, and I don't want either of us to end up dead." He put it bluntly, hoping to startle her into backing off a bit.

"As long as you're with me, I don't think either of us is really in mortal danger," she said.

He stopped in midstride and looked at her. Was she actually telling him he could rely on *her* to protect *him?* Irritated, he began walking again. "You can be infuriating at times, do you know that?"

"Right back at you," she replied.

Their eyes locked and, for a gut-clenching moment, he felt the attraction between them increase to a new level. He looked away quickly. The last thing either of them needed was for him to get distracted now. The woman was a walking danger zone.

"Be quiet until we're back in the car. I have to stay focused," he said.

Her eyes flashed with annoyance but she did as he asked, and he breathed a silent sigh of relief. He kept her close beside him, knowing that she was his responsibility—whether she knew it or not. But feeling the gentle warmth from her body stirred something in him. The more he fought it, the more restless he became.

By the time they reached his sedan, his hands had clenched into fists and his body felt coiled. He would have loved a physical confrontation right now and the chance to work off that steam. But there'd be no such luck for him today.

They were underway within seconds. After they'd left the farmhouse far behind them, he finally relaxed again. She wasn't going to be easy to protect—not while she had this fool notion of helping him to do his job.

"You know what worries me most?" she asked, then, without waiting for an answer, continued. "What if the break-in has nothing to do with Al? Do you see how that opens a door to a whole bunch of other questions? I don't even know in which direction to look next."

"We'll find a lead," he said. If Laura's troubles really weren't related to Al, that meant there was another dangerous player he had yet to uncover—one with a probable connection to his friend Doug.

"Since I'm at the center of whatever's happening," she mused, "I'm going to have to give things some serious thought and see what I can come up with. Then we'll start looking into all of it together."

Somehow he managed to suppress the oath forming on his lips. "Listen, Laura, for the record, I said I'd help you. I never said that we would be partners."

She smiled slowly. "I know. Isn't it wonderful how things worked out? Now you don't have to go it alone on this case."

The look he gave her would have cut most men off at the knees, but her eyes were bright with determination and it was clear she had no intention of backing down.

Burke focused on the road, wondering how he could be so attracted to such an annoying woman. It had to be hormones. Nothing else made sense.

Doug would owe him big time for all the aggravation this case was causing him. If he ever caught up to his buddy, he'd collect, even if he had to take it out of his hide.

IT WAS CLOSE TO TWO in the afternoon when Burke saw Laura and Doña Elena leaving the house. He'd waited for this chance since Laura had told him she'd be giving a talk on the craft of writing at the senior center today.

The moment Burke saw Laura's car disappear around the corner, he signaled Wolf and walked over to her house. The front door was constantly opening and closing as workmen came and left with their tools and repair materials. Since the housekeeping crew wasn't scheduled until later today, this was the perfect chance to finish what he had to do.

As he strolled inside the house no one gave him or the dog a second glance. Most of the workmen had already seen him earlier and probably assumed he was welcome.

Burke headed for the living room, studying the partial chaos around him. Elena and Laura had already started picking up the books and placing them back on their shelves. The first thing that struck him was the multitude of foreign language paperbacks. From their covers—many with similar images, but with titles in different languages— it appeared that Laura's books had been translated widely.

Curious, he flipped through one of the English editions. He'd never read a romance novel in his life, but for her, maybe he'd make an exception. If he bought a copy at the store, and brought it back to her to sign, he could then tactfully point out that she was the writer and he was the P.I.

Though the idea was a sound one, he knew in his gut she'd ignore him and continue to try to investigate. It was obvious to him now that it was her nature to be irritating when she was after something.

He admired tenacity, but not in women who weren't in the business. Why was it so difficult for her to let him just do his job? He would never try to tell her how to write. Why couldn't she be reasonable about this?

Burke began to sort through the next stack and almost immediately spotted a book with an imprint he recognized. On the spine was the inverted triangle with a star in the middle he'd seen on Doug's stationery. Two years ago, when Doug had first gotten the job, he'd written an honest-to-gosh letter on real stationery and sent Burke a bunch of business cards along with it. It had been his way of ribbing Burke, who usually didn't carry business cards because of the secrecy that surrounded Gray Wolf Investigations.

Burke took the book in his hands, verified that it was the logo of a publishing house in West Medias, then, carrying the book, went to the sofa and sat down. He couldn't read a word of Rumanian, so his attempt to leaf through it was totally unproductive.

He considered what he'd found. The West Median government was a military dictatorship. Everything was censored, particularly books, to fit the controlling regime's philosophy. The link to Doug's company was interesting, but hardly remarkable. Looking up at the shelves, Burke saw at least four more books from the same West Median publisher, with different titles. What had at first seemed a possible clue now faded into nothing more than a coincidence.

Then he felt someone approaching and stood up. He wasn't sure how he'd felt her presence so clearly even before looking, but before he turned his head, he knew it was Laura.

"Hi. I thought you wouldn't be back till later," he said.

"I come back unexpectedly, find you going through my stuff, and that's all you have to say?" She saw the book in his hands. "Don't tell me you were looking for reading material to bone up your foreign language skills."

"Are you kidding? I only speak three languages—Navajo, English and good-ole-boy."

Suddenly a loud, annoying electronic buzzer went off. Wolf jumped to his feet, his ears pricked forward, his lips curling in a snarl as men, some of them grumbling under their breath, walked past him, heading for the front door.

"What's going on?" Laura asked one man.

"You need to get out of here. The second I installed the carbon monoxide detector, it went off. If you stay inside, it could make you sick, or worse."

"Didn't you check the gas heater?" Burke asked as he headed to the door, Laura beside him and Wolf trailing behind.

"That's not my job," the man answered. "One of the guys had a wrench with him and shut off the gas, but we still need to clear out until the carbon monoxide level drops."

Burke moved ahead of Laura, shielding her as they stepped outside, and leaving the door open behind them to vent the house. Her enemies were playing a deadly game. He had to find answers before it was too late.

HAVING CALLED the furnace installer from Burke's house, Laura now stood outside along with the four workmen, anger coiling inside her. Someone was doing his best to turn her life upside down, and it was high time she started to fight back, and fight back hard.

As she watched Burke questioning the men, she remembered how she'd found him searching through her books. An ally with secrets wasn't an ally she could trust or rely on wholeheartedly.

What bothered her most was that she probably wouldn't have ever known what he'd been doing if she hadn't returned unexpectedly, because the auditorium at the center had required some emergency plumbing repairs. At least Elena had remained behind to speak with friends, and hadn't been around to see Burke's behavior for herself.

Tension made Laura's body ache. She hated having her life spin out of control like this. As a writer, she already had more than her share of insecurities to deal with. She could pour her heart out in the pages of her books, but there were never any guarantees the readers would like what she wrote. It often made for sleepless nights right before a book was scheduled to hit the stands. She put herself on the line every time a new title came out. Uncertainty was as much a part of what she did for a living as was owning a computer. Her way of compensating for all the self-doubts that came with creative work was to keep things at home running on an even keel. But now, all that was vanishing before her eyes, and there seemed to be little she could do to put a quick stop to it.

Laura swallowed and gathered her courage. Answers needed to be found and she'd never get anywhere standing here. She'd just decided to join Burke and help him question the other men when a white van with the furnace installer's red logo pulled up. A man stepped out of the vehicle and strode toward her house, carrying some kind of instrument she supposed ''sniffed'' the air for carbon monoxide.

Laura caught up to him, then followed him to the furnace in the hall compartment. ''This heater is brand-new. How could it be leaking already?'' she asked.

He shook his head and wrote some notes on the paper fastened to his clipboard. ''Ma'am, when I left two hours ago, this unit was properly installed and adjusted, and worked perfectly. I'm very careful at my job. Someone must have tampered with the air balance after I left. The adjustment is way off. That's why the burners were giving off a lot of carbon monoxide.''

''Just how bad was the carbon monoxide leak?'' she asked, amazed that her voice sounded so steady.

He paused, considering his words carefully. ''Providing you're in good health, it would have made you sick, but the carbon monoxide might not have killed you for several days. It's a different story when it comes to children or an older person, like the woman I saw here this morning. It might have killed her by morning, if she'd spent the night here. Elderly people are more…fragile.''

Laura felt her legs turn rubbery. She took a step back, intending to lean against the wall, but she suddenly collided against a rock-hard chest.

''Easy,'' Burke said gently, his hands coming to rest on her shoulders as he steadied her.

The warmth of his touch eased the icy chill that had spread all through her.

Burke began talking to the technician, his voice crisp and businesslike. ''Tell me, the arson investigator who was here earlier—do you know him?''

''Sure. His name is Springer. We've dealt with him off and on the past few years. Back at the shop today, he asked me a lot of questions about the furnace.''

''What kind of questions?''

Burke's tenacity seemed unshakable as he pressed the man for answers. He was supremely confident as an investigator, and every word he uttered, and even his intonation, attested to the fact that he knew exactly what he was doing. For a moment, Laura found herself wondering if he would also be that self-assured in bed. Would he be a patient lover, or wildly passionate and demanding?

As the installer moved away, Burke leaned down to

speak softly in her ear. "Are you all right? I felt you shiver."

Her thoughts had betrayed her. Embarrassed, but determined to cover it up, she moved away and forced her thoughts back to the business at hand.

"Whoever messed with my furnace gambled with Elena's life. The thought of losing her... That scares me more than I can possibly tell you. Coming after me is one thing—I'll fight back. But Elena...she doesn't deserve any of this."

"Maybe you two should go away for a while," Burke suggested. "In the meantime, I'll keep looking into things here for you—"

"No way I'm letting this creep run me out of my own home. And though I'll certainly ask her, I doubt Elena will agree to leave, either. She doesn't like bullies, and giving in to one would be unthinkable to her."

"All right. In that case, I better get down to work. I want to check with all the workmen here and find out if they saw anyone messing around the furnace—besides the installer, of course."

"I'll help you," she said.

Most of the work crew had been too busy to notice much of anything except their own tasks, but an elderly man, one of the carpenters repairing some holes poked in the wallboard by overturned furniture, approached Laura while Burke went to question two men taking a break outside.

"I heard you asking questions about the furnace," he said tentatively, "and I may be able to help you. A guy came in earlier today, but it wasn't Artie, the man who'd done the installation for you. I assumed it was a gas inspector, but in retrospect, I guess I should have checked. I'm sorry."

"That's all right. You couldn't have known," Laura answered. Seeing Burke coming up, she filled him in.

"Can you tell me what the man looked like?" Burke asked.

The carpenter considered for a moment, then nodded. "He had a dark blue baseball cap and glasses—the kind aviators wear, with the thin rims. He had a thick, black mustache, too. I also seem to recall that he was wearing a light blue service shirt, and that it had some kind of company logo on it—but I can't remember what it looked like. I wasn't paying close enough attention."

"You did just fine. Thanks so much for your help," Laura said.

As he walked away, she looked at Burke. "I don't remember seeing anyone who fits that description. Do you?"

"The cap, dark glasses and the mustache...I have a feeling it was all part of a disguise. People would notice that instead of him. He came in wearing a standard uniform and easily passed himself off as a workman."

"It's just so...planned. I don't get it. Why is someone doing this to me?"

"Let's go back to my place," Burke said, cocking his head toward the door. "We need to talk someplace where we can have some privacy."

"Okay." She had a feeling he wanted to ask her more about Ken. Burke was probably wondering if there was something more she hadn't told him. But the truth was she hadn't kept anything from him. He was the one who was keeping secrets. She still wanted to know exactly why he'd been looking through her books. "You're right about one thing. It's time we laid our cards on the table."

She saw the flicker of wariness that crossed his features, but he remained quiet as they walked down the sidewalk to his home.

As soon as they were alone in his living room, he gestured to the couch, silently inviting her to take a seat. "First, I want you to know that I *will* catch whoever is doing this. But I'm going to need you to be brutally honest. Is there something you haven't told me about Ken Springer?''

''No, there isn't.'' She paused, then continued. ''He told me on our second and last date that he never gives up on what he wants. I didn't realize at the time what a curse that would become.''

''Think hard about this before you answer,'' Burke said. ''Is there any chance he may have joined forces with Al Baca?''

She gave him a startled look. ''I really doubt it. As far as I know, they've never met.'' As she held his gaze, sexual awareness seeped into her mind with the gentleness of a lover's touch.

She looked away quickly. ''You're on the wrong track, Burke. There's something else going on here. And unless I miss my guess, you know a lot more than you're saying. Maybe you'd like to start by telling me what you were doing in my home, looking through my books.''

Burke considered his answer carefully before replying. ''I could lie to you, Laura, but I won't. I think you deserve to know the entire truth. But be prepared. This case is a lot more complex than I've led you to believe.''

Chapter Seven

Silence stretched between them for a long time as he gathered his thoughts.

"I've been hired to protect you," he said at last.

For a moment all she could do was stare at him. "I don't understand. Who hired you? And please don't tell me it was Ken. If it is, I think I'm about to sock you in the nose."

"No, not him." Burke took a deep breath, then began to explain, giving her the highlights. When he finished, he studied Laura's expression as she tried to take it all in. She was scared, but she was also angry. "The reason I'm telling you this now is because you need to know exactly what you're up against and that this is no time for you to try your skills as an amateur sleuth. This is a bad business, Laura."

"This friend of yours—Douglas Begay—he's the reason you were searching my books when I wasn't there?"

Intelligence and curiosity sparkled in Laura's eyes. Burke had a feeling she'd throw herself even deeper into the case now. Suddenly he had another startling realization: as annoying as it could be, he really liked that fire in her, the spirit that compelled her to keep trying until things were right again.

Oh, yeah. He was losing it. He forced himself to focus,

and using his best no-nonsense, professional tone of voice, continued speaking.

"Doug Begay works in publishing. The reason I was looking through your books was because I was trying to find a professional connection between you two. Are you sure you've never met him? He used to live in this area. Would you like another look at his photo?"

She shook her head. "That's not necessary. I don't know him—professionally or personally. Why don't you just call him right now and ask him why he hired you to protect me?"

"It's not that simple," he said, explaining Doug's situation as best he could.

It was tougher than Burke had ever imagined, seeing her trust in him falling apart. But he didn't have any other choice. "I didn't just happen to move in next door. The agency leased the house to help with the case," he said at last.

As silence stretched between them, he didn't press her to tell him what she was thinking. He didn't have to. It was etched on her face.

Hearing his cell phone ring, and knowing it would be Handler, Burke excused himself and stepped into the next room. It was time to fill him in on the latest events.

AS HE LEFT THE ROOM, Laura remained where she was. She'd thought she could handle whatever Burke told her— that nothing could be as bad as having secrets between them. But she'd been wrong. She felt sick inside. Facing an unpleasant truth always hurt, but this cut deep enough to reach her heart. She'd let her feelings—and her fantasies—run away with her. Although she'd told herself to fight the attraction between them, she'd lowered her guard. Now she felt like a fool.

People—women—probably came in and out of Burke's

life constantly, all part of the cases he worked. The bottom line was that she'd simply been part of a job he'd been hired to do.

Angry with herself, she paced around the room. Burke had never really been interested in her. She had to accept that.

She gazed down at Wolf, who lay on the floor watching her. "At least you didn't lie to me."

"I never lied to you, either," Burke said, coming back into the room. "I just didn't tell you everything."

"Your intent was deception." Her answer struck him with the force of a blow, and she felt some satisfaction when she saw him wince.

"Remember that, when I first met you, there really wasn't much point in making what you were facing a lot worse with speculation—and that was all I had," Burke said. "Even now I don't know what's going on—except that you're in danger."

"That doesn't cut it for me. You still deliberately misrepresented yourself." She really couldn't stand the thought that she'd been so nutty about a man who saw her as nothing more than part of his job. It was too humbling, and humility wasn't a virtue she wanted to acquire.

"I did what I had to do," he said flatly.

"All right," she replied, her voice cold and businesslike. "We'll work together because we both have a common interest. You want to solve your case and then move on, and I want you to find answers so I can get back to my life."

"In the meantime, we can also be friends," he said.

His voice was a deep rumble that reached all the way to her bones. There was a raw maleness about Burke that would excite any woman on earth. Laura pushed the thought back. She'd never lower her guard around him again. She learned from her mistakes.

"Friendship isn't something available upon request or on demand. It develops because of a deep-seated trust between people—and, under the circumstances, there's no chance of that ever happening." She paused as she looked around. "Of course Elena and I will be moving out of your house as soon as possible."

"It would be a mistake for you two to leave. This is the safest place for you both to stay," he said, his voice as level as his gaze. "With Wolf and me on the job *no one* will harm you."

She shook her head. "I wasn't quite sure of you before, Burke, but I'm even less sure of you now."

"You're angry and I understand that, but listen to your instincts," he said. "Deep down you know you can trust me to look out for you."

She *wanted* to trust him, and that's what scared her the most. "I'm sorry, Burke. I just don't feel comfortable around you anymore."

"What's between us has nothing to do with comfort."

Those eyes. They sparked with a fire that touched her soul. He stirred many emotions inside her, but he was right—there was nothing comforting about any of them.

"We'll talk about this later," Laura said, reminding herself sternly that his real interest was the case, not her. Because of that, her attraction to him was, at best, misguided. "The book you were looking at with the West Median publisher's imprint is only one of many foreign copies I've received, and there are at least four others from West Medias, if I remember correctly. I just don't keep track of them anymore. But as far as the case goes, if you think someone's after one of my romance novels, you're really heading down the wrong track."

"Why?"

"People can buy those easily enough," she answered with a shrug. "The only ones that might be of any great value are ones I've written that haven't been published yet. But copies of those are already with my editor, so if one of my novels were to show up with someone else's name on the cover, my publisher's lawyers would be all over their case. And as far as first editions for collectors—mine aren't worth much more than the cover price.''

She paused for a moment. ''But there *is* something else we might consider. Do you think it's possible that your pal Doug decided to try and pair up his bachelor friend with a romance novelist and concocted the whole thing? Does he have a quirky sense of humor?''

''He wouldn't have made the situation sound so dire if it was all part of a joke. Doug is one of the most direct people I know. If he wanted to set me up, he'd be as subtle as a brick. There's more to what's going on, Laura. I feel it in my gut, and my instincts seldom prove to be wrong.''

''Okay, but let's reason this out. If he thought I was in immediate danger, Doug would have probably contacted the police, or asked you straight out to do it for him. Since he didn't, I think it's safe to assume that he *feared* something might happen, but wasn't sure it would. What he was actually doing by hiring Gray Wolf was taking precautions.''

There was admiration in Burke's eyes as he considered her supposition. ''That's a logical argument.''

''Don't sound so surprised. I write books, remember? I'm used to dealing with logical progressions.''

''But you don't write mysteries or thrillers.''

''And romances don't count?''

''I just don't think logic and love have anything to do with each other,'' he said.

''No, they don't,'' she conceded with a wry smile. ''But events in a novel have to make sense. That requires logic.''

''Then you have my respect. It must take a ton of skill to write about an emotion that never makes the slightest bit of sense—and in most cases is just plain crazy—in a way where it actually seems like a rational move between two adults.''

Laura looked at him for a moment, understanding something for the first time. ''You don't believe in romantic love, do you?''

He hesitated before answering. ''I've never been in love, not unless you include the crush I had on Mary Ann McAllister in the fourth grade. And I generally don't believe in anything I can't touch or feel.''

His answer saddened her, though it shouldn't have. There was nothing between them—and this just proved it. ''You're missing out on a lot, Burke.''

''I don't think so. There's a world of comfort in things that can be touched, and felt,'' he said, his voice low and seductive.

''Oh, please. I thought you were a few levels above the Neanderthal me want woman type.''

''No guy is above that.''

''Ugh. That's discouraging news for a romance writer. Let's get back to business.'' She took a deep breath and looked away, trying to force herself not to respond to that devastating smile of his.

Hearing a vehicle pulling up, Wolf went to the window and, parting the curtains with his snout, looked outside.

Catching a glimpse of the senior center's van, Laura stood up. ''There's Elena now. I better go talk to her. I don't want her to learn what happened to the new furnace from one of the workmen.''

Burke and Wolf stayed with her as she headed across Burke's front yard.

''Elena,'' she called out. Laura hurried forward, stopping her before she could go inside.

The minute Elena turned to face her and Laura saw the

pallor on her face, she knew something had happened to her godmother. "Are you all right?"

Elena nodded. "It's that new driver, Michael Enesco. He's so hard to take at times."

"What happened?" Laura asked quickly.

"First of all, he drives like one of those big-city cabbies. He scares most of us half to death with his sharp turns and the way he comes right up behind other cars, then slams on the brakes!" She shook her head. "Mrs. Kline very nearly lost her dentures!" she added in a conspiratorial whisper.

Laura tried not to laugh. "I'm sure the ride home was frightening—"

"Oh, it was far more than just his driving. He said some things that were just not right."

"Like what?" Laura pressed, worried.

"It was all so embarrassing…" Elena gazed around nervously.

Although Laura wanted to shake Elena and force her to get to the point, she knew that her godmother would have to tell her at her own pace. Glancing at Burke, she saw impatience mirrored on his face and, catching his eye, she shook her head, cautioning him not to try and rush her.

Mercifully, he understood and didn't press. A man willing to wait… That was rare. Tantalizing images teased her, and soon her imagination began racing down a path she knew could lead only to trouble.

She shifted her gaze and her attention back to Elena.

"After he'd dropped everyone else off and we were alone in the van, he told me that if I didn't stop meddling in his business, I'd be really sorry. The worst part is that he speaks very little English, so it's hard to understand him. But the way he looked at me…" She shuddered. "I tell you, it gave me goose bumps. That man is just plumb crazy."

"What was he talking about? Do you know?" Burke asked.

Elena nodded as they went inside Burke's living room and sat down. "He obviously believes that I was the one who started that gossip about him, but I would never do something like that."

"What gossip?" Burke pressed, sitting across from her in one of the easy chairs.

"People are saying that Mr. Enesco is having an affair with Nicole Maurer, the wife of the senior center's director of operations."

"I hadn't heard about that," Laura said. She glanced over at Burke, trying to figure out if he was thinking what she was—that Enesco might have had something to do with the break-in. But Burke's expression was inscrutable. She would have had more luck trying to read the rock structures at Stonehenge.

"And for some reason, he blames me for all the talk going around," Elena said, her expression bewildered. "But I've never discussed the subject with anyone.... Well, I did express my opinion to Mrs. Kline about it briefly one time. But she started the conversation. Honest."

"Enesco might have overheard you," Burke said, deciding right then to have Handler do a full background check on the man. "But try not to worry about it anymore. You're home safely now, and I'll have a talk with the driver just to make sure it doesn't happen again."

"*We'll* go talk to the driver," Laura corrected.

"It'll be easier if I go alone," Burke said flatly. "I can convince him to show some respect to a lady in a way that every man understands."

"Like volunteering to grind his face into the pavement?" Laura asked, and saw the amusement that suddenly sprang up in Burke's eyes.

Elena laughed. "All right, you two." She stood up. "I'm

going to take a shower, then I'll walk over to our home and see if there's anything I can do. The housekeeping service should arrive shortly," she said, looking at her watch.

As Elena ambled off down the hall, Laura glanced over at Burke. "I'm glad we made her laugh. She was so pale when she came home, I was—"

Suddenly there was a dull thud and a groan from the far end of the house. Instantly, Laura was on her feet, racing down the hall. Burke was right behind her. They found Elena on her knees, leaning against the wall, her breathing unsteady.

"Did you fall?" Laura asked quickly.

"No. My legs just...gave way." Her face, pale before, was now flushed.

"Burke, call an ambulance," Laura stated.

"No, absolutely not," Elena said firmly, trying to stand up, but wavering. "Call Dr. Anderson. He'll come over."

Laura looked at Burke. "Do it, please. He's in the book."

THE TIME BETWEEN Burke's phone call and the doctor's arrival was only thirty minutes, but it was the *longest* half hour of Laura's life. Now, as they waited for him to examine Elena, she paced the hall.

Seeing how worried she was, Burke instinctively tried to take her hand, but she moved away. "You don't have to face fear alone, Laura," he said quietly. "Whether you accept it or not, I *am* your friend."

"I'm not afraid," she mumbled, then was horrified when a tear spilled down her cheek. "Okay, I'm terrified," she admitted, wiping her face with her hand.

"You know she'll be all right," he said in a quiet voice.

"I don't *know* anything—not until the doctor finishes

examining her!'' she said, struggling to keep her voice low for Elena's benefit.

He brushed his knuckles over her wet cheeks. ''My people believe that the spoken word has power. She *will* be all right,'' he repeated.

''Yes,'' Laura answered, understanding. ''I'm sure she'll be fine.'' As she looked into his eyes, she felt a tug on her heart. She moved away quickly. Burke wasn't a friend. Nothing between them would last beyond the end of the case. To lean on his strength, to depend on him now would be too easy—and too heartbreaking, knowing what she did. There was nothing real between them. He was only a stranger who would soon disappear from her life.

Twenty minutes later, Dr. Anderson finally came out of Elena's room.

''Is she all right?'' Laura asked him quickly.

''She'll be fine, but she needs to take better care of herself. It seems that with all the upheaval in her life these past few days, she hasn't been taking her medication as often as she should. You'll have to make sure that she does, and that she takes it easy this coming week. I've given her a sedative, so she'll sleep for several hours. Rest is the best medicine for her now.''

After the doctor left, Laura sat down heavily on the leather couch in the den. ''It looks like we won't be moving out right away,'' she said as Burke came into the room.

''I'm sorry that Doña Elena is sick, but I'm not sorry that you're staying.''

Wolf came over and put his massive head on Laura's lap, gazing up at her with his big amber eyes. She scratched his ears and smiled. ''He's a smart animal. He seems to know when a person needs a pal.''

''He's lucky, too. People never expect him to be anything except what he is.''

Laura looked at Burke, understanding what he was telling her. "I accept what you are—a P.I. working a case. That's your priority, and rightly so. Let's not try to save a relationship that never existed."

"You don't really believe that."

Laura shook her head, then glanced over at her house through the living room window. "The housekeeping crew is finally here, and so is the furnace guy," she said, changing the subject. "He's got some tubing or flexible pipe with him. I better get over there."

"Good idea," Burke said. "By the way, I'd like to borrow those books that came from West Medias."

"Why? You can't read Rumanian."

"The agency can find someone who does. We'll also check out the publisher there, just in case."

"Take them then. I think there are five in total. Three arrived together about a month ago."

"I'll need the English originals, too."

"All right. Just take the New Zealand or Australian versions with the same titles. You can check inside, on the copyright page, where they usually put the original titles in English, and match them up that way." She paused, then added, "Someday you might want to broaden your horizons and read a romance novel yourself. It wouldn't even have to be one of mine."

"I'd like to read one of yours. But not yet," he answered.

"Why? Are you afraid you'll like it?"

He smiled, then shook his head. "I'm not ready to peer down the roads you take when you work."

"Why not? I'm seeing yours."

"You travel with your heart and I may see more—or less—than you intended me to." Burke paused. "Let's leave it at that for now."

Those eyes, and the way he looked at her, made her feel both vulnerable and wildly excited. She clamped down on her thoughts quickly. "All right. Let's go over to my place and, if I get a chance, I'll help track down the books you need."

As they went outside, her mind returned to what he'd said. She created stories from the heart, and bits and pieces of her always found their way into the pages of what she wrote. It was inevitable. From that perspective, he'd been right to decline her offer. But it bothered her to know that he'd realized how much of herself really went into the books and that he'd now be able to cut through the story and look into her heart anytime he chose.

LAURA LOST SIGHT of Burke as she continued the task of restoring order to her house. Working along with the house-keeping service, she found the job seemed to go quickly.

She'd just finished in her office and moved out into the living room when the gas company representative appeared at the front door.

Seeing her, he came over. "I'm back again, ma'am. I'm here to check out the new furnace and confirm that it's been properly installed and adjusted."

Burke came out of the kitchen and joined her as she led the man down the hall. "The new back door's in place," Burke said, "And with that big brass dead bolt, it's as solid as brick."

"Good." Hearing a vehicle pulling up outside, Laura stopped by the front window to get a look at the new arrival. Ken Springer was coming up the walkway to the house. "Will you escort this gentleman to the furnace for me, Burke?"

"No problem."

Bracing herself, Laura went to meet Ken before he came inside. "I don't want any more problems with you, Ken," she said quickly. "We've already established that what happened here has nothing to do with arson."

"Sorry, but the furnace contractor asked me to check out the installation. You've had two gas-related accidents here now." He brushed past her and stepped into the living room.

He started down the hall, then stopped and faced her. "By the way, I checked out your neighbor for you. I can't find out where he works, but he's from the reservation. You should avoid him if you can. Those people think differently than us."

"Us who? You and I don't think anything alike. Don't try to find things in common between us that don't exist."

"He's Navajo."

"No, really? And I'm Hispanic and you're Anglo. So what?" she retorted. "Now that we've had this cultural affirmation, will you leave?"

"Laura, listen to me." Ken grabbed her arm and pulled her toward him.

"Let go of me this instant." She was ready to raise her knee and watch him crumple, when she heard Burke's voice behind her.

"Do as she says." His voice was barely more than a whisper, but she'd never heard a deadlier sound. She felt a cold chill touch her spine.

Ken's gaze was fixed on Burke, but he didn't let go of her arm. "Get lost. This isn't your turf."

Burke's move was surprisingly effortless. With his gaze locked on Springer's, he took hold of Ken's index finger and unwrapped it slowly from Laura's arm, bending it back at an unnatural angle.

Ken's reaction was nearly instantaneous. He released her and stumbled back a step. His eyes had narrowed with pain, but he didn't make a sound.

Burke moved between her and Springer, his gaze never leaving his adversary.

"This isn't over, Silentman," Ken said, his voice low.

Navajo Justice

The room had grown still and Laura saw the others had stopped their work and were watching both men.

Ken glanced around at their faces, his hand bunched into a fist, but he found no allies. "We'll settle this soon—on my terms." With one last glance at Burke, then Laura, he strode past them and out of the house.

Burke watched from the front porch until Springer got back into his department vehicle and drove off. "He lost face here today. That'll eat him up inside and make him dangerous," he said softly, turning to look at Laura.

She was no match for Springer, but he was, and now it was personal. There were two things guaranteed to rile his temper—a man who mistreated kids, and a man who roughed up a woman. "But to get to you, he'll have to go through me. What happened here today will never happen again. That's a promise."

Chapter Eight

Laura walked back into the house with Burke. The workmen, who'd all come to the door or window to watch what was going on, were oddly silent as Burke came in. They nodded and gave way—partly out of respect and partly out of common sense. Burke looked as if he was itching to break someone in half.

"Ken said he'd been asked to follow up on what had happened here because I'd had two gas-related accidents. But he was right on the heels of the gas company inspector. Did you notice that?"

"Yeah, and his timing does raise some interesting questions. Let me talk to the gas man and find out if either he or his office called Springer or the fire department."

"And if they didn't?"

"Then Springer may be watching your house."

When Burke looked down at her, his eyes were bright with a fire that made her heart start pounding in her throat.

"But remember what I said, Laura. You'll never have to worry about that guy getting close to you again."

The strength she saw reflected in his gaze reminded her that, like the mountain lion, he knew how to fight and how to win.

The gas company man finished his inspection and came up to meet them. "Everything's working fine now. If no one tampers with the adjustments, you shouldn't have any more problems.''

"Did you or someone else at the gas company call the arson investigator?" Burke asked.

"I called Lieutenant Springer on my way here because you'd had problems before, and he'd asked my office to keep him updated on any new business or service calls at this address.''

"Okay, thanks," Burke said.

As the man walked out, Laura looked up at Burke. "Well, that's settled." She glanced at the bookshelves. "Did you find all the books you wanted to look over?"

"I have them in my jacket. I didn't want them just lying around with all the people coming and going.''

"Okay." As she started to walk away, he reached out and grasped her hand.

A jolt of excitement raced up her spine and, as she looked at him, she saw that he'd felt something, too. Dangerous—that could sum up the way things were between them. She tried to make her voice sound casual, and by some miracle succeeded. "Yes?"

"Listen, I'm going to go to the furnace contractor's office. I want to know if Springer also asked them to notify him if something went wrong here. I want to see to what extent he has engineered things so that he'll have a reason to keep coming around. If he's stepped over the line in any way, I want to make sure I'm in a position to put a stop to it.''

"Then I'm going with you."

"Are you sure you don't want to stay with your godmother?"

"The doctor said she'll sleep for hours, but I'll leave her a note, just in case. Can we also leave Wolf with her?"

"Sure."

Back at his house, while waiting for Laura to write Elena a note, Burke changed Wolf's collar.

"What are you doing?" Laura asked, coming back into the room.

"It's a signal to Wolf that he's on sentry duty," Burke said. "No one who comes in uninvited will leave without teeth marks."

"Are you sure Elena will be safe?"

"You can count on it. He won't harm anyone unless it's an intruder."

THE NEIGHBORHOOD WHERE the contractor's office was located was rougher than he'd remembered. "This area's gone down a lot in the last few years," he said, looking at some young street thugs standing beside a storefront awning.

As he got out of his car, Burke made it a point to stand perfectly still and make eye contact, his gaze hard and expressionless. Seconds passed as steadily as heartbeats, but the thugs finally moved away, walking in the opposite direction. Satisfied, he went around and opened the door for Laura, then walked with her into the contractor's office.

The beefy man with an anchor tattoo on one of his hairy forearms looked out of place behind a desk, tapping on an adding machine.

"Can I help you?" Seeing Laura, he stretched out his hand. "I'm Joey LaSalle." Then he gave Burke a nod. "I believe your tribe doesn't like to shake hands."

"True enough," Burke answered.

"I sure hope you're not here because one of my servicemen missed an appointment," he said.

"No, we just came to ask you a few questions," Burke said. "My lady friend has been having some problems with a guy who keeps harassing her. He's a fireman and he's got some official clout. Guess he thinks that make him immune.''

"Yeah, guys like that can be a real pain.'' He looked at Laura, then back at Burke. ''But what's this got to do with me?''

"Do you know an arson investigator named Ken Springer?'' Burke asked.

The man scowled and nodded. ''Yeah. He was here earlier and came on real strong for someone without a warrant—like he was the fire marshal or something.'' He paused for a second, as if trying to get a better handle on things. ''Hey, are you the lady who had the furnace that some lowlife tampered with? Laura Santos?''

She nodded, but before she could say anything else, he continued.

"Look, for the record, my installer is a pro. He swears everything was adjusted properly the first time.'' LaSalle rubbed the back of his neck with one hand. ''But when our man went back out the second time, things were way off. We had to notify Springer and the gas company inspector. We were in a tough position legally, you understand? When a mishap like that happens, we have to cover all the bases. Then Springer came by earlier today and told us that he was already investigating a case of attempted arson at that address. At his request, we agreed to notify him immediately if we were called out to your home again.''

"There was no attempted arson—or at least no evidence to indicate that,'' Laura said, her voice quiet. ''Springer is just using that to get to me. He wants me to depend on him for protection, I guess.''

"That sorry son of a gun.'' LaSalle's jaw clenched and a muscle jumped in his cheek. ''I'll tell my employees not to give out any information about you unless there's a court order involved. You shouldn't have to put up with any guy pushing himself on you just 'cause he wears a badge.''

"Thank you," Laura said. "That's very kind of you and I appreciate it."

As they walked out, Burke looked down at her. "Springer has overstepped his authority. You could get him fired—or at least in a heap of trouble. But getting people to testify can be tricky."

"I'd rather not go that route. I really don't want to ruin his life. I just want him to leave me alone. But if he keeps pushing it, I'll talk to his bosses. I think one or two guys at the house will come forward as witnesses if I ask them."

She slipped into the passenger's seat, then waited until they were under way. "Not to brag or anything, but I hope you realize that the reason we got answers back there so quickly and without any fuss was because *I* was with you. My talking to Mr. LaSalle and explaining what was going on made him want to help us even more, because I wasn't just a name or a statistic then. All in all, I'd say I did very well."

"No, the proper term is 'I done good.' You need to learn to speak good-ole-boy if you're going to work the case with me," he teased.

"Of course. I'll be sure to remember," she said, trying, like him, not to crack a smile. "And don't worry. I'm a very quick study."

"Somehow I figured that."

It was difficult sitting in the car with him. As much as she wanted to treat him as just another guy, everything about Burke marked him as one of a kind. He was rugged, and dangerous, and if he was rough at times, that just heightened his appeal.

She stole a furtive glance at the way his powerful hands gripped the wheel. For a moment, she pictured those hands on her body and, to her horror, she almost sighed.

"You okay?"

No, she was losing it. Just being around Burke made her

heart beat so fast it was hard to breathe—and the lack of
oxygen was killing her brain cells. Clinging to that bit of
logic, she stared out the window. "I'm fine. Why wouldn't
I be? I done good today."

He burst out laughing.

AFTER THEY ARRIVED BACK at her home, Laura went
through the house taking note of the progress. The back
door worked and the heater was installed. Workmen were
now busy patching the holes in the living room wall, created when the original intruder had toppled a large armoire
during his search of the house. There was similar damage
in Elena's bedroom and throughout—everything ranging
from scuff marks to gouges in the plaster.

At the moment, the damp odor of curing plaster and dry-
wall, coupled with the sealer coat on the back door and the
trim, was almost overpowering.

Eager to get some fresh air and wanting to check on
Elena, they left her home and walked across the way to
Burke's house. "It won't be long now before Elena and I
can move back home," she said. "And as soon as she's
ready and the final coat of paint has had time to dry, we're
leaving—just so you know."

"Okay, but until then, let's take it a day at a time."

As Burke opened his front door, Wolf came to greet
them, licking his chops. "Hey, Wolf," Laura said, crouching down and scratching him behind the ears. "Whatcha
got in your mouth?"

"That's bread," Burke said, crouching in front of the
dog. "Wolf, if you grabbed anything off of the counter,
you're in serious trouble," he said, and hurried toward the
kitchen.

Just then Elena came through the open doorway. "No,
Wolf's been a very good dog. I made myself some toast
and, since he looked hungry, I made him a piece, too."

Seeing her, Burke grew concerned. "The doctor said you'd sleep for hours! What happened? Aren't you feeling well?"

She smiled. "I napped for as long as I needed to, but then I woke up hungry. I was never that sick, you know. I just needed to relax and calm down after that scary ride home."

"We haven't had a chance to talk to that idiot driver yet, but we will," Laura assured her.

"Now that you're both here, I can cook supper," Elena said.

"Absolutely not," Burke said.

"I second that. Hey, wow, a miracle—we agree on something." Laura reached for the phone. "I'm calling Pizza Pizzazz. A day like today calls for fine dining on the best paper plates money can buy."

DINNER WAS A SIMPLE affair, but it felt good to have both of the women safe under his roof. There was something about Laura that exasperated Burke and got under his skin. He didn't want to like her, but he couldn't seem to have one clear thought that wasn't somehow wrapped up in her. The worst part was that the whole experience made him feel so good, he didn't want to run for cover.

"Tell me what's happening at the senior center," he asked Elena, forcing himself to focus on business.

"There's a lot more going on at the center than people realize," she said pensively. "For instance, have you heard of John Foster and what happened with him?"

Laura nodded. Everyone knew the town's leading real estate developer. "Didn't he promise to make a generous donation to the center? I think I read something like that in the papers."

"Yes, the offer was made, but it came with strings attached—ones that no one was eager to make public."

"Like what?" Burke asked, his curiosity piqued.

"The center would get the money only if we didn't interfere with his plans to build a four-story apartment complex on the land adjacent to the center—a parcel that Foster had originally promised to sell to the city for a nominal price so they could turn it into a much needed recreational park."

"How did you find out about this?" Laura asked.

"I overheard a conversation one afternoon when I was in the office," Elena answered, then with a glance at Burke, added, "I work at the center part-time." She took a deep breath, then continued. "When I realized what was really going on, I knew that everyone who would be affected by the apartment complex had a right to know what was being done behind their backs. The other seniors felt the same way I did, so we decided to fight Foster's plans.

"I got everyone organized, and we fought the development on the grounds that an apartment complex would mean an increase in traffic and noise, not to mention take away a much needed neighborhood park. We got the support of parents who lived in adjacent areas, we circulated petitions, and the end result was a lot of bad publicity for Mr. Foster."

"When did all this happen?" Laura asked, stunned.

"While you were busy finishing your last book. I never said anything because I knew you were really fighting to make your deadline," Elena said. Then she looked at Burke. "When she's going over the last draft of a book, she's totally lost in her own world. Before I moved in, she would run out of everything from milk to toilet paper and not even notice."

Burke's eyebrows arched and he looked about ready to laugh. "How do you *not* notice you're out of toilet paper?"

"I'm creative," Laura snapped.

Burke burst out laughing at that.

"Okay, so I'm not exactly domestic goddess material," she muttered. "Go back to your story, Elena."

"Well, once Mr. Foster was forced to abandon his plans for the complex because of public pressure, he also reneged on his donation to the senior center. Karl Maurer, the director, blamed me for the whole thing and fired me from my job. He even tried to bar me from using the center's facilities, but I fought back. Once everyone learned that I'd been fired, all the seniors protested and threatened to stop using the center and paying their membership fees. Needless to say, I got my job back."

Laura shook her head. "How long was all that going on?" Her last draft often took weeks, and it was inconceivable to her that Elena had handled this for that long without her noticing.

"The whole thing happened in a matter of days—two weeks at most. Then it was over," Elena said. "Of course, Karl has continued pressuring me to apologize to Mr. Foster in the hopes that he'll change his mind about making a donation."

"And have you apologized?" Burke asked.

"No, of course not. I did nothing wrong. If anyone should apologize, it's Mr. Foster. He tried to pull a fast one on all of us in the community."

Laura sat back in her chair, totally dumbfounded. "Is there anything else you haven't told us?"

"Now I've hurt your feelings," Elena said remorsefully. "But when something upsets you, sometimes it takes you days to get back into your writing. That's why I didn't say anything."

"How are things between you and Karl now?" Burke asked.

"In a word? Tense. The fact that I stood up to him is like a thorn in his side."

Laura glanced at Burke. "What do you think? Could he be the person behind the break-ins?"

"Whoever broke in was looking for something specific." He turned to Elena. "Can you think of anything you have that Karl Maurer might want?"

She considered for a moment. "Well, now that you mention it, awhile back he really wanted me to return a nasty memo he'd written me. But he wouldn't break in to get it now. It's not worth that much to him anymore."

"What memo?" Laura pressed.

"Once he found out I was organizing the protest against Foster's development project, Karl was furious. He tried to talk to me several times, but one of us was always getting called away. Finally, one day, right before leaving on a business trip, he scribbled a hurried memo and left it on my desk. In it, he told me that if I didn't stop interfering with Foster's plans, he'd fire me and make sure no one in this town ever hired me again. He threatened to tell people I was growing senile—can you believe it? I'm sure he figured that memo would stop me in my tracks, but of course, it didn't. Eventually, he fired me. That's when I told him that I still had the memo and if he gave me a bad reference or tried to keep me from getting hired elsewhere, I'd show it to the first newspaper reporter I could find, and declare that Karl had been in a conspiracy with Foster."

"Where's that memo now?" Burke asked quickly.

"I threw it out after he hired me back," Elena said with a shrug. "I'm sorry I didn't remember this when we had the first break-in. My memory sometimes plays tricks on me."

Laura sat back in her chair, trying to make sense out of everything. "We have to find out if Karl's implicated in what's been happening to us."

"Honestly, you two, I really doubt it," Elena argued. "Image is everything to that man. That's why he didn't want me to fight Foster. He knew what a toll that would take on his reputation.''

"That argument would also explain why he'd risk breaking in to get the memo back," Burke said.

"We need to take a closer look at the people who work at the center and the things happening there." Laura glanced at Burke, then back at Elena, an idea forming in her mind. "Tomorrow's the center's annual fund-raising banquet and dance. Didn't you tell me that everyone was encouraged to bring guests?" When Elena nodded, Laura looked at Burke. "Bring steel-toed boots, 'cause I'm a rotten dancer."

Chapter Nine

This was supposed to be a fact-finding mission—not a date. But it *felt* like a date.

As Burke strode across the room toward her, Laura had to admit that he looked incredibly sexy and masculine in his dark slacks and black leather sport coat. He wound his way confidently through the dozen or so couples dancing to a Glen Miller tune popular with the seniors, then gave her one of his drop-dead-gorgeous smiles.

Her heart rate went up a notch. A cocky grin like that should be outlawed. She took a deep breath. Burke was used to women fawning over him. Guys like him knew what they had and used it. But she had no intention of playing that game.

"Thanks for the punch," she said as he handed her a plastic cup.

"Karl Maurer is across the dance floor talking to those ladies." He motioned with his head and spoke just loudly enough for her to hear. "Elena told me that as soon as he breaks free of them, she'll introduce us. In the meantime, try to relax. You look like you came here on business, and that doesn't fit our cover. Elena has told everyone that I'm your boyfriend, so I think we should make it look convincing," he said, placing his arm around her waist. Leaning over her seductively, he whispered in her ear. "If it helps you to get the right look in your eyes, you could try picturing me naked.''

A vivid image of Burke that day she'd caught him just out of the shower suddenly popped into her mind—but then her imagination kicked in and she saw him dropping the towel he'd had wrapped around him. Her mouth went dry and her heart began to pound.

Burke gave her an utterly charming smile. ''Ah, I see it worked. Your cheeks are flushed.''

''They are not,'' she protested quickly, then, looking around, saw they were being watched by a couple dancing past. Laura forced herself to smile.

''That's better. Keep smiling and let's dance. That'll help,'' Burke said.

''No, it won't. I'm an awful dancer. I'll step on you.''

''I'll risk it.'' Burke grabbed her hand and led her out onto the dance floor. As the music system began playing a romantic ballad from the forties, Burke wrapped his arm around her waist and twirled her until she was in his arms, swaying gently with the music.

Power and strength defined him. The outdoorsy scent of his cologne and the hardness of his chest as it pressed against hers made her feel wonderfully alive and feminine.

''I thought you said you couldn't dance,'' he murmured into her ear.

His intimate tone and hot breath made her skin prickle. ''I said I wasn't very good at it,'' Laura corrected.

''But you are.''

As he drew her closer against him, she tried to stop him, but his arm was completely unyielding. ''Make it look good, beautiful.''

A special warmth wound around her, though she assured herself that she was acting like a fool. She knew that there was danger in Burke's arms, as well as pleasure. But that realization only made it all the more exciting.

"If you want to make this look really good, then let's go for it," she said, taking charge. If nothing else, stealing away some of his control would make her feel loads better. Looking up at him, Laura curved her hand around his neck and stretched up to meet his mouth.

Her lips played over his, tempting him, but when she tried to draw back, he opened his mouth hard over hers, taking over. His kiss was all hunger and possession...and heaven.

When he drew back, his eyes were blazing with passion. "That's enough for now," he whispered, his voice raw. "In another second or two, I'm damn well going to forget where we are and why."

She ran the tip of her tongue over her lips, tasting him there. The fires inside her could have warmed the entire North Pole, but she forced herself to smile as if nothing out of the ordinary had just happened. And for that, she figured she deserved an Oscar. "See? I can work undercover. I'm a very good actress."

"That was no act," he murmured, holding her close. "Any man who is a man knows when he's given a woman pleasure."

His words were silky, searing a path through her center. "I'd argue with you, but I'd blow our cover." She rested her cheek against his chest. "So what now?"

"We wait. I don't want to go talk to Maurer and possibly tip our hand. I want him to come to us."

"How are we going to manage that one?"

"I'm going to take you out the side door onto the veranda. Let's see if he strolls out to say hello to us."

Burke curved his hand around her shoulders, his fingers brushing her neck in a casual caress that made shivers cascade down her back. Every breath she took was filled with anticipation as he led her outside.

Stepping into the shadows with her, he suddenly pulled

her into his arms. "One more time," he whispered, taking her lips.

He plundered her mouth with the skill of a lover long denied. Shudders ripped through Laura as he tasted her, drawing her tongue into his own mouth, then plunging deep into hers.

It was a dance as primitive as the moonlight that illuminated them.

When Burke eased his hold, she had to lean against him. So much for being in control. "How's this going to get Maurer out here?"

"Beats me, but it felt real good, didn't it?"

She stared at him, then suddenly laughed. "You're an arrogant son of a gun."

"Maybe," he replied with a grin.

As she stepped back, the lights from inside the building fell upon her face and he suddenly saw that her lips were swollen and almost bruised. The realization stunned him. He should have been more careful with her. A woman like Laura deserved a man who knew how to be gentle.

"I'm sorry," Burke whispered, lifting her hand to his lips and brushing her fingertips with a kiss. "Was I too rough?" As he ran a work-hardened thumb over her mouth, she parted her lips slightly. He had to bite back a groan. She was enough to drive any man crazy.

"I like being kissed hard like that," she said unsteadily.

The desire he heard in her voice made new fires spread through him. He released her and took a step back. If he touched her again, he'd go crazy. He'd never felt anything this strong—anything this intense—with any woman he'd ever known. And the truth was, he had no idea how to handle it.

"There you are, you two," Elena said, bringing out Karl Maurer according to plan. "Come on back inside now. There are people you lovebirds have to meet."

Burke forced himself to focus, and tried his level best to ignore the pounding heat that was coursing through him.

"Elena is so happy that you've found someone at last, Laura," Karl Maurer said, smiling at her.

Elena introduced the men and Burke forced himself to shake hands with the Anglo. He wasn't a traditionalist, but some Navajo customs were deeply ingrained, like the aversion to touching a stranger. Shaking hands was an Anglo custom he'd forced himself to accept and adapt to, since he lived and worked outside the rez, but he'd never really grown used to it.

Elena then introduced Nicole Maurer as she came out to join them. Burke noticed that as she greeted her husband, she was clutching her evening bag so hard her knuckles were white. Curious, he studied her expression, wondering what had made her so tense.

Several moments later, Michael Enesco came out. Burke was surprised to see the center's driver join his employers so readily.

Karl introduced him offhandedly though it wasn't clear if Enesco even understood what was happening, his English was so poor. Then Maurer focused on Burke as Enesco wondered off. "I don't think I've seen you around town before," he said. "Are you new to these parts?"

"No, not really. I've lived in and around the Four Corners almost all my life," Burke commented. "But I have to admit I never paid much attention to this center. You run a nice operation here."

"Thank you," Karl said. "We're always short of funds, but I guess it's that way everywhere these days."

"Does the city or county support the center?"

"No, we're privately funded."

"By whom?"

"Several businesses here in town. It's a tax write-off for them. Every member also pays a small user's fee."

Burke continued to press him casually about operations, asking Maurer to show him the facilities. Catching Laura's eye as he moved away, Burke saw her nod, then focus on Nicole. She'd work alongside him tonight. But the stakes were high, and he had no intention of letting her out of his sight for long. She was highly intelligent, but still an amateur, and lack of experience in a game like this could lead to a deadly mistake. Whether she liked it or not, he'd have to watch her back.

LAURA SAW BURKE WALK AWAY. The farther Karl Maurer went, the closer Enesco drew to Nicole Maurer's side. But if anything, it only served to make Nicole even more nervous than she was before. Once or twice, Laura caught the unguarded look Nicole gave Enesco. It was not the furtive glance of a woman in love; rather, it was one of revulsion. More intrigued than ever, Laura sidled closer, wedging herself between Enesco and Nicole. Enesco gave ground only grudgingly.

As Elena moved off to talk with a board member of the center, Delbert Hutton, Laura concentrated on Nicole.

"I think you've all done a great job of planning this social tonight," she said lightly, trying to make conversation.

"Well, the actual planning and the details were all attended to by Shaunna Williams. She's our activities coordinator."

"You're lucky to have her then."

Nicole gave a tight-lipped smile. "It's difficult these days to keep our staff happy. Our funding...well, it isn't what it used to be. I suppose you've heard that we lost a huge donation we'd been expecting," she said pointedly.

If Nicole had hoped to put her off, she failed. Laura smiled, undaunted. "My godmother always follows her highest sense of right. And once she sets her course, there's no stopping her.''

"So I've noticed.''

As Nicole moved to the refreshments table, Enesco remained nearby. Laura, trying to get some time alone with her, concluded that the only safe haven would be the rest room.

"Could you show me to the ladies' room?" she asked quietly.

"Sure.''

Nicole led the way down the hall, and still Enesco followed. Annoyed, Laura turned around and gave the man the haughtiest look she could muster. "There are some places ladies prefer to go unescorted," she said, then followed Nicole into the rest room.

"That man is so annoying. Why do you keep him? I heard that the seniors hate the way he drives," Laura said. "He really frightens the passengers.''

She nodded. "Both Karl and I have already spoken to him about that.''

"There are other rumors going around, too," Laura said slowly.

Nicole stopped freshening her lipstick and glared at Laura. "It's malicious gossip, and I don't care to discuss it.''

"Ignoring it won't make it go away. You'd have a better chance of squashing that kind of talk if that guy didn't stick to you like a shadow.''

"I don't appreciate the sarcasm," Nicole said coldly.

"I was only being truthful. How could anyone not notice it?''

"It's too bad your family aren't as tactful and discreet as they are honest." Without giving Laura a chance to reply, she strode out of the rest room.

By the time Laura returned to the dance, Nicole was

standing near the music system among a small crowd that had gathered there discussing their favorite musicians and songs. Enesco, like the parasite he appeared to be, was less than an arm's reach from her again.

Elena came up to Laura. "Well? Did you learn anything interesting while you were with Nicole?"

"And her evil twin, Enesco? Not really. Where's Burke?"

Elena pointed to the far corner. Burke was standing with two women who seemed to be oblivious to everything except him.

"Looks like Mrs. Turner's daughters have him cornered," Elena said. "Both are still single. Aren't they beautiful?"

"Yeah, they are," Laura answered, a bit irritated. Burke looked completely at ease. The women, on the other hand, were clearly competing against each other for his attention, inching closer with every word they said, and laughing loudly every time he answered. "Let's go rescue him."

"He doesn't look as if he needs rescuing," Elena pointed out. "I think he's enjoying the attention."

"Yeah, well, they look far too young."

"They're at least in their twenties," Elena said.

"IQ doesn't count."

Laura walked across the room and flashed Burke her most innocent smile. "There you are! I was wondering where you went off to." She nodded to the women.

"Burke was just telling us all about his Army Special Forces training. Did you know only one in ten soldiers are tough enough to get accepted?" The leggy brunette glanced at Laura, then gazed adoringly at Burke.

Laura gave him a completely guileless look. "Burke, you shouldn't try and get these girls interested in enlisting. They probably have plans for college after they graduate."

Burke started to laugh, but seeing the spark in Laura's

eyes, thought better of it, and quickly said goodbye to the two young women. A brave man always knew when to disengage.

As they walked away, Burke glanced at Laura casually. "If I didn't know better, I'd think you were a tiny bit jealous."

"In your dreams."

His chuckle was oddly disturbing. Determined to take her mind off him, she glanced around the room and spotted Elena sitting alone on the opposite side of the room. "We better get her back home, Burke. I have to make sure Elena doesn't get overly tired," Laura said, hurrying across the room.

A moment later, she sat beside Elena. "We've done all we can tonight. What do you say we go home?"

"All right. Did you get a chance to talk to Michael Enesco?" Elena asked.

"Tonight's not a good time for that," Burke said. "It'll be better to wait until we can catch him alone."

As they walked back to the car, Laura glanced at Burke. "Did you find out anything useful?"

"Only that Karl Maurer is very tight-lipped about the center's business operations," he answered. "What about you? Did you get anything out of Nicole?"

"Not really. But I can tell you that she finds Enesco revolting. No way she's having an affair with him."

"Maybe they had an affair, Nicole decided to end it, but Enesco wouldn't let go," Burke responded.

"Could be, but the only thing we can be certain about is that Karl and Nicole are both real uneasy around Enesco."

"If you ask me, they're all hiding something," Elena said. "I was talking to Shaunna Williams and she told me that several of the center's members have been hit by residential burglaries recently. The police have speculated that the thieves may have gotten the addresses from the center, or by following our members to their homes. Karl was extremely upset by the allegation. And, since the burglar apparently knew when people would be away from home, it must have occurred to Karl, just as it did to Shaunna, that Michael might be behind the break-ins. Michael knows where all of us live and when we're here.''

''I don't like Enesco,'' Laura said, ''but it's unfair to lay this on him without any evidence.''

''I'm just saying that the possibility may have occurred to Karl and that he'd be very worried about it. If Michael's involved, the scandal would cause many of the seniors to withdraw their membership. That would, more than likely, lead to the center's closure. Karl would do just about anything to keep that from happening.''

''Until we know for sure what's going on, avoid being alone with any of them, particularly Enesco,'' Burke advised.

''You don't have to ask me twice. That man makes my skin crawl,'' Elena exclaimed.

The drive back to the house helped them relax, and soon their conversation shifted to other topics.

''I was surprised to see Wolf didn't make a fuss when we left him alone tonight,'' Elena said. ''He's such a special animal and so well trained! He didn't even bark.''

''He's probably glad to have the house to himself. It's downtime for him.''

''He's really smart,'' Laura commented. ''I think you're lucky to have him.''

Burke nodded slowly. ''He's a great partner. When we're out working, he's one hundred percent reliable.''

But when he was left on his own...well, he'd have to see how the house had stood up to a few hours with Wolf.

They arrived a short time later. The enormous German shepherd cross, who was lying on his side, didn't bound up to greet them. He merely raised his head and looked at them as they came in the front door.

"So much for 'welcome home,'" Burke muttered.

"I'm going to make some herbal tea. Would you two like some?" Elena stopped in the doorway to the kitchen and gasped. "Burke, Laura, you better get in here."

"I knew it," Burke muttered, glaring at the dog.

Burke hurried into the kitchen and discovered that the refrigerator door had been pulled open. A carton of milk lay on the floor on its side, empty, but there were no traces of milk on the floor. Several plastic wrappers that had contained cheese and cold cuts had been torn open, emptied and scattered about. The bread wrapper had been chewed through, and most of the bread, except for a few soggy slices, had vanished.

"Wolf!" Burke roared.

The dog trotted up, then sat before him, licking his lips.

Burke knew he couldn't punish the dog now. After-the-fact didn't count in dog training—you had to catch an animal misbehaving in order to make sure it linked behavior with consequences. Yet every instinct Burke had told him that the dog knew precisely what he'd done.

Laura tried not to laugh. Wolf was staring at Burke almost as if he found Burke's predicament incredibly entertaining.

"You *know* what you did," Burke said sternly.

"Let it go, Burke," Laura said, unable to suppress a chuckle.

"Do I have a choice?" he grumbled.

At Laura's insistence, Elena went to bed, while Burke and she tackled the mess. By the time they'd cleaned up the kitchen, they were more than ready to call it a night.

Tired, but wanting time to unwind a bit and think, Laura opted for a long soak in the tub before going to bed.

"I may be in the bathroom forever, just so you know."

"Take all the time you want. You've earned it. I'll be at my computer for a while, then I'm going to bed."

While Burke headed to the den, Laura went back to her room, stripped off her clothes, then wrapped her favorite blue silk robe around herself. It was time to indulge herself. Bubble bath bottle in hand, she went to the bathroom. To her surprise, Wolf followed her in, then lay down almost like a sentry by the doorway.

"Trying to avoid Burke, are you?" Laura looked at the beast and sighed. She considered sending him back out, but no harm would come of his staying, and in the mood Burke was in, the dog was probably better off with her.

"Okay, Wolf. You can stay in here with me, but scoot aside a bit, 'cause I need to close the door."

A few minutes later, Laura lowered herself into a pool of lavender-scented bubbles. Closing her eyes, she relaxed, enjoying the first moments of peace she'd had in a long time.

Soothed by the warm water and the quiet that enveloped the house, Laura drifted off to a peaceful sleep and dreamed of dancing in the moonlight with a Navajo man whose touch was like velvet and whose kisses tasted of seduction and the dangers of the night.

BURKE SAT IN FRONT OF the computer. He'd hoped to hear from Doug tonight. It had been a small eternity since the last time he'd had any word from his friend.

He leaned back in his chair and rubbed his eyes. He just couldn't shake the feeling that Doug was in major trouble. Too tired to sort it out, Burke decided to call it a night, but first he wanted to go next door and make sure Laura's house was locked up and secure. He went down the hall, searching for Wolf, and called the dog's name softly.

The hall was dark, but he could see that the light in the bathroom was still on. Then he heard a soft scratch on the other side of the closed door. It didn't take a genius to figure out that the idiot dog had gone into the bathroom with Laura while she bathed.

The walking furball had it made. Women always adored him, and they went out of their way to coddle him, much as Laura had tonight. She'd no doubt allowed Wolf to stay in there with her in order to keep the dog out of his way.

He knocked lightly on the door, but she didn't answer. Laura had probably fallen asleep, as she'd warned him she might.

Moving slowly and silently, Burke grasped the doorknob and turned it. The lock clicked faintly, but as he pushed the door open a crack, the hinges squealed.

"Wolf," he whispered. He promised himself that he wouldn't sneak a peek at Laura, even though the thought of her silky body wrapped in nothing but soapy bubbles made every muscle in his body tense up.

Cracking the door open a little bit more, he saw the front half of the dog a foot away. The animal stared at him curiously, but ignored the whispered command.

Annoyed, Burke snaked a hand inside, reaching for his collar, intending to haul him out.

Suddenly he heard a soft, strangled cry—from Laura. The choked sound was filled with blind fear, and Wolf reacted instantly, bounding to his feet. Using his nose to push the door wider, he ran past Burke into the hall, searching for trouble.

As the door flew open, Laura jumped to her feet. Then, in an attempt to cover herself, she gathered the clear shower curtain around her.

She was so beautiful she took Burke's breath away. Her creamy, wet skin glistened in the soft light of the bathroom.

"Easy, it's just me," he said. The terror on her face sliced through him. "I'm so sorry. I didn't mean to startle you awake like that." He stepped in, and was reaching for a towel to hand her when Wolf suddenly rushed back into the bathroom, bumping him aside.

Burke slid sideways on a wet spot on the floor and went sprawling over the rim of the tub. He hit the water with his shoulder, splashing it everywhere. He cursed and shifted to a sitting position in the tub, wiping the soapy bubbles from his face.

When he looked up, he saw Laura standing naked before him. For a moment he couldn't breathe. He wanted her, *now.* To his credit, he didn't even try to touch her. She still looked completely bewildered, and he wouldn't take advantage of her like that.

"Laura, I'm so sorry. I'll climb out of the tub right now and go kill the dog." He tried to stand, but slipped and went tumbling back down, splashing water onto the floor.

"Just get out of here," she managed to gasp through clenched teeth. "And take that moose of a dog with you. And don't you dare look at me."

"I wouldn't dream of it." Well, not much anyway. "I'm just going to stand up first, then I'll get out of your way."

Laura tried to reach for the towel rack, but as she leaned forward the hooks of the shower curtain unsnapped from the rod and she went tumbling down in the tub, landing with a splash atop Burke, in his lap.

Desire, black and powerful, slammed into him. Laura was exquisite, and with her naked bottom pressed against him, he was lucky he could breathe without drooling.

She shifted, trying to recapture her balance so she could stand, and he groaned.

"Wait, let me help you." He gripped her waist, intending to help her up, but her skin was like silk and honey. At that moment, he knew he was lost. He was a man and a man could take only so much.

He pulled her against him and kissed her, long, hard and deep. Streaks of fire raced through him. She tasted so good.

Her soft moan ripped into him with a force that would have knocked him off his feet if he hadn't been sitting already.

Before his thoughts melted away, he drew back, lifted her to her feet and stood, wrapping the closest towel firmly around her.

As Laura looked at him he saw both desire and outrage in her eyes, fighting each other.

"Say something, for God's sake," he begged her.

Instead, she punched him in the stomach. "That's for being an oaf! Now *leave!*"

Catching his breath, he stepped out of the bathroom, dripping water everywhere. As he tried to close the door behind him, he saw that his hands were shaking. Hell, his entire body was about to burst. But it had been worth it.

Out in the hall, he rubbed his stomach. She had one heck of a punch for such a little thing.

As he started toward his room, leaving a stream of water with each footstep, he saw Wolf sitting in the doorway, his tongue lolling out the side of his mouth. He looked inordinately pleased with himself.

"Mutt, if I didn't know any better, I'd swear you did that on purpose," Burke said slowly.

Then he shook his head. "I'm going nuts. That's all there is to it." He stripped off his wet clothes, then toweled himself off and slipped into dry ones. "I've got some water to mop up, then we've got to get busy, partner. We have work to do."

Chapter Ten

Burke was up again at dawn. Alone with Wolf, he stood outside in the cool desert air and watched the sun rise over the high mesas of Carson National Forest far to the east.

No matter what it cost him, he had to keep his distance from Laura from now on. His feelings for her were growing too strong, and there was no way he could allow that to interfere with the job he had to do. She deserved one hundred percent from the Gray Wolf operative assigned to protect her, and he'd make damn sure that's what she got. He wouldn't fail her, not as he had his brother. The weight of that broken promise, though it seemed a lifetime ago now, still haunted him.

As the soft first rays of the sun bathed the earth, he remembered his boyhood days on the reservation. Every morning his mother would rise to say her prayers to the dawn. She'd take a pinch of pollen from her medicine bundle, touch it to her lips and then throw it upward as an offering to the sun. It surprised him how clearly he could still see the image in his mind, despite the many years that had passed.

He now followed a different path, making it his mission to fight for those who couldn't or wouldn't fight for themselves. He equalized the odds in a world where evil often overwhelmed the good—and in that was his redemption.

Burke took Wolf to check the grounds around his house and Laura's, as he'd done late last night, then returned home. Hearing the two women in the kitchen, he went inside to join them.

Elena served them freshly brewed coffee while Laura concentrated on something she was writing in a small notebook.

"She's always like this when she gets an idea for a new book," Elena said softly.

After several minutes, Laura glanced up. "I'm going over to my house this morning to work on my computer. The last work crew won't arrive until this afternoon."

"And while you're doing that, I'll drive to the market just down the street and get some staples for us, like milk and bread," Elena said. "I'm afraid Wolf didn't leave us much for breakfast."

Burke nodded. Elena would be all right. The trip would take her less than five minutes and she'd be in public view most of the way. He'd stay with Laura, who appeared to be the real target. "I'll go over to the house with you," Burke told her.

"I need to be alone if I'm going to work," she said.

"With all the crazy things that have been happening, you also need to be protected, Laura," Elena said.

Burke thanked her silently. Laura would accept that from Elena far easier than she would coming from him.

"Wolf and I will stay out of your way. We'll keep watch and let the workmen in when they arrive." She was acting decidedly cool this morning—not that he blamed her.

"You both have a half hour. After that, I want to see you back here for breakfast," Elena said firmly. "Later, we'll see about moving into our own home. The essential repairs should be finished by the end of the day, and I think we can put up with the smell of whatever painting still needs doing."

Laura nodded. "Yes, I think it's about time we all get back to our own lives."

"You can go back to your own home, but this case is not over," Burke said. "You can't just ignore it."

"Do whatever you have to, but Elena and I will be going home today," she answered.

He didn't argue with her. It was clear she'd already made up her mind, and he couldn't blame her for wanting to be more in control of her own life.

Laura handed Elena the keys to her car. "Here you go. Be careful."

Burke walked Elena outside and helped her into the car. As she slipped behind the wheel, she glanced up at him. "Laura isn't always easy to deal with, but I trust you to watch over her. I know you care for her—I can see it in your eyes. Promise me that you'll make sure she's not hurt, in any way."

He remembered the weight of another promise made and broken so long ago, and hesitated. "I don't—"

"Give me your word you'll do everything in your power to see to it," Elena insisted.

Burke nodded. That he could and would promise. "You have it." And no matter what it cost him, this was one promise he'd make sure was kept.

ALTHOUGH SHE'D AVOIDED looking at Burke this morning over coffee, Laura knew that he hadn't taken his eyes off her. She tried not to think about last night, yet the memory stayed at the edges of her mind, taunting her. Just remembering how his gaze had seared over her as she'd stood naked before him made her mouth go dry.

Burke walked her home after Elena left. Desperate to put some distance between them, she hurried into her office as soon as they got there, and shut the door behind her.

Alone, Laura walked across the room and dropped down

into a chair. She needed to get back to the things she understood, such as her work and her lifestyle. Piece by piece, she was giving away her heart to a man who only wanted to toy with it for a while before he moved on and out of her life.

Laura leaned back in her chair, trying to sort everything out in her mind. Suddenly she heard a car pulling into the driveway, and then the screech of tires and doors slamming.

Laura jumped to her feet. A heartbeat later, she heard Elena scream.

Laura ran to the window and saw Elena struggling with a man who was trying to pull her into a van. Someone else was at the wheel of the vehicle.

Laura raced to the front door, but Wolf and Burke were already outside, and the van was racing away. Elena had fallen to the grass beside the driveway, and Burke was crouched beside her. Wolf was chasing the fleeing van, but Burke gave out a sharp whistle, and the dog stopped in the road, panting, and returned.

Laura ran toward them but, seeing her, Burke held up his hand. "Go back inside and call 911. We need an ambulance and EMTs right now. She's having a heart attack."

Laura did as he asked, despite the almost paralyzing fear that gripped her. By the time she returned, Burke was pressing down on Elena's chest rhythmically, alternating with mouth-to-mouth resuscitation.

She knelt down by Elena and joined Burke's efforts, breathing air into Elena's lungs intermittently as Burke continued to try and get her *madrina*'s heart to respond. After almost six minutes, Burke checked her pulse, looked around for the ambulance for the tenth time, then shook his head slowly.

Laura felt herself drowning in a sea of blackness and despair as they continued their efforts to revive Elena. Losing her mother so many years ago had been devastating, and she'd thought nothing could ever hurt her that much again. But pain, never ending, sucked her down into despair with every breath she took.

Tears streaming down her face, Laura never even heard the paramedics arrive. The emergency medical team took over the effort and tried everything, including the paddles, but there was nothing more to be done.

As if watching a dream unfold, Laura remained on her knees and watched the emergency crew cover the body, then put their equipment away as Burke spoke to someone on his cell phone.

He came up to her and helped her to her feet as men took the body away. Moving automatically, Laura walked into the house, then stood in the living room, staring outside but seeing nothing. Her sadness and anger had turned into a cold, numbing feeling that nothing seemed able to penetrate.

Burke came up behind her, turned her around gently and cupped her face in his hands. "I'm going to be right here with you and I'll help you every step of the way. You don't have to face this alone. I know you're a strong woman, but we all need someone to help us through the rough spots sometimes."

She shook her head and stepped back. "It would be too easy to become dependent on you right now."

"I can handle it," he said, trying to pull her into his arms.

"I can't." She stiffened and moved away.

To open herself up to the comfort he could offer her was tempting—but also impossible. Once the case was finished, he, too, would leave her, and her heart was too shattered to take another loss. Wordlessly, she turned and walked away.

TEN MINUTES LATER the police arrived. Burke had called them, she learned. Laura gave the young Hispanic detective a statement, answering questions automatically.

"I didn't get a look at the face of the man who tried to drag Elena into the van," Laura said. "I just saw what was going on, then ran outside. I know there were two people involved, the other one being the driver, but I don't even know if it was a man or woman behind the wheel."

"What do you think they were after?" he pressed.

"All she had were groceries in the car," Laura said, trying to make some sense out of it.

"Are you sure they weren't trying to push her *toward* the house instead of into the van?"

She heard his words clearly, but she couldn't understand what he was asking her. "What difference does it make which direction they wanted her to go? She was not going by choice. Isn't that enough?"

Burke came forward then. "Look, she's told you all she knows. You're asking for conclusions she can't make. Let me describe what I saw. Maybe it'll help you track down the assailant and his partner."

The cop nodded and closed his notebook. "We can talk outside. I'm sorry for your loss, ma'am," he added, and walked toward the door with Burke.

As Burke accompanied the officer outside, Laura forced herself to pick up the phone. She had duties to attend to and arrangements to make.

THE FUNERAL SERVICE was held two days later. There had been a close examination of the body because Elena had died during an attempted kidnapping, but, as Laura had suspected, her heart condition had been simple to detect, and the body had been promptly released.

The day of the funeral turned out to be the worst day of her life. Beneath the suffocating sadness that filled her was anger—a quiet, cold rage that wouldn't end until the man who'd caused Elena's heart attack was brought to justice.

Burke stayed with her at the cemetery as the minister said the final prayer over the crypt, where Elena's ashes were interred beside her husband's.

After the service was finished, most of those who'd attended met at the Romero's home, in Elena's neighborhood, for coffee and a light buffet. There, Laura accepted the condolences of Elena's many friends. After she'd spoken with everyone and thanked the hosts for their hospitality, Laura walked with Burke to his car.

"I know how hard it is to accept a senseless death, Laura. But no matter how it seems to you now, you *will* get through this."

"We have to catch the man who terrorized her and brought on her heart attack. It's the only way I'll be able to live with what's happened."

"We'll find him," he said.

"I heard you on the phone last night talking to the police after the coroner declared the cause of death. Did the detective have any theories?" Laura asked.

"They believe it was a pair of thieves that have been targeting seniors from the center. The full story hasn't been released, but apparently there were three other cases where seniors were terrorized in their own homes. The robbers would force them to reveal their bank account numbers and passwords, then one would keep the victim hostage while the other depleted the entire bank account through automatic tellers."

"But anyone who'd watched Elena's routine would know I'm home during the day."

"I pointed that out and they told me that the daughter of one of the seniors was raped during one of the incidents. They like having family members there. It gives them added leverage. These guys, I'm told, strike after most people in the neighborhood have gone to work in the morning—always in broad daylight. Seniors are less guarded, and, from the evidence, these guys like the added rush of working a high-risk operation.''

''So what do we do now? Any ideas?''

''We let the police work their angle. For all we know, they're right. But in the meantime, we'll investigate the case using another approach. I thought we'd start by concentrating more on Al Baca. We visited his home and found that trap, remember? I'd like to talk to him next. Do you know where we can find him at this hour of the day?''

''He hasn't had a job in months, but I can make a few guesses where he's likely to be, based on things Elena told me.''

''Good. Your godmother didn't trust or like him, and she had good instincts about people. I think this is a good lead to start with now.''

''Give me a chance to go home and change clothes. I'd rather be wearing slacks to the places we'll be going.''

''No problem.''

''By the way, is it my imagination, or are you avoiding mentioning Elena's name?''

''It's the Navajo way.'' Seeing that she wanted more of an explanation, he continued. ''I was born and raised on the reservation. Although I left as soon as I could—there was nothing for me there except bad memories and poverty—our traditions stayed with me.'' He paused to gather his thoughts. ''Our people believe that everyone and everything has two sides. When someone dies, the good in them merges with universal harmony, but the earthly side— all our lower tendencies—remains earthbound. To use the name of one who has passed is to call their *chindi*, the earthbound side of human nature, and no good can come of that.''

"Then out of respect to you, I'll avoid using her name around you."

"That's not necessary."

"I know, but I'd like to do it."

Burke nodded. The more he got to know Laura, the more he was drawn to her. In these days where the whole point of everything, from a business deal to an affair, seemed to be to dive in, get what you wanted, and then bail out, Laura Santos was nothing short of amazing.

"Laura? Could I speak with you a moment?"

She turned and noticed Ernest Martinez, Elena's attorney, approaching. He had nodded to her earlier, and she had acknowledged his greeting with a silent thank-you. The stoop-shouldered old man had been Elena and her husband's friend and attorney long before Laura was ever born, and she had expected him to be at the service.

"Thanks for being here, Mr. Martinez." Laura introduced Burke to him, then waited for the old family friend to get to the point.

"I'm sorry to have to bring up this topic under these circumstances, but there are some things you need to know right away about Doña Elena's estate, and the lawsuit filed by her brother-in-law." Ernest spoke softly, his voice shaking with emotion and age.

Burke looked at him with speculation.

"I understand," Laura replied. "You already know the difficulties we've been experiencing, and undoubtedly have heard about the police investigation into her death." She looked to Burke, who nodded.

"Yes. That's why I feel you should know, before all the legal matters begin, that Elena left all her estate to you alone. That means that Al Baca's lawsuit will be thrown out, but it also means that if he's going to contest the will, and I think it likely that he will, you're going to become involved in this matter of the deed and all related business.

You're going to need to be very careful around Al, and you're going to need an attorney.''

"I have an attorney who specializes in publishing matters, but this isn't his area of expertise. Will you represent me on this, Mr. Martinez?''

"I certainly will. I just thought you should know what you're getting into, young lady. But you're in good hands with me, and I'm sure Mr. Silentman will be keeping you safe.'' Ernest looked hard at Burke, who nodded.

Mr. Martinez took Laura's hand. "If there's anything you need, please call me. In the meantime I'll be taking care of all the necessary paperwork concerning the transfer of property and other assets.''

Laura nodded. "Thanks again, Mr. Martinez. My godmother was wise to trust in your friendship.''

"And yours. I'm sure you and Burke here will be very successful in answering all those questions we have about what happened to the sweet lady. I'll be in touch.'' Mr. Martinez nodded to Burke, squeezed Laura's hand gently, then walked away.

"Nice man. And he knows I work for Gray Wolf. I recognized his name as being connected to a previous client of ours.''

"Him I trust." Laura nodded.

They climbed into Burke's car, and he drove her home. Then he waited in the living room while she changed, noting that the scent of fresh paint had nearly disappeared. The workmen had finished their tasks yesterday afternoon at Laura's insistence. It had been her way of distracting herself from her own thoughts, he suspected.

As he looked around, he wondered if she'd adapt well to life alone. But then again, he couldn't see a woman as beautiful as Laura having any problem finding company. Men would trip over each other running to console her. The thought irritated him, and he pushed it aside.

A moment later, she came out wearing dark slacks and a loose fitting, ivory-colored cotton sweater. The clothes were not intended to be sexy, but on her, anything at all would look that way.

"I'm ready to go," she said, grabbing her purse.

LAURA HAD ONLY KNOWN the bar by name, but Burke had recognized it instantly. It was the last place he would have wanted to take her—or anyone else not skilled in hand-to-hand combat.

He mentioned the bar's reputation for fights and that it appealed to every lowlife around, but one look at her face assured him nothing short of tying her up would keep her from going in.

"You'll need me to point Al out to you," she said. "There are a lot of people who fit his general description—brown hair, medium build, brown eyes. I have to go."

Burke yielded reluctantly. "We could wait and try to catch him at home."

"No. Let's finish what we started."

He knew she needed to work the case—now more than ever. But he'd have to watch her like a hawk.

They arrived at the bar near the edge of town a little after four-thirty, but pickups and older model cars had already filled up most of the parking lot. The bar was an ugly, square, cinder block building painted either gray or black a long time ago, with an even uglier, faded sign that read Poker Face Bar.

"Okay, let's go," Burke said.

As soon as they walked inside, Laura was glad he was with her. The crowd was a rowdy one, comprised mostly of men and women in their later thirties and forties clad in jeans, Western-style shirts or T-shirts from concert tours, and boots or athletic shoes. A few of the men wore baseball

caps with team or company logos from businesses related
to local trucking, or the oil and gas industry.

Laura stopped just inside the entrance, beside the grungy
wall paneling, looking around for Al while her eyes adjusted to the dim interior. There were no windows.

She spotted him after a few minutes. The middle-aged
man was leaning against the far wall, beer bottle in hand,
watching a tall, hard-looking blond woman engaged in a
game of darts.

Laura slipped through the gathering, turning sideways at
times to avoid patrons who were watching the game and
oblivious to her presence. Burke followed.

When she got close enough for conversation and called
his name, Al looked up, surprised to see her. "What are
you doing slumming in my neighborhood?"

"I need to talk to you about my godmother. Can we go
outside where we can speak in private without having to
shout?"

She saw his gaze shift to Burke, who was standing directly behind her. "Tell Elena to come talk to me herself,"
he said, then looked back at the tall blonde with the darts.

Laura bit back her anger. "I think you should reconsider.
You're going to be very interested in what I have to say."

Curiosity flickered in his eyes, then with a shrug, he took
one last swig of beer, set the empty bottle down on the bar
and followed her and Burke outside.

She felt better the moment they were out of the building.
At least here the air wasn't stale with the scent of liquor
and cigarettes. And the silence was startling.

Al leaned back against the side of the building, scratching his arm absently. "The only thing I'll ever want from
Elena is the deed to the land that belonged to my brother
and me. It's mine and she knows it."

"Her lawyer doesn't agree, and neither will a judge."

"If that's all you came to say, then you're wasting my

time." He turned and started to walk toward the entrance. "I'll see her in court."

"I don't see how. Elena's dead," Laura said.

He stopped abruptly and turned around. His eyes were alive with calculation but there was no hint of sorrow there. "First *I* heard of it. When did she die?"

"Two days ago," she answered. "Her funeral was earlier today."

Al allowed the silence to stretch. "Well, I can't say I'm sad to see her go. She was a self-righteous witch."

"Show her some respect." Laura's voice cracked through the air like a whip, making Al look up in surprise. "We're here to ask you a few hard questions, so think carefully before you answer. Someone has broken into my home several times recently, and we all know how eager you are to get your hands on that deed." Laura paused and, never taking her eyes off him, added, "Also, you should know Elena died because her heart gave out during a kidnapping attempt right in front of our home."

"Wait one minute," he said quickly. "I had nothing to do with any break-ins or kidnapping or anything like that. There's no way you can pin that stuff on me."

"We tried to pay you a visit at your home a couple of days ago, and nearly ran into a very nasty surprise you left behind," Burke said pointedly. "Who's got you so afraid that you're willing to risk killing some innocent kid who happens to wander in?"

"It was *inside* my home. I can do whatever I want there. Traps aren't illegal."

"Maybe so, but burglary and manslaughter are," Burke said. "We all know you want the deed to that land, and that there was only one person keeping you from it."

"I still want it, but I'm not guilty of burglary *or* kidnapping." He looked at Laura. "But now that Elena is gone, that deed should come to me. It shouldn't be yours, that's for sure. My brother was nothing to you."

"Her attorney, Ernest Martinez, says that I'll inherit all her property. It's in her will, apparently. I intend to see that you never get that deed. You made her life miserable and this will be your payback."

"I'll take *you* to court then. I'll never give up fighting you on this."

"Knock yourself out." Laura turned and walked away.

As soon as they were out of earshot, Burke broke the silence between them. "You shouldn't have told him about your godmother's will. All you've done is turn yourself into his new target."

"I can handle threatening phone calls, and I can afford Ernest Martinez. Al Baca picked on Elena because he sensed that her age and heart condition made her vulnerable. But he has no advantage over me. Besides, I've got friends—big friends—close by," she added with a hint of a smile.

"And I *will* protect you, darling."

The softly spoken words made a thrill race through her, but she pushed the feeling back. "What next?"

"I want to do a little more checking on Springer."

"You don't really think he's involved, do you?"

"I don't know. That's why I want to check it out. But first I need time to make some phone calls and organize my thoughts."

"I'm going to move back home today," Laura said as they got under way. "It's time for me to start getting used to living alone again."

"You won't be alone—not while the case is still open. That would be too dangerous, particularly after everything that has happened. These men are playing hardball and, if you're by yourself, you'll be easy prey."

She paused, considering her options. "You know, if we

work it right, my moving back home will give us the break we need. All we have to do is make it *look* as if I'm alone. If these people think I'm defenseless, they'll come after me, and that's the best way to catch whoever's behind this mess.''

''Making yourself a target isn't the answer. There are other ways to accomplish what we need to do.''

''Maybe, but so far we aren't having much luck,'' she said, disheartened.

''Investigations take time, Laura. Trying to speed things up usually ends up creating more problems than it solves.''

Truth be told, he knew how she felt. The impatience, the frustration—those were things he'd experienced himself. But what worried him most was her desire to *make* things happen.

When a client reached that stage, trouble always followed. That was why Burke had no intention of letting her out of his sight. Trouble found Laura too easily as it was. But one way or another, he would protect her. The woman had a piece of his heart, and he'd never let anything happen to her.

AFTER THEY ARRIVED at Laura's place, Burke left her in the living room and stepped into the kitchen to call Handler. It didn't take long for them to connect.

''I've got a problem,'' Burke said. ''I'm going to need some backup on this case. I've got two suspects I need to keep under surveillance.'' Although Gray Wolf operatives normally worked alone, support operatives could be made available under special circumstances. Burke explained what had happened since his last report.

''So you want one of our operatives to keep an eye on Al Baca, the deceased's brother-in-law, and another to concentrate on Laura Santos's boyfriend-wannabe, Springer,'' Handler verified. ''Let me check our rosters.'' There was a pause, then he continued, "I can spare only one operative, just barely. To give you backup, I'm going to have to take someone off a case. I'm sorry, but the way it shapes up, one man will have to split his time."

"In that case, if at all possible, I'd like the job to be given to the operative code-named Wind. I've supervised his cases in the past, and he's great with disguises. I can't remember him ever losing a person he's been assigned to tail."

"You're in a unique position. As the agency's supervisor, you know the skills and talents of all our other operatives—a very rare privilege in an agency where, for security reasons, we seldom meet."

Burke was well aware of the agency policy that dictated the investigators remain anonymous, even to each other, except under emergency situations. Their ability to go undercover, as well as their safety, would have been compromised if those steps weren't enforced. As an added precaution for the investigators who lived and worked in the same area, operatives were prohibited from actively trying to identify each other or fraternizing in public. That was meant to prevent anyone who knew one of them as a Gray Wolf investigator from identifying the others by checking on his associates.

The small tattoo normally hidden beneath their wristwatches carried the most risk, but in a crisis insured that an operative would know an ally immediately—without the need for an ID or explanation.

"That's why I'm certain Wind's the man for this job, unless he's currently on another assignment and you're supervising him yourself."

"He's doing preliminary work on a new case, so I can have another operative fill in for him on that part," Handler answered. "I'll get in touch with Wind today and get him on the job effective immediately."

After hanging up, Burke took a few moments to himself. Fieldwork was always uncertain, no matter how experienced the investigator. Visceral reactions had to be tempered with knowledge and confidence. But the most important quality was having the guts to follow through—to see a case to its conclusion.

Love had never been part of the equation—until now.

He focused on the job, distancing himself from his feelings. His professional duty was clear. He had to keep Laura safe and catch whoever intended to harm her. For now, nothing was more important than that.

Chapter Eleven

When Burke went to join Laura, he found her in her office with Wolf, sitting in front of the computer. But she hadn't bothered to switch it on.

"Are you okay?"

She shook her head and wiped a tear from her cheek quickly with her hand. "I know I should push my feelings and thoughts aside until we find answers, but I can't do it. It's my fault Elena's dead, and I don't know how to deal with that."

"What are you talking about? You had nothing to do with what happened." Burke stared at her, trying to understand what was going through her head.

"I should have insisted Elena go away and stay with relatives in Albuquerque right after the first break-in. I knew there was something very wrong going on, and should have seen it would be too much for her."

Now he understood. He'd been there himself. Hindsight could be a devastating enemy. It had nearly destroyed him once. He remembered going over things in his mind, telling himself that if he'd done things just a little differently, his kid brother would still be alive. Burke had driven himself into a downward spiral that had nearly broken him, replaying what-if scenes in his head.

"Don't go there," he said, his voice filled with a rawness

he couldn't hide. "Second-guessing yourself like that will destroy you a little bit at a time. You'll dig a hole so deep for yourself you'll never get back out intact. Believe me, I've been there."

She looked up at Burke, surprised by the pain in his voice. "You've suffered a loss, too, one that tore you up inside," she said slowly.

"Yeah." The memory felt like a knife to his gut. "That's why I'm warning you. Let it go. What happened wasn't your fault, and deep down you know that."

"In a way it *is* my fault," she whispered in a broken voice. "There are things I didn't do…things I should have done."

Burke took Laura by the hand, led her to the living room couch and sat beside her. The cry for help he saw in her eyes had ripped through him. He couldn't stand to see her in pain. He had to help her even if it came at a high cost to himself.

"I've never spoken to anyone about what I'm going to tell you," he said. The words already left a bitter taste at the back of his throat. "Losing someone you love, someone you feel responsible for, can burn a hole right through you. I lost my little brother when I was seventeen. I was supposed to keep him safe, but I failed. To this day, I still remember every single detail of the day he died."

Laura reached for Burke's hand, deeply touched by his willingness to share his past with her. It was a gift she'd never expected. Although to the world he was tough and hard, he was now letting her see the vulnerable side of him—one he kept hidden from everyone else.

For a moment, they simply held hands. The gentleness and warmth of that touch bound them and strengthened their broken hearts.

Laura broke the silence first. "I don't imagine I'll ever forget anything about yesterday, not for as long as I live."

"In time, you'll put it in a place inside yourself where it can't overwhelm you. But if you cling to the belief that you're responsible, that will trap you in time and you won't be able to move forward."

To help her, he had to tell Laura the whole story, even if it meant letting her see him as he was—flawed. That's when he felt it—that first spidery touch of fear. He wanted her to accept him—no, it was more than want. He needed her to see him for who and what he was, and to know that she still cared for him.

Burke gazed at her, wondering how she'd respond to what he was about to tell her. With a burst of courage, he continued. "I remember coming home from high school. I'd just begun my senior year. Hoops, my kid brother, was already home playing basketball—that's how he'd gotten his nickname. Dad had been drinking, just like every day since our mom died."

"Did he feel responsible for her death?" she asked, trying to understand.

"No, it wasn't like that. My mom died of lung problems, and no one could have saved her. But his heart was broken. He got through the days by drinking until he passed out. He'd work occasionally, but then he'd spend what he made on cheap booze and leave us to fend for ourselves. Our relatives were on the other side of the rez, so we had no family to turn to." Burke shrugged. "But Hoops and I got by. I learned to hunt, and got a part-time job after school so we could buy our own groceries. But we never had enough food." He met her gaze. "You have no idea how hard it is to go to bed and try to sleep when you're so hungry your stomach hurts. But we struggled through it one day at a time, and we got free lunches at school when it was in session. Then things got worse."

"Worse?" She couldn't imagine anything going downhill from there.

"My dad went from helplessness to anger. Eventually, we learned that the best way for us to stay in one piece was to avoid him when he came home drunk, at least until he passed out. I wanted to run away, someplace off the rez, but I couldn't leave Hoops behind and I knew we both couldn't make it living on the streets." Each memory bit into him, slicing him up inside. "You see, I had to honor the promise I'd made my mother. Before she died, she asked me to take care of Hoops. She said that I was stronger than my dad, so she was depending on me." He paused, then in a slow, heavy voice added, "I made that promise to her never knowing how hard it would be for me to keep it—or that I'd ultimately fail."

"What happened to Hoops?" Laura whispered.

Burke took a deep breath. Bringing this into the light, baring his soul to Laura, was the hardest thing he'd ever done. But he wouldn't stop now. If he could spare her one moment of the hell he'd gone through, it would be worth it. "One night my dad stayed out later than usual. By the time he got home, he was roaring drunk and meaner than he'd been in a long, long time. He shoved me into the wall and nearly broke my jaw. I knew Hoops would be his next victim, so I stole the keys to Dad's pickup and left with my brother. I figured we'd spend the night out with a street gang in Farmington I'd been hanging with instead of going home. One of the guys was bound to let us crash with him."

Burke lapsed into a long silence, and Laura held his hand in both of hers. Finally he went on.

"I pulled up into the shopping mall parking lot where the gang sometimes hung out, and noticed one of the guys waiting in his car for the others. Hoops and I got out and walked toward him. Just then another car filled with guys from a rival gang pulled up between us and our friend.

"I gave Hoops the truck keys and told him to run for

the truck while I held them off, but they had plans of their own. Three of the guys kept me occupied while two others grabbed Hoops and shoved him into their car. My friend came over, but he got decked with a baseball bat. They had me down, kicking me, and I never had a chance. Before I could stop them, they took off with my brother. Without even thinking, I ran after them on foot. They'd slow down until I got close, then speed up again, knowing I'd never give up. I thought they were just having fun with me and, eventually, they'd let him go. But the driver was watching me instead of the road, and ran a stop sign. A truck hit them broadside.''

He paused. He felt cold all over, but her hands hadn't left his and he focused on the warmth of her touch. At long last, he continued. ''I got to my brother, but by the time the paramedics arrived, Hoops was gone. He died in my arms.''

''You couldn't have known what would happen,'' she said, tears filling her eyes. ''You were only a kid yourself, and you were trying to protect your brother from your dad.'' She felt a rush of empathy. Everything feminine in her wanted to ease the pain of that memory.

''But my judgment got him killed instead.''

Burke's voice was flat, but she could see from the rigid lines of his body that it was taking a great deal of effort for him to sound calm.

''That night I failed my kid brother *and* myself. The promise I'd made my mother—everything I'd believed in— changed in the twinkling of an eye. I seldom went home at all after that. I sank deeper and deeper into depression because I couldn't let go of the guilt. I just wanted to die.''

''You were so young to have to deal with so much,'' she said, her heart aching for him.

He couldn't bring himself to defend what he'd done, so just kept talking. ''Then my dad paid the price for all the drinking he'd done. His body began shutting down. He quit drinking, but by then it was too late. I saw him die a little bit at a time, like my mom had, and that's when it hit me. He'd thrown away his life, but I didn't want to do the same. So I got my act together and finished high school.''

"Then you went into the military?"

He nodded. "I was a born fighter because that's what I'd had to do all my life. I decided to use the warrior side of me to protect those who wouldn't or couldn't fight for themselves. As soon as I could enlist I joined the army, and eventually ended up in the Special Forces, specializing in Intelligence. Being part of an elite force suited me for a while.''

"But you didn't stay," she observed. "Was it because you learned to forgive yourself?"

"That came with time, but it wasn't the reason I left. I knew I'd been running from myself and that, to square things, I'd have to come back. I'd intended to join the police department, but before I could, I was contacted by Gray Wolf. Handler was interested in my Intelligence background and special skills. I liked the opportunity he was offering me, so I took the job. To this day, I have no idea how Handler knew about my military experience—it was all classified and still is.''

"But you found your calling."

"You can say that. My mother used to tell me that a Navajo could only find peace by 'walking in beauty.' That meant living life in a balanced and harmonious way. But my life still wasn't balanced—I had to make amends for the life that had been lost while under my care. So I made it my mission to fight for others who had the odds stacked against them.''

"Until I make sure that the ones who came after my godmother are in prison, I'll have no peace," Laura murmured. "I can't even try to move on and let go until that's accomplished."

"We *will* find them," Burke said firmly. "But in the meantime, you have to protect yourself. You can't continue second-guessing yourself." He drew her into his arms and held her against him. "I've been to the hell that you're just starting to know. If you don't fight it, Laura, it'll destroy you."

"I'll try, but you know what? I sure wish I could run away from the terrible pain inside me, if only for a little while," she said. "Too bad I could never go fast enough or far enough for that."

He tugged at her hand and she stood. "Where are we going?"

"To greet the wind." Leaving Wolf to protect her, Burke asked her to wait at her door with the lights out as he jogged over to his house.

Wondering what he was up to, she remained where she was. There was a full moon tonight, and the soft silver light dappled the ground in shimmering hues. It was late and the neighborhood was quiet. She liked listening to the breeze rustling through the tree branches, and taking in the scent of burning piñon logs from neighborhood fireplaces.

Hearing the roar of a powerful motorcycle engine, she smiled, suddenly realizing what Burke had in mind. Making sure Wolf had a fresh bowl of water and a biscuit, she left him inside the house. The dog didn't protest, almost as if he'd understood, after hearing the sound of the motorcycle engine, that he wouldn't be going.

Burke pulled up in front of her a few moments later. He was wearing his leather jacket and had another one over his arm. "This one's for you. Leather blocks the wind and you'll stay warm."

The jacket held that powerful sexy scent that seemed to define him—and excite her.

"Let's go," he said, putting on his helmet and handing her his spare.

They left the neighborhood quickly, then he turned and headed down a deserted road at the edge of town. Taking advantage of the lack of traffic, he pushed the motorcycle to top speed.

She felt the power of the bike and his control over it. It was freedom, pure and wild, and as they raced into the night, the speed was exhilarating—and the rightness of the moment intoxicating.

Her body was pressed to his, her hands wrapped tightly around his waist. The leather jacket he wore was open; he hadn't bothered to zip it. She worked her hands beneath the smooth leather. His shirt was light and she felt the muscles of his chest as she tightened her grip.

She would never forget this moment. For now, they were simply man and woman with nothing to guide them but the road before them and the night.

A long time later, when the night air turned icy, Burke finally headed home.

As they pulled into her driveway, Laura felt a twinge of disappointment. Wordlessly, she handed him the helmet he'd loaned her.

Their eyes met for one moment and he glanced into her broken heart. On the road, when she'd rested her head against him, he'd felt a wave of tenderness and protectiveness that had caught him by surprise. When she'd slipped her hand beneath his jacket, showing him that sharing the taste of the night wasn't enough—that she needed to touch him and feel the warmth of his flesh—it had nearly knocked him senseless. He'd wanted to stop the bike, to love her, and push back the pain that was breaking her in two.

Following an impulse he couldn't resist, he leaned over and brought his mouth down on hers. Her lips parted easily and her soft sigh of surrender tore right through him.

"Make the sadness stop for tonight, Burke," she said, drawing in a breath. "Make me feel alive. I've wanted you for so long and I can't stand feeling so alone."

The words slammed into him, making the fire inside him grow. His need for her never stopped—but knowing she needed him, too, sealed his course. Before he knew it, he was kissing her again and carrying her inside.

Wolf gave them one look, then went to lie down again on a throw rug across the living room.

"I've never felt this way about anyone else, Laura. You're in my blood."

He took her down the hall, set her down on her bed and held her close to him. Tonight would be an awakening and a healing. For her. For him.

Her breathing was unsteady as he mated his tongue with hers, teasing her, drawing her into his mouth, then plunging into hers. The little catch in her breath as he rained kisses down her neck, and the way she clung to him, drove him wild.

"We'll be a part of each other tonight. You'll feel me inside you, touching your soul, loving you. Ask for whatever gives you pleasure, and take whatever you want." He caressed her, opening her blouse and kissing the softness of her breasts.

She shuddered and whimpered, bathed in impossible sensations she didn't want to fight. Needing even more from him, Laura tugged open his shirt and ran her hands over his skin, feeling his muscles bunch and tense as she caressed him. She loved the hardness of his chest and the way his heartbeat pounded against the palm of her hand.

With one impatient tug, he stripped off his shirt and tossed it aside. Her hands felt like silk, and the trail of fire her touch left in its wake made it impossible for him to think.

"I want to be gentle with you, to take all night and

beyond, but if you keep touching me like that—'' He sucked in his breath as she slipped her fingertips beneath the waistband of his jeans. Before he could try and cool the heat that tore through him, she shifted and positioned herself over him. With slow and deliberate intent, she drew a long line with the tip of her tongue down the center of his chest.

He brought her mouth to his. The way her body pressed against him, the moist, scorching trail she'd left on his chest, made him crazy.

With a groan, he eased her back. "I want you too much...I need to cool off. I want to be gentle with you."

Still straddling him, she slipped off her shirt and bra, then leaned over until the tips of her breasts touched his chest. "Don't hold back," she whispered. "I want tonight to be wild, with no rules. Just us—needing, wanting, taking...and loving."

She whispered the last word and he suddenly knew that the strength of the feelings flowing through her scared her just as they did him. But there was no turning back. This was love—nothing else could be so powerful, so encompassing.

Rolling over, he positioned her beneath him, then murmuring her name, he took one of her breasts into his mouth. He ravaged her softness, loving the way she arched back, begging for more. Instinct and need drove him, for his mind was drugged with passion.

He unfastened her slacks and pulled them down over her hips, baring her, his gaze greedy as he kissed and tasted the areas he exposed, like a man who'd gone hungry too long.

Then suddenly and unexpectedly, he lifted her to her feet.

"No, don't stop," she pleaded.

"Never." With his hands firmly on her waist, he steadied

her as she stood naked before him. He wanted her to remember tonight—remember him—always.

"More," she begged, her eyes smoky.

In answer, he trailed long, wet kisses down her body.

She gasped as he found the core of her womanhood. "I'll
fall."

"I'll hold you. You won't be hurt. Fall...in love," he
murmured, his hand parting the moist petals he'd tasted.
"Lean on my shoulders," he said, then knelt before her.

It was magical, this mind-rending pleasure. She couldn't
think. She could only feel.

He felt her shatter as pleasure rocked her with unrelent-
ing intensity. Nothing had ever been sweeter or more sat-
isfying. Burke pulled her back down onto the bed and
kissed her lovingly.

When he drew back, she whimpered softly.

"No more waiting," he murmured.

Standing by the side of the bed, he peeled off his jeans,
and for one breathless moment let her gaze at him. There
would be balance and harmony between them. Then, his
body aroused beyond imagination and his blood raging, he
parted her legs and lowered himself over her. "And now
hold on to me."

The night became a journey of discovery for them both.
He filled her completely, loving her and letting the power
of their lovemaking rebuild her broken heart. He held nothing back from her. He took her higher than she'd ever been,
and in endless cycles of gentleness and roughness, showed
her pleasures she'd never tasted.

At long last her body arched and she cried out his name.
He followed her a heartbeat later and, with a cry ripped
from his soul, collapsed against her.

She held him then, and for long moments there was only
peace and love.

An eternity later, he stirred. "I'm too heavy for you,"

he murmured, his voice raw and deep. As he shifted to one side, she reached out to him.

"Don't go."

"I won't." He pulled her against him until her head rested on his chest. "Sleep now."

As Burke held her, he knew tonight would be a part of him forever. He loved her—more than he had a right to. Somehow, sometime, she'd made a permanent place for herself in his heart.

But he was a realist, not a romantic. What they'd shared had been born of desperation and unbearable pain. And that would taint and eventually destroy what they'd found.

Love without commitment from both man and woman couldn't survive, and Laura had made no promises. She'd never told him she loved him, not even during those mindless moments when passion had shuddered through her. She'd only come to him because she'd wanted the ache in her heart to stop—even if only for a little while. Once morning came, what they'd found in each other's arms would become a bittersweet memory, never separate from the pain they'd both wanted to outrun.

Laura had wanted comfort, and he'd given her everything a man who loved her could. But in the process, he'd lost his heart to a woman who would one day, probably very soon, leave his life forever.

Chapter Twelve

As the sunlight peered through a crack in the curtain, playing upon her pillow, Laura awoke. She was in her own bed, tucked under the covers. Burke lay beside her.

For a moment, she smiled, remembering, and allowing herself a moment to watch him. He lay completely naked on top of the covers, looking very male and endearingly rumpled.

She sat up, careful not to wake him. Men looked cuddly in the morning, but women invariably looked like something out of a teen horror flick of the sixties. At least she did.

Getting out bed, she reached for the first article of clothing near her. It turned out to be a light blue sweater that had fallen to the floor. She slipped it over her head as she got to her feet. Realizing that she was still bare from the waist down, she went to the dresser, searching for underwear.

"You look sexy," he murmured.

She gasped. A woman's least flattering attribute was her derriere. She turned, then, realizing that she'd just offered him an even more private look, she tugged at her sweater, forcibly stretching it down. Then, muttering something about a shower, she bolted into the bathroom.

Moments later, alone in the shower, she leaned against

the tiled wall and allowed the warm water to trickle down
her body. She didn't regret last night, but it wouldn't happen again. None of the relationships she'd had with men
had ever really grown. And everyone she'd really loved had
been taken from her. Her father and mother, now Elena...
How could anyone ask for love when every day that passed
brought only one certainty—it would not—could not—last.

It was better not to open her heart at all. Love led to
loss, and there was no way to avoid it. If she truly cared
for Burke—and she did—the best thing she could do for
both of them was to protect them from the pain that would
follow as inevitably as the end of each day.

By the time she emerged from the bathroom, a floor-
length robe wrapped tightly around her, Laura felt more in
control. As she stepped out into the bedroom, she saw that
Burke had gotten dressed. He stood by the window, Wolf
at his side.

"I need to take him for a run and go get dog food from
my house. Will you be all right?"

"Yes, of course. I'll fix breakfast for us, then we can
figure out what needs to be done today."

"Laura, about last night..." His voice was rough and
hard—a tone she'd learned meant he was feeling uncertain
about something. "Do you have any regrets?" he asked at
last.

He hadn't wanted to ask the question; she could sense
it. Her heart went out to him, because by asking, he'd made
himself vulnerable.

"No regrets at all," she said.

She saw him relax, then brace himself. "It can't happen
again, you know. I have a job to complete," he said in a
firm, quiet voice.

Laura watched him walk out with Wolf, then sat on the
edge of the bed. Once again he'd reminded her that what
kept him with her was the case. And now, in the clear light

of day, he'd drawn away from her. His expression and his voice had become distant. Though it had been exactly what she'd wanted, and she should have been relieved, the truth was all she felt now was hurt and desperately alone.

AFTER A BRIEF and quiet breakfast, they headed for the senior center. Leaving Wolf in the shade on the grass, they went inside.

The plan called for a change in tactics. Laura would concentrate on Karl Maurer, while Burke questioned Nicole, Maurer's wife. Burke was convinced that, hidden among the many secrets the center housed, were the answers they were searching for.

A short time later, Laura sat across from Karl's desk in a small, cluttered office with tired-looking wood paneling covered with tacked-on memos. "My godmother's death has raised a lot of questions," she told him. "The police think that what happened to her is related to the thefts and burglaries some of the center's members have experienced lately. That's why I'm here. I need to talk to you about that."

"Laura, I know you've suffered a terrible loss, but you need to remain patient and let the police do their job. The people you're looking for and trying to identify are probably very dangerous. I don't want to see anything happen to you," Karl replied.

"I appreciate your concern, but I'm not going to back off. I need to know why this happened to Elena."

"I wish I could tell you, but I assure you, it has nothing to do with the center," he insisted. "The addresses and phone numbers of our members are stored in our files and in the computer. The file cabinet is kept locked, and you need two passwords to access the membership files. I'm not saying it's unbreachable. I'm just telling you that the time and effort it would take would make it very unappealing to an intruder. And since most of our members are on fixed incomes and live modestly, the payoff wouldn't justify the considerable risk of discovery.''

"How thorough are your background checks on the center's employees?''

"Do yourself a favor. Drop this before you embarrass yourself or some innocent person, and get sued.''

"We're talking about a serious crime that led to someone's death," Laura protested. "I would think you'd be eager to do everything in your power to find out what part the center played in this.''

Karl's eyes darkened with anger. "We've played *no* part in what's happened. This conversation is over.'' He walked to the door and held it open. "You'd better leave now.''

Laura left the office reluctantly, hoping that Burke would have better luck. She'd batted zero. Seeing Burke talking to Nicole in the recreation room, she hung back, waiting just outside the entrance. Nicole's face was pale and her eyes looked wide and alarmed. She kept trying to turn away from Burke, but he stayed with her, asking questions. Finally, anger flashed clearly over her features, and she turned and strode away from him. This time Burke didn't go after her.

Seeing Laura, Burke walked over to meet her. "I have a real bad feeling about this place.''

"Did you get anything out of her?''

"Not directly, but the way she was acting spoke volumes to me. Innocent people don't react to simple questions that way. That woman is just plain scared.''

"Maybe we should try and talk to Enesco," Laura suggested. "He's in the foyer watching us," she added, cocking her head toward the soft-drink machine in the small room adjacent.

"Let's give it a try," Burke said, walking across the recreation room with her.

"After that, we should talk to the seniors, and John Foster, the real estate guy. He has ties to Karl Maurer because of the land deal my godmother soured for them."

When Enesco realized they were coming to talk to him, he tried to slip away, but Burke jogged forward and caught up to him before he could get out the door.

"Mr. Enesco, I wonder if you'd mind answering a few questions for me."

"English not good," the wiry, dark-haired man said in a thick accent Burke couldn't quite place.

"How long have you worked here?"

"No understand," he said. Then, seeing Nicole, he waved at her.

Nicole came over nearly at a run. "Mr. Silentman, I thought you were finished here," she said sharply.

"I still have a few questions I'd like to ask the center's driver."

"I'm sorry, but you're not with the police. You have no legal authority here, and we've already answered enough questions."

Burke's gaze was cold as steel. "You're acting like you've got something to hide."

"No, Mr. Silentman. What we're doing is forcing you to respect our privacy. We need to get things back to normal around here as soon as possible, and answering endless questions isn't going to help any of us."

"Mrs. Maurer, I also work for Gray Wolf Investigations," he said. "If you're in trouble, I can help you."

The news seemed to stun her, and her mouth dropped open. She stepped back, turning pale. "No one here needs or wants your help, Mr. Silentman."

"Even if you refuse to cooperate, we *will* find answers. Whatever you're hiding won't stay hidden for long," Burke said.

"Why are you pressing this? Do you think we had something to do with Elena's death?'' When neither Burke nor Laura answered, Nicole looked at them, horrified. "How could you believe that?"

"We're not accusing you or anyone else, Nicole," Laura said. "All we know is that something is being covered up here—something that may have begun with the deal your husband tried to cut with John Foster, the real estate developer."

Her eyes grew wide. "You're so wrong. Please leave right now. If you have any more questions, you'll have to go through our attorney. His name is Eric Cruise and he's in the book."

Michael Enesco looked at both of them, and then silently followed Nicole as she walked away.

"Why did you tell her you were with Gray Wolf?" Laura asked.

"I wanted to rattle her, and I think it worked. Now we'll wait and see if that leads her to make any mistakes we can take advantage of," Burke said. "Now let's go talk to John Foster."

BURKE DROVE ACROSS TOWN to the real estate developer's office. Now that he knew for sure that they were onto something, he had to dig deeper until the pieces of the puzzle started falling into place.

Burke and Laura went in together, and this time they took Wolf with them. The dog stayed beside Burke, at heel, as they were shown into Foster's office.

"I think bringing the dog was a stroke of genius," Laura said when they were left alone in the plush office. "The receptionist took one look at Wolf and decided not to make us wait."

Burke looked down at the dog, who had a panting grin on his face. "Yeah, furball. I think you've earned your dog food today."

Wolf licked his chops, and when he opened his mouth again, his canines gleamed.

Laura chuckled softly. "I think he's reminding you not to tease him too much. He considers some things, like his dish of kibbles, sacred."

Before Burke could respond, Foster strode into the room. He exuded the self-confidence and arrogance of a man used to power. Everything about him—the expensive cut of his suit, the casual attitude and even his custom-designed office furnishings—spoke of prestige and position. A photograph of Foster, the New Mexico governor and the president engaged in conversation hung above the man's desk in a large gold frame.

Introductions were brief. There was a restless energy about the developer as he walked to a built-in sideboard and poured them both mineral water in silver-rimmed glasses. Although he'd acknowledged Wolf's presence with a brief glance, once the dog lay down it was clear Foster no longer felt the animal merited his attention.

"I'm sorry to hear what happened to Doña Elena, Miss Santos," he said, his pronunciation practiced and flawless.

"Thank you. It's been a difficult time. There are so many things I still don't understand."

"Which brings us to the reason why we came." Burke presented himself as an investigator for the Gray Wolf agency, then waited patiently for the man's response.

"I had a feeling that your interest in this case was more than personal," Foster said. "What can I do for you?"

His words stabbed at Laura, but she pushed the feeling aside.

"I'd like you to give me the particulars of the deal you made with the senior center," Burke said.

Foster regarded him coolly. "I normally don't discuss my private business dealings with anyone."

"We believe there may be a connection between the

business deals conducted by the center's administrative officer and an attempted kidnapping that led to a death.''

"My godmother's, to be precise," Laura added.

For a moment Foster said nothing, staring across the room, gathering his thoughts. "Elena Baca became my greatest nemesis," he finally admitted, "but I don't see how you can link an attempted kidnapping or her death to the business deal I had with Karl Maurer."

"Cases come together in strange ways," Burke said, deliberately being vague. "Why don't you tell me what you know? Your cooperation will make things easier on everyone involved, and maybe help clear up matters before there's a lot of ugly publicity."

Foster jumped at the chance to avoid bad press. "It started when Karl asked me to become a sponsor for the center. That operation has always been on the verge of bankruptcy, but it's even more so lately because the building needs some renovations."

"I don't understand. How can they be so critically short of money? They've always had such a large membership," Laura said.

"The fees they can charge are moderate because their membership is, by and large, from a lower-income clientele. This isn't, after all, the Cherry Ridge Country Club. Right now, the center needs to upgrade the facility to meet the standards for handicap access, and they're desperate for a corporate sponsor."

"I had no idea," Laura said.

"The Maurers bought the center in a mortgage foreclosure arrangement about three years ago. They've worked hard and have turned a lot of it around by getting prominent business interests in the community to make donations and become sponsors. In exchange, the senior citizens are encouraged to use the services the businesses provide. It's worked well, but it still didn't give the Maurers the funding necessary to meet all their objectives.''

''And you offered to make a substantial donation in exchange for some cooperation,'' Laura said.

''Precisely. I wanted to buy the land adjacent to the center and turn it into a low-income apartment complex. But I knew that people generally oppose new developments they perceive as lowering property values, so I had to move fast before neighborhood associations got their people organized. Maurer offered me a deal. He promised me the support of the center in case I needed it to fight neighborhood opposition—in exchange, of course, for a substantial donation. The deal was for a high five figures, and that money would have put him in the black again.''

''But then he found out he couldn't deliver the support,'' Burke said.

''Right. When Elena Baca found out about the building project, she did precisely what we wanted to avoid—she organized everyone into opposing the development, asking that the land be used as a park, as promised. When Maurer tried to get the seniors to support his stand on the issue, he failed. Mrs. Baca's arguments were far more persuasive, it seems. My development fell through. Of course I rescinded my offer to make a donation, because Maurer hadn't met his side of the bargain.''

''Did you take a big loss on the deal?'' Burke asked.

''In the long run, no. I just chose another site, and construction is already under way. Unfortunately, the affair resulted in some negative publicity for my company and that did trouble me.'' He opened his hands, palms up, and shrugged. ''But that's hardly enough reason for me to have her kidnapped. And to what end? Ransom? Hardly likely, don't you think?''

''What about Karl Maurer?'' Burke pressed.

''I hear he's still in financial trouble. My guess is he'll

have to shut down or file for bankruptcy in another six months unless he gets a sponsor with deep pockets to back him." Foster paused. "But it's partially his own fault, you know. His bookkeeping is a disaster, and he's frittering away his investment."

"Explain," Burke said.

"I had a complete check done on the center's finances before I agreed to do business with Maurer. In the course of that, my accountant found some routine but substantial debits listed as miscellaneous expenses. Those really cut into his operating budget. At first we suspected he was skimming money, but if he is, I don't know what's become of it. I had a credit report done on him and the man's personal finances aren't in much better shape."

"I'd like a look at those files," Burke stated.

"Absolutely not. Those are confidential reports my business obtained under the condition that they remain private."

Burke stood. "Then I'll have to find another way to get those reports, or similar ones. And I will. You can count on that."

Foster met Burke's gaze and held it as he weighed his options. "Your company has a solid reputation," he said at last. "If Gray Wolf can guarantee that they'll keep the reports entirely confidential, I might be persuaded to cooperate."

Burke considered it, then nodded. "Agreed. We'll only use the reports to generate leads. We'll substantiate the data we need independently."

"Fair enough." The developer walked across the office and unlocked a file cabinet. After a moment he found what he was looking for, then headed over to a small copy machine. He placed the papers from the file folder into the feed tray and began to make copies. "Having you put your firm's reputation on the line is all the guarantee I need."

As they walked out minutes later, Burke looked at Laura. "He's a very smart man. Without belaboring the point, he just warned me that if I violate our agreement, he'll make sure word gets around that Gray Wolf Investigations can't be trusted. Our reputation—and our business—would suffer irreparable harm."

"But we got what we wanted," Laura said as she followed him out to the car. "So what now?"

"I want to stop by my office at Gray Wolf Investigations. I'd like to get the name, address and telephone number of the translator who's working on your foreign editions. But to do that, I'll have to talk to Handler, my boss, and access our computer records there. Some things never leave the office database."

As Burke drove to the outskirts of town, he wondered what she'd think of the agency, or more to the point, Handler. That electronically altered voice often rattled people.

For a moment, he considered taking her home, but then nixed the idea. She was safer with him. And the truth was, he wanted her to see his world and the part of his life no one else ever saw. That was, for some inexplicable reason, suddenly very important to him.

Chapter Thirteen

They pulled up to a stark-looking warehouse on the eastern outskirts of Farmington. Burke parked near the side door and, with Wolf by him, walked over and pressed a small buzzer. The windowless metal door opened, and they went inside.

They entered a small office area equipped with four over-stuffed leather chairs and a large desk with a computer and multifunction copier. "Have a seat. I need a few minutes at my desk," Burke said, sitting down behind it.

"Mr. Silentman," an electronically altered voice stated from a microphone in the corner near the ceiling, "I'm surprised to see you here today."

Burke turned in his chair to face the video camera attached on the opposite wall. "I've had some new developments," he said, and filled Handler in about Foster and the other recent events. "What I'd like to do next is talk to the translator who's been working on the foreign editions."

"I'll have to clear it with him first. His agreement with us guarantees him anonymity unless there are extenuating circumstances," Handler said. "But as of his last report, the first two novels he read seem to be a relatively accurate, but censored translation of the English original."

Laura looked at Burke. "I told you," she mouthed.

"He'll keep at it, however, until all five books are checked out," Handler said. "If he finds anything unusual, you'll be notified immediately."

"I would still like a chance to speak to him. I want to get his impression on word usage and other subtleties, and possibly the editorial alterations. What we're looking for may be an out-of-place phrase, a series of what appear to be typos, or a misspelled word or series of words that make up an anagram. I'd like to impress upon him that this might be more complex than a simple translation job, and I think it'll help if I discuss this directly with him."

"Then I'll clear it with him and let you know as soon as possible," Handler answered. "Please upload the files you brought us from Mr. Foster into the computer."

"I'll do it right now, sir."

The room grew silent as Burke began scanning pages into the computer. Laura came up to stand beside him.

"Who's Handler, and why all the secrecy with his voice?"

"I don't know the answer to either of those questions. All I can tell you is that he prefers to keep his identity hidden. Agency rules prohibit any operative from trying to learn who he is, too."

"How do you know he's not a criminal on the run?"

"Because of the backing this agency gets from law enforcement agencies—federal and local—whenever we need it. We even have access to several restricted databases. Handler has some serious high-level clearance."

"How many people work here?"

"I'm honestly not sure. There are operatives and support personnel, but everyone, including me, works on a need-to-know. I have access to more information than most because my job is to coordinate the field operatives, but I'm restricted to certain areas of the business."

After he was finished scanning the information, he turned

and faced the camera. "The papers have been scanned and uploaded."

"Our accountants will check everything out. We should have a report for you within twenty-four hours."

Burke signaled Wolf, who'd been lying on the cool concrete floor, and motioned Laura toward the door. "We're finished here for now. Let's return to your home."

Later, as they drove back, Laura glanced at Burke. "I'd be screaming with questions if I worked there."

Burke laughed. "Our investigators are people who, by profession, don't trust anyone and don't take things at face value. But here, everything about the operation assures you constantly that you're on the side of the good guys. The work we do sets things right for people who wouldn't have had a chance without us."

"And that's why you stay?"

"Every time we close a case I know I've played a part in restoring harmony and I can walk in beauty."

"You have nothing to atone for. You know that now, don't you? You're not to blame for what happened to Hoops."

"You, of all people, should know how some tragedies become a part of everything we are. The past guides our present. We can't escape what came before—the only choice we have is how we use the experience."

When they pulled into her driveway, the senior center's van was parked there at the curb, waiting. "This is an interesting surprise," she said.

Michael Enesco stood beside an elderly woman who sat in a motorized wheelchair.

"Do you know her?" Burke asked.

"That's Shaunna Williams, the activities coordinator," Laura said.

Seeing them get out of Burke's car, Shaunna waved.

"I'm glad you're here. I didn't want to give up and leave without talking to you."

"Come into the house. We'll be more comfortable there."

Shaunna glanced back at Enesco. "Please wait for me here, Michael," she said, then pushed a small lever on a control box, setting the battery-powered unit into motion.

Burke helped maneuver Shaunna's chair over the threshold, and they all entered the living room. Laura and Burke took a seat on the couch, and Shaunna took a position facing them.

"Now tell me what we can do for you," Laura said.

Shaunna took a deep breath, then let it out slowly. "I worked at the center before the Maurers took over. I was a receptionist and clerk, working for minimum wage, though I'd been there for three years. But when the Maurers came on board they promoted me and made me activities coordinator. My handicap didn't matter to them at all. They simply trusted me to do the job." She looked at Burke, then at Laura. "The reason I'm telling you this is because I want you to know that they're very good people. You've misjudged them completely if you think they've done something illegal."

"I'm not judging them," Laura said. "I'm just looking into a few things."

"You're investigating the center, trying to find a link to Miss Elena's death, but you have no idea the harm you're doing to the Maurers' reputations. And without their good name, they won't be as successful soliciting donations and raising funds to keep the center open. Between the police and you two asking to see our records and trying to find a connection between the thefts, things are growing increasingly difficult. The Maurers failed to get any more funds from sponsors recently because they're underneath this cloud of suspicion."

"Then we all need to work together to clear this up quickly," Laura answered.

"But innuendo is destroying the center, don't you see? And the seniors desperately need it to stay open. The elderly become invisible to the rest of the community. Many people are uncomfortable around older folks. There are dozens of labels attached to us—too slow, too grouchy, too feeble. The end result is that we're isolated. We need a place that's for us—one where there are no labels, only understanding from our own contemporaries. Friendships we can count on."

"You're right about all that, but the investigation can't be dropped until the truth comes out," Laura said.

"No matter what the cost?"

Burke spoke at last. "What you have to remember is that the seniors have been victimized by robberies that happened in their own homes, and they deserve answers and justice. There's a question of their safety, too. Do you understand?"

Shaunna nodded slowly. "All right. I knew I couldn't talk you out of dropping the case, but will you at least investigate more discreetly?"

"We'll do our best," Burke answered.

Shaunna Williams thumbed the lever on the wheelchair's control box and made her way slowly toward the door. Burke moved ahead of her to help her get over the threshold again. "Thank you for taking time to listen," she said.

Laura watched from the window as Enesco met her and helped her into the van, using a power-lift platform.

Burke had come up behind her, and when Laura turned around, her breasts brushed his chest. She heard him suck in his breath. His eyes were stormy with desire and, for a heartbeat, she couldn't tear her gaze away.

Burke stood his ground as need and desire slammed into him with the force of a speeding car. She made him crazy.

In a moment of recklessness, he tangled his hand in her hair and drew her toward him.

His kiss was like the man he was—hard and demanding. His tongue danced with hers until the blood rushing through his veins turned into a river of fire. He would have traded everything for the chance to take her again, to feel her come alive beneath him as he entered her body.

He released her seconds later, before his control vanished. As it was, his breathing was harsh, and his body throbbed fiercely.

Laura moved away from him. "I can't play this game. I'm not yours and you're not mine. All we're doing is making it harder on ourselves when the time comes for us to move on."

Burke allowed her to walk away because he knew that his duty was to guard her, and he couldn't do that while kissing her senseless. As she left the room, he remained still, waiting for the fires inside him to cool.

"A man fights for what he wants, and I *will* fight for you," he whispered in the emptiness of the room. "What's between us is right, and one way or another, I'll have to make a believer out of you."

TWENTY MINUTES LATER, they sat in Laura's kitchen. She'd brewed some coffee for both of them, desperately needing something to do.

The desire to give in to the torrent of feelings that had cascaded through her when Burke kissed her had been overwhelming. But fear made for caution. How could she forget that every relationship she'd ever had had failed? And Burke's profession was a dangerous one. She couldn't watch him leave every day, knowing he might not return.

"She was sent here, you know," Burke commented, interrupting her thoughts.

It took her a moment to figure out what he was talking about. "You mean Shaunna?"

"Yes. I'm certain the Maurers sent her, hoping she could persuade us to drop the case. The fact that they're trying so hard could mean we're getting close to something they don't want us to know."

"Then I think we should go talk to Delbert Hutton. He was a really close friend of Elena's, and he's on the board of directors at the center. He might know more about the Maurers and their current associates."

"Do you have his address?"

She shook her head, but went to the phone book and looked it up. "Got it. Let's go."

Just then, Burke's cell phone buzzed. He listened to the caller for a moment, exchanged a few words, then hung up. "It's an associate of mine who has been keeping an eye on Springer. Since he's been strictly business for the past day, my man is going to trail Al Baca for a while."

"Good. Maybe Ken finally got the message."

They drove to a large residence a few miles up La Plata Canyon on the western side of Farmington. Inside the walled property was a large two-story house, and beyond that, a small white cottage with a matching picket fence. "Mr. Hutton lives in the cottage, his daughter and her family in the house. He's very independent, though he's nearly ninety, so this arrangement suited everyone."

They found Mr. Hutton on his knees, gardening, beside the cottage. He glanced up, pushed his glasses into place and, recognizing Laura, smiled. "How wonderful to see you!" he said in greeting, standing up slowly and leaning on a cane. "Come into my house. We can talk there."

The two-room cottage was cozy and the walls were covered with photos, as were nearly every tabletop and shelf. He showed them to the kitchen area, then washed his hands in the sink.

"Would you prefer iced tea or colas?" He waved them toward chairs around a small wooden table.

"Whatever is easier," Laura said. "Can I help?"

A few minutes later they sat down around the kitchen table.

"Now tell me why you've come. This is more than a social visit, isn't it?" he asked.

She nodded. "It's about the center and what happened to my godmother."

His expression grim, Delbert leaned forward and placed his hands palms down on the table. "To tell you the truth, we're all very worried. Everyone on the board of directors regrets that we didn't keep closer tabs all along on what was going on there. We've been told that finances are a mess at the moment."

"I've heard the center's having a financial crisis," Laura said.

He nodded slowly. "Apparently, Foster's promised donation was critical. Now, on top of everything else, the police think the center's involved somehow with the thefts the seniors have experienced." He shook his head slowly. "If there have been improprieties of any kind, the members of the board are just as responsible as the Maurers, in my opinion. We didn't pay enough attention to what was happening there."

"Tell me about Karl and Nicole. Do you think they're on the up-and-up?" Burke asked.

The elderly man hesitated. "I don't know for certain, to be honest. They formed the corporation and handpicked each board member. Allowing someone to oversee your activities doesn't sound like a good strategy when you intend to hide something, but you never know. We accepted because we knew that it would be easier for the center to solicit sponsors if there was a board on record, overseeing the operation. And, truth is, we all have a vested interest in having the center remain solvent. But now…well, I can tell you that we've decided to get more involved, and we've started by ordering a full audit of the books. It'll begin next week, I'm told.''

"Do you think it's possible my godmother found out that the center's funds were being misused, and that's why there's a financial crisis there?"

"If Elena discovered something of that nature she'd have come directly to me. I was her friend. When she found out about the deal the Maurers were cutting with Foster, I was the first person she told, and I helped her organize things.''

"Did the board look into the Maurers' activities then?" Burke asked.

"There was some talk about doing that, but, eventually, it fizzled out and nothing happened." He shrugged. "The board's main function has been to take care of disputes members have with management. We're given financial reports every quarter, mind you, but they've always seemed to be in order, and aren't very detailed.''

"If you find out that there's been illegal or criminal activity, would you call me and let me know? I'll keep it confidential," Laura said.

He considered for a moment, then nodded. "I shouldn't, but I will—for Elena's sake. She would have wanted me to help you.''

After saying goodbye, they started home. Lost in thought, Laura stared off into the distance as the day yielded slowly to night. "We've been working practically nonstop for days now, but we still don't have any real answers.''

"We have some, just not enough.''

"What part do you think your friend Douglas Begay plays in all this?"

"I wish I knew," Burke mused. "But my gut feeling is

that once we answer that question, we'll be able to see the whole picture clearly.''

His cell phone rang, and he brought the unit out and flipped it open. "Silentman." Listening for several seconds, he acknowledged the caller with a thanks, then disconnected, frowning.

"Your contact?" Laura asked and, seeing him nod, added, "Is something wrong?"

"Probably not. He just can't find Al Baca right now, so he's going to prowl the taverns on East Main near the Poker Face Bar to try and locate him. If that fails, he's going to go by the fire station and check again on Springer."

Burke pulled into her driveway and parked. "On a much less serious note, I was thinking of getting a pizza for dinner. Are you up for it?"

"Sounds fine. Delivery around here takes forever, so let's go pick it up after I take a shower."

"No more bubble baths, huh?" His tone was light, but his eyes darkened and flashed with an eroticism all their own, and she knew he was recalling the night he'd interrupted her bath. A special awareness shimmered between them—his very essence calling to hers.

A tremor shot through her, and he instinctively reached for her hand. "Are you okay?"

Though it had only been a casual touch, heat flared between them.

She drew away. "Let's go inside. Wolf's probably starving, right boy?" She glanced behind her and, without warning, Wolf leaned forward and licked her face with his wet tongue.

"Aack!" Laughing, she jerked back, then scratched the dog's head. "That's some kiss."

Burke laughed. "At least he hadn't just had his canned dog food."

She wrinkled her nose. "Eeeuu! With that charming thought I think I'll hit the shower. I won't be long."

Laura went to her room and undressed, listening to the clang of the dog food plate and Wolf's excited bark as Burke fed him in the kitchen.

She had stripped off most of her clothing, and was down to her panties, when a flash of movement outside the window caught her eye. The gap in the curtains was less than three inches across, and the possibility of an intruder seemed unlikely because the backyard was fenced and padlocked.

Unsure, but deciding to ask Burke to check, anyway, she went to get her robe. Before she could reach it, a figure approached the glass. Moonlight and shadows distorted his features, making them appear dark and sunken, like an apparition straight from hell.

Laura screamed, turning away.

Chapter Fourteen

In an instant, Burke crashed into the room. Seeing her wearing only panties, he froze.

"There was a man right outside my window!" she blurted, reaching for her robe.

Her words broke through to his brain, and a rage as dark as night filled him. Running to the window, he yanked it open, then pushed out the screen.

"Get him!" he ordered Wolf.

The animal didn't hesitate. He leaped out the window like a bolt of lightning.

"Get dressed," Burke growled, jumping out of the window after Wolf.

As the intruder climbed up the fence, Wolf lunged and barely missed his flailing leg. Burke heard the man cursing as he scrambled over the top and dropped with a thud on the other side.

Grabbing hold of the top of the six-foot fence, Burke pulled himself up and over in one powerful effort. Before he could get to the curb, however, the intruder had jumped into his car and was racing down the street. The license plate was unreadable, probably splashed with mud to conceal it, and it was too dark to see the exact make of the car. Burke stalked back to the house, his hands clenched into fists. It would feel good to beat on something now. He thought of the heavy body bag at the gym, and had a feeling he would put his fist right through the leather.

Wolf was in the living room, having obviously come back in through the window to guard Laura once it was apparent he couldn't jump over the fence.

"We missed an opportunity tonight, furball. I would have loved tearing that guy apart, then tossing you what was left over."

Wolf barked and licked his lips.

Laura was waiting in the kitchen, hugging her robe to her. "I called Wolf back inside. The creep got away?"

"Yeah." The word left a bitter taste in Burke's mouth.

As he glanced over at her, he saw that she was trembling, and without even stopping to think, he pulled her into his arms.

Laura didn't struggle as he held her against him, stroking her hair and murmuring reassurances. But it was hard for him to be gentle now when what he wanted most was to find the creep and pound his face into the dirt.

As he held her, he slowly became aware of the soft curves of her body, which the thin fabric of her robe did little to disguise. To the touch, it was almost as if she were wearing nothing at all.

It became torture not to push the robe away and make love to her over and over again until nothing else mattered—to her or to him.

"I will never feel safe in my home again," she said.

"He didn't touch you—and he never will," Burke said, his voice filled with raw conviction.

When his cell phone rang, he forced himself to release her, but the heat of her body remained with him and the soft scent of her perfume remained on his clothes. "Go get dressed. I'll answer this call, then contact the police. They'll want to ask you some questions."

As she moved away, he flipped open the phone. He

spoke to Handler, updating him, and was surprised to hear how steady his voice sounded, when every muscle in his body felt coiled with tension.

With effort, Burke pushed his personal needs aside, knowing they had no place in what he had to do now. It was time to take care of business.

SHE'D HAD VERY LITTLE sleep and lots of time to think. By the time Laura left her bedroom the following morning, she knew exactly what she had to do. The police had come by briefly last night, but since she hadn't been able to make an ID, there'd been little for them to go on. Now, it was her turn.

The more she'd thought about it, running through the events of last night in her mind, the more convinced she became that the person she'd seen could have easily been Ken Springer. The Peeping Tom's height and shape were about right for Ken. Of course, that didn't prove anything, but she intended to find out one way or another this morning. Burke, of course, wouldn't like her plan at all, but she'd see it through.

As she stepped into the kitchen, Burke was feeding Wolf. His shirt was open and hung loose over his pants. He hadn't shaved, was barefoot and had obviously just woken up, but he looked incredibly sexy.

"Good morning," he said gruffly, glancing up.

She went over to the counter and began to fix coffee. "After we're both awake, I want to go to the fire station where Ken has his office," she said. "I'm going to force a confrontation with him. I've thought of little else all night, and I believe it might have been him outside my window."

"I'll handle this." Burke's face became hard, anger flashing like fire in his eyes.

"No. This is something I have to take care of myself."

Seeing him start to argue, she held up a hand. "I know you can take care of this, Burke, but I need to do this for myself. You won't always be there."

Her words cut him like a knife. He *wanted* to always be there. Then, as he studied her face, he suddenly understood what was driving her. Laura needed to face her fears. She had to prove to herself that she could handle a creep like Springer, and that no one had the power to make her cower. Her courage never ceased to surprise him. "All right. But I'm going with you. No, don't bother arguing. I'll stay out of it, but I'm going."

As he walked out of the kitchen, Laura dropped down onto a chair. For a minute or two, she'd seen only anger on Burke's face. He'd wanted to handle this himself. But he couldn't always have what he wanted—no more than she could.

As she heard the sound of an electric razor coming from one of the bedrooms, her gaze fell on the wallet and keys he'd left on the table. It was almost as if he belonged here now.

Pushing back the longing that wound through her chest, Laura poured herself a cup of coffee, then sat down and tried to think practical thoughts.

By the time Burke emerged, showered and dressed, his mood had worsened. "I've changed my mind," he announced. "This guy is unbalanced, and I don't want you anywhere near him. So I'll go. You stay."

"Monosyllabic orders might work when you're dealing with Wolf, but I find that irritating. And, in case you haven't noticed, I don't take orders. At most, I listen to suggestions."

He wanted to throttle her. He really did. How on earth had he fallen in love with such an exasperating woman? "Listen very carefully—"

"No. *You* listen. I'll either go alone, or you can come

with me. But I *am* going. Now let's get cracking,'' Laura said.

Muttering vile things under his breath, Burke snapped an order to Wolf and followed her outside.

"We're taking the agency car," he said, heading her off as she strode to her small sedan.

"Are you sure? If you're having doubts, I'll be happy to drive myself."

He swore softly. Gone was the sweet, vulnerable woman he'd held last night. Maybe aliens had kidnapped *that* Laura and left him with a substitute. Roswell wasn't all that far away.

"We're *both* going in *my* car," he roared.

She seemed to sense he meant business, because she followed him. But the second he turned north instead of south when he backed out of the driveway, she sat up abruptly.

"You should have gone the other way. This isn't the quickest way to the station."

"That's because we're going to get breakfast. I want you to think about this first."

"I don't need to think—"

"Oh, yeah you do. Trust me." As he halted at the stop sign just two blocks from Laura's home, he saw Springer's vehicle parked by the curb just ahead, with him in it. "Son of a—"

Seeing there was no oncoming traffic, Burke pressed down hard on the accelerator, swinging his vehicle around sharply so it blocked Springer's. The move surprised Laura, and she gasped.

Springer, who'd ducked down to avoid being seen, looked up, startled that Burke was so close now.

Burke jumped out of the car.

Springer also stepped out of his car, and came forward, his hands clenched into fists.

He threw a punch immediately, but Burke ducked. Grabbing Springer's outstretched arm, he twisted it behind his back and forced Ken up against the hood of the department's car.

"News flash—there are laws against stalking," Burke growled. "You're busted."

Ken groaned, tried to wiggle free, then realized he was going nowhere. "I'm watching for an arsonist who might be in this area. Check it out with my captain if you don't believe me."

Laura walked over to Springer's car and, looking inside, found a pair of binoculars. Sitting behind the driver's seat, she raised the binoculars and looked off in the direction of her house. Through a gap in the trees, she could see her living room window and all the way to the coffee urn in her kitchen.

Swallowing back her anger, she put down the binoculars and walked up to him. "Ken, I'm pressing charges this time. I've had enough of this. I know it was you looking in my bedroom window last night."

Springer's face went pale. "Laura, please don't do that. I was only trying to protect you! All I wanted to do was make sure you were still okay. But if you turn me in, I'll probably lose my job, and nobody will ever hire me as a fireman."

She saw the fear in his eyes and hesitated.

"Don't do it, Laura, please. I won't cause you any more trouble. I swear."

She hated what he'd done, but she didn't want to destroy him, either. "I'm going to give you a second chance, Ken. Those are rare in life. Use it well. But understand one thing. I *never* want to see you again, not even by accident in a store. Am I making myself clear? If I do, I'll press charges. And I'll have witnesses. It won't just be my word against yours."

"Agreed. I promise." He tried to break free of Burke's grip, but it didn't work.

Burke stared at him, anger still etched clearly on his face.

"Burke, let him go," Laura said firmly, unsure he would do as she asked. It didn't take a mind reader to see that he was itching for a fight.

Then a car drove by, slowing down as it passed them and distracting Burke for a heartbeat. An elderly man with long white hair gave Burke a nod, and as the car continued on, Burke seemed to ease up.

"Get out of my face," he snarled. "The lady has given you a chance—which is more than you deserve. But if you screw up, you'll answer to me."

Springer rushed to his car without looking either of them in the eye, then backed away quickly and drove down the street.

"Thanks for doing what I asked," she said.

"Don't thank me too much. The only reason I let him go was because he may yet come in handy to us."

"Huh?"

"He doesn't know it, but as of right now, he's under surveillance for the second time," Burke explained.

"Who's watching him? No one followed him. I'm sure of it," she said, looking around. "The only car around here that went in the same direction was the one driven by that old man, and he went by first. He certainly didn't follow."

Burke smiled at her, but didn't answer.

"Even if you tell me that Gray Wolf hires senior citizens, the fact is he wasn't *following* Ken."

"There are some things an operative can't discuss. You'll just have to trust me."

Men were strange creatures, she suddenly decided. Attractive and appealing, but definitely strange.

As they finally got under way again, heading to the restaurant for breakfast, Burke dialed his associate's cell number. "Wind, thank you."

Laura stared at Burke. "Do you thank the clouds and the trees by phone, too?"

He smiled. "Actually, I do."

AFTER A HEARTY BREAKFAST, they drove back in the direction of Laura's home. They hadn't gone a mile before Burke glanced into the rearview mirror for the second time.

"What's wrong?" she asked.

Wolf, who'd been eating a plate of eggs she'd insisted on ordering for the dog, had left his food and was sitting up straight, ears pricked forward.

"I think we're being followed by that blue van about two hundred yards behind us. But hang tight. I need to make sure this is more than coincidence."

Burke turned and headed toward the main highway, but at the final intersection before the ramp, swerved to his left and headed straight down a narrow access road. Slowing as if to make a right turn, he accelerated at the last minute and drove on into a residential area.

He checked the rearview mirror every few seconds, and made a series of random left and right turns, circling several blocks. Finally, he stopped by the curb beside a vacant lot.

After a five-minute wait without spotting the blue van, they pulled back out onto the access road. Burke checked in the rearview mirror again and finally relaxed.

"You either lost him or the van was never following us, right?"

"I'm not sure yet." Burke continued back uphill toward the main highway.

Slowing for a red light, he glanced in the side mirror and cursed. "That guy's a pro."

Laura glanced back and saw that the blue van was once again behind them.

"Now what?"

"I'm going to turn the tables on him and see how good he is at avoiding *us*. Just keep your seat belt on and brace yourself for a quick move." Burke pulled over to the shoulder of the road and stopped the vehicle. He stepped out of the car and popped the hood open, as if to check the engine.

Laura saw the blue van suddenly pull out of the row of cars waiting for the light, and turn completely around, slipping between two cars headed in the opposite direction.

"He's running for it." Burke slammed down the hood and jumped back into the car. "That's one smart cookie. He anticipated me, and we'll have a hard time catching up to him now. So we won't try. Let's just get out of here while the going's good."

Pulling back out onto the road, Burke took the light on a yellow and sped up the ramp to the highway.

"Who do you think could be following us?" Laura asked. "It isn't Ken Springer, that's for sure, unless he's a better actor than I thought."

"You're right, it can't be Springer. Whoever that was is no amateur. But we must be making the right people nervous. Let's get back to your house so I can check out a few things using the computer. I want to know if anyone's reported a blue van stolen, or if there are any crimes connected with a vehicle of that make, model and year."

On the way, Burke decided to speed the process up, and phoned in the query to Handler.

Moments after they arrived at Laura's, Burke's cell phone rang. Handler had found nothing on the police databases concerning a blue van, but he said he'd keep looking. "What I do have for you is the information you requested on the driver at the senior center, Michael Enesco," Handler added. "He hasn't been in the States very long— less than two months. That's why we had a problem turning up anything. He's here on a work visa from West Medias."

"Another link to West Medias..." Burke muttered. There was something going on, but only Doug had the answers and he was nowhere to be found.

"We're still trying to find a connection between Enesco and Douglas Begay, our client, but so far we've come up empty."

By the time Burke closed his cell phone, ideas were racing in his head.

"What's going on?" Laura asked.

He told her about Enesco.

"That's interesting, but there's no way he's the guy who broke into my house. The intruder I ran up against had *no* accent, and Michael Enesco's English is barely understandable."

"But we can't ignore his connection to West Medias. Doug knew you needed protection. That's the key—and the only link I can see between you and him are those foreign editions." Burke placed another call to Handler. This time, he managed to get the translator's name and address. "Tomorrow we're going to pay him a visit," he said after hanging up. "Handler has him working overtime tonight so, with luck, by tomorrow we'll have answers."

Burke spent the rest of the day finishing up background checks via computer on the rest of the staff at the center. With the exception of Enesco, there was nothing out of the ordinary to be found. The only person who didn't seem to have much documented background or work history he could check on was Karl Maurer's wife, Nicole. The only thing he could dig up about her was that she and Karl had been married for ten years. And, from what he could see, Nicole had been a stay-at-home wife. It all seemed straightforward, but he just couldn't get rid of the feeling that he was missing something.

More determined than ever, he continued digging. On this ground, he was sure of himself. No matter what it took and no matter what the cost, he would break this case wide open.

Chapter Fifteen

Laura tried to begin the outline of her new book, but it was impossible. She sat in front of the computer for hours, trying to put something—anything—down, but the ideas weren't flowing today. Even letting in some cool, fresh air by opening the window didn't seem to stimulate her mind.

Knowing from experience that this was something that couldn't be forced, she tried to catch up on her e-mail instead. There was a letter from her editor, asking when they should expect the proposal for her next book, and several notes from readers.

After responding to each of the thirty or so messages, Laura sat back, mulling things over. She'd have to get back to her regular work schedule soon. Writing for a living was a difficult proposition. Whether or not ideas came, bills always did.

She looked at the blank word-processing screen again. The problem was that it was hard to let her imagination soar when reality kept pulling her back. Knowing that she couldn't even guarantee she'd be alive tomorrow made it difficult to think of anything else.

It was dusk when she finally gave up and wandered out into the living room. Burke was still in front of his laptop, and it was clear from his rapt concentration that he didn't want to be disturbed.

Laura brought out a stuffed frog she'd picked up at the state fair once and began playing tug-of-war with Wolf. Letting him turn it into a drool-covered lump seemed a small price to pay for everything the dog had done to protect her so far.

Some time later, after Wolf lost interest, she went into the kitchen to get something to drink. As she pulled a box of chamomile tea from the cupboard, the smoke-scented breeze coming through the window over the sink diverted her attention. Brushing the café curtains aside, she glanced out into the night and gasped.

"Burke, fire!"

Moving quickly, she picked up the household fire extinguisher and ran out, Wolf at her heels.

"No, wait!" Burke ran after her, but she was already in the middle of the yard.

The rosebed was in flames, and Laura knew the small fire extinguisher she was holding would never be enough to contain it. The strong odor of charcoal-starting fluid told her the blaze had been deliberately set, and could spread to the wooden fence unless they worked quickly.

Hooking up the garden hose, Burke turned on the water and came to her side, soaking the flames with a heavy spray. Working together, they took less than five minutes to extinguish the burning plants. "Good thing you caught it before it got worse," he said after soaking the ground and fence thoroughly just to make sure no embers remained. "There's almost no damage to the fence." He shut off the spray, then turned off the faucet. "Come on. Let's go—"

Suddenly Wolf growled, a low throaty sound that sent a chill up Laura's spine. In a heartbeat, the dog shot back into the house.

"Stay outside," Burke ordered, drawing his weapon and running after Wolf.

As soon as they were inside, Laura followed slowly and carefully. She would stay out of their way, but she had to see what had triggered Wolf. It was her house, after all. She walked through the kitchen on tiptoe, but when she entered the living room came face-to-face with Burke's gun.

"I told you to stay put!" he said, quickly tucking his weapon away.

"What happened? Did you see anyone in here?"

"No, but I figure the fire was a diversion. In the ten or so minutes we were outside, someone climbed through the open window into your office and went through the bookcase. I think he also downloaded some of your computer files, because the screen showed the main directory, but you'll have to check on that yourself."

She ran to her office and switched screens to the computer log, which showed recent operations. What she found made her blood run cold. Most of the text files in her word processing directory had been copied onto floppy disks.

"I think I'm going to be sick," she muttered, telling him what had happened. "You know, after all this is over, I've decided to move as far away from here as I can."

"That would be a mistake," he said, his voice suddenly hard. "You shouldn't allow anyone to run you out."

"You don't understand. Too much has happened here already. The memories alone..." She shook her head.

"There are good memories here for you, too, Laura. Don't let these people rob you of those. If you do, they've won." And the truth was, he had his own reasons for wanting her to stay. The thought of never seeing her again left him feeling as if she'd reached inside him and torn out his heart.

"It's not that simple. When I look around my home, I really feel my godmother's absence. And then I remember that everyone I've ever loved leaves. Loving brings great happiness, but it always exacts an equal or greater amount of pain. From now on, I intend to go it alone. If I build my own security and happiness, it can't be taken from me.''

Burke understood what she was feeling—but, even more importantly, he now knew that he had to let her go. In his type of work, there was *never* any security. Risk went hand in hand with having to strap on a gun every morning. He could try a nine-to-five office job, but he knew he'd be miserable. He wasn't cut out for that.

The bottom line was that she deserved a different kind of life than what he could offer her. Pushing back the hurt that ripped through him, he focused on the job. It was all he had now.

Bringing out his cell phone, Burke called Wind, and learned that his fellow operative had kept tabs on Springer until he'd seen him heading down the interstate on his way out of town. He'd followed him for a while, making sure it wasn't a ruse, then had headed back into town. Switching targets, he'd then concentrated on Al Baca, who tended to be more mobile at night.

Burke hung up, frustrated, and wishing that two operatives had been available, to watch both suspects full-time.

"I need to go see if Springer is at home," Burke announced. He wouldn't put it past the man to have pulled a fast one, though the likelihood that he'd spotted Wind was undeniably slim. "The person who was watching Springer has spent the last few hours staking out Baca, so we don't know what Springer's been up to. If he's home, I'll feel the hood of his car and see if he's just returned from somewhere."

"You think he might have set fire to my garden? But why?"

"Revenge."

Laura shook her head. "You're wrong. This wasn't his doing. It's not his style."

"Probably not, but I still have to check."

"I'm going with you. And if Ken's really behind this, I'll punch his lights out myself. I loved those roses."

Burke forced himself not to laugh, certain that if he did, she'd slug *him*. But she was so small he had a hard time seeing her as a serious threat to a guy the size of Springer.

"Let's go then." He'd take care of her, and she deserved a chance to see this through.

Burke grabbed a flashlight from his gear, checked in with Handler to get Springer's address, then drove across town with Laura and Wolf. For a short while, Burke thought he saw a blue van tailing them, but then the vehicle disappeared.

He was starting to get paranoid, that's all there was to it.

The moon was high in a clear night sky as he drove to a newly developed area dotted with inexpensive cottages set on small lots. As they approached the house, he saw that there wasn't a vehicle anywhere near the L-shaped, pueblo-style home.

Burke parked around the corner, three houses away from Springer's house, and looked about for curious neighbors. Everyone seemed to be inside, minding their own business or asleep. "I'm going in on foot," he said, reaching into the glove compartment and pulling out a pair of thin leather gloves. He signaled for Wolf to accompany him, and they got out of the vehicle.

"Ken's obviously not there," she said, climbing out quietly to join them. "The lights aren't on, and his car's not in the driveway or at the curb. What's the point?"

"I still want to take a look around. There don't appear to be dogs on this block, so I won't disturb anyone, hopefully."

"I'll go with you," she said.

"I'd much rather you stay at the corner and be my lookout. You can warn me if you see headlights approaching from either direction.'' He handed her the car keys.

''You've got it,'' Laura said. There was a telephone pole at the corner, and she could stand behind it, if need be, while keeping watch.

Burke looked around again to assure himself there weren't curious neighbors peeking out their windows, then rounded the corner. He went up the driveway, then circled the house, which, like most of the homes in the area, still didn't have a fence or wall around the yard. Wolf, used to sentry duty, was alert to sounds and movement, and worked quickly with Burke.

Assured at last that no one was home, Burke put on the leather gloves, went to the back door and tried the handle. It was locked.

Seeing a large, flat rock beside the concrete pad that served as a back porch, he looked underneath. Sure enough, there was a key, placed inside a flattened plastic pill bottle to keep it from rusting.

He unlocked the door, then placed the key back where he'd found it, making sure everything looked undisturbed, then went inside, Wolf leading the way.

Burke used the flashlight he'd brought with him to make a cursory search of the house. It was sparsely furnished. The leather recliner and sofa in the den seemed most used, and on the far wall opposite the recliner was a wide-screen TV and expensive-looking sound system. With a bookstand full of sports magazines and a remote control device containing as many buttons as a computer keyboard, the place looked like a typical bachelor's home. Nothing merited more than a glance as Burke went to the only room furnished as a bedroom, and opened the closet.

Inside he found clothing, and a camera bag on a shelf—nothing out of the ordinary. He was thinking of checking elsewhere when the beam of his flashlight fell on the back of the closet door. It was filled from top to bottom with tack holes.

Curious, he took a closer look. Springer had fastened something here, where it couldn't be seen unless the door was open, and Burke was determined to find out what it was. As he stepped back to get a better perspective, something shiny on the carpet caught his eye. He picked it up and saw that it was a corner of a photograph, with a tack still attached to it.

Burke looked around and found a wastebasket beside the dresser. He dumped the contents onto the carpet and saw that the basket had been filled with dozens of photos of Laura, all with tack holes in their corners. The photos had been taken with a telephoto lens, and showed Laura in several places—shopping, at the post office and working in the front yard.

Several showed her inside the house, and one shot was of Laura standing outside the shower, naked. The dark lines cutting across her body told him that the picture had been taken by carefully aiming the camera through the blinds.

Burke fought the anger that swelled inside him. Hearing a vehicle in the driveway, he put the last photo in his pocket, returned the rest to the wastebasket and put it back in its spot.

Calling to Wolf, Burke hurried through the house and went out the back door, locking it from the inside. As they went around the corner, he saw the agency car. Laura was at the wheel. She'd left the headlights off, but she was obviously coming to warn him.

He and Wolf were in the car within ten seconds.

"I saw headlights in the distance," Laura said. "We don't have much time."

She backed out of the driveway quickly, then drove around the corner, driving two more blocks before turning on the headlights.

"Did you find anything?" she asked excitedly.

He hesitated.

"You *did* find something." Her voice went up an octave. "What?"

"First, let's get out of this neighborhood, then we'll talk. There's a through street ahead. Take a left, and keep going until we eventually reach Main Street. After that, pull into the first parking lot you see and I'll take the wheel."

Laura didn't argue, and that was a major win as far as he was concerned. He kept his eyes on the road behind them as she drove through the sparsely populated, hilly area on the northeast side of Farmington. No one seemed to be following them, so they must have made a clean getaway.

Then he saw headlights. There was a van a few hundred yards behind them on the isolated road. An icy chill touched his spine. After they'd left Laura's neighborhood, he'd thought he'd seen a van, but it had turned down a side road and he'd dismissed it. Yet spotting another dark-colored van behind them now on this nearly rural stretch of road worried him.

She glanced at him. "Give me a hint, at least."

"Excuse me?" he asked. She couldn't have read his thoughts this quickly. If she had, maybe it was time to hand in his P.I. license.

"What did you find in Ken's house?"

"He was obviously obsessed with you. But what I saw there suggests he may have changed his mind, and is finally getting his head together and moving on."

"What makes you think that?"

"We'll talk later," he said, pointing ahead to a convenience store beside an intersection. "Pull in there and I'll take the wheel."

As she entered the parking lot, Burke looked ahead, then behind them. They appeared to be alone, except for the night clerk inside the store. Burke breathed a silent sigh of relief. There was no doubt about it, he was getting paranoid—an occupational hazard for cops and P.I.s.

"You sounded upset when I picked you up at Ken's house. Something you found there really bugged you. What was it?" she pressed.

He gave her the quick version, then pulled the photo from his pocket. "I was going to destroy this, but I'm going to show it to you first because you've got a right to know, and because it'll show you what you need to watch out for in the future."

She stared at the photo he'd taken from Ken's house. It wasn't a clear, high quality photo, but despite the dark lines that crisscrossed her body, she was completely exposed. In the bright lights of the convenience store parking lot, it seemed all the more shocking.

"That slimeball!" She shredded the photo until the tiny pieces lay on her lap like confetti. "He must have sneaked right up to the blinds and angled it precisely. I usually leave them cracked a bit so I can still get some outside light." Rage filled her. "Well, that does it. I'm pressing charges."

"You can't," he said firmly. "At least not with this as evidence."

She looked at the scattered fragments. "Oh. Right. Maybe I can tape it together—no wait. Then I'd have to show it to other people, like lawyers and policemen." She shuddered. "I can't do that."

"It's not just that, Laura. I got it during an illegal search. I found his house key and let myself in. He could prosecute me just as easily for being in his house." Burke paused. "That was the worst of the lot. But the good news is that he'd already thrown all of them into the trash. If he'd gotten rid of them just because he was afraid someone would find them, he would have burned them. What this indicates is that he's decided not to focus on you anymore—in more ways than one. I doubt that you'll have any more problems with him.'' In fact, Burke intended to see to it personally. If Springer so much as came within a mile of Laura, he'd pull him apart limb from limb.

Laura said nothing for a long moment. ''All right. What you've said makes sense. I hate that he did this, but it's over—at least as far as Ken is concerned,'' she added. ''Let's get out of here.''

As they got out of the car to switch seats, Burke heard the sound of an engine revving up. Suddenly the van came out from behind the building with a roar, squealing its tires as it turned sharply toward them. Burke grabbed Laura and shoved her back inside the car.

Pulling out his gun, he braced himself, locking his hands into firing position as the van bore down on him.

''Burke, run!'' she screamed.

He blocked out the sound of her voice and rapidly fired two rounds. The windshield of the vehicle shattered, but the van continued toward him.

Burke dove underneath the agency car just as the van sideswiped the passenger side, ricocheting off with a loud thump.

Burke rolled and came out on the driver's side, unhurt. He was inside the agency car a few breaths later. The van was hurtling away at high speed.

''Are you okay?'' Burke looked Laura over quickly, and seeing her nod shakily, breathed again. ''We're going after him. Hang on.''

Chapter Sixteen

Despite his best intentions, by the time they reached the next intersection, a mile down the road, the van was nowhere to be seen. The van driver had turned off his headlights, and in the darkness, surrounded by hilly terrain, the vehicle was all but invisible now.

Burke drove down both streets, searching, in case the driver had merely pulled off the road. After about five minutes, it was obvious they weren't going to find him.

"Did you get a look at the driver?" Burke asked her. He had, but he wanted to know if she'd be able to corroborate his statement.

She shook her head. "All I really saw was the van barreling down on us. And when I realized it was going to sideswipe us, I dove across the seat and closed my eyes. Sorry. It was an automatic response."

"It's okay."

"No, it's not. I should have handled this better, Burke," she said, clearly annoyed with herself. "You stood up to him. You didn't duck and close your eyes."

He grinned. "Are you kidding? Sure I ducked! I didn't cover my eyes, but that's just 'cause it's not in my nature."

Laura nodded, her expression grim. "I'll do better next time."

Burke smiled. Somehow, he didn't doubt she would.

"Who was the driver? Ken?" she asked.

"No. It was Michael Enesco."

She stared at him for a moment, the knowledge sinking in. "Are you sure?"

"Yeah. All the way down to his cold expression. I believe running over someone comes naturally for him."

"Then we have to call the police. He tried to kill us. The man can explain his reasons from a jail cell."

"I'm not calling the cops—not yet, anyway. First I want to see if I can track him down. I need to find out who else is working with him, and if he's behind bars, there's little chance we'll get any answers. If he's a foreign agent, the cops aren't going to get much out of him. He's been trained to withstand an ordinary interrogation."

"An agent..." she repeated quietly. The words hung in the air ominously.

"Yes. With his skills at tailing people, breaking into homes, and behind the wheel, it's obvious this guy's a pro. And we've seen at least one other person with him when they tried to kidnap Elena, which means Enesco isn't working alone."

THE FOLLOWING MORNING they went to the center. By the time they pulled into the parking lot, Laura had psyched herself up to do whatever it took to get answers.

"Enesco may know you saw his face," she said. "The center's van isn't here, but Nicole and Karl's vehicle is right over there."

"Let's go talk to them and see what they have to say."

As they walked into the outer office, Nicole was behind one of the desks. Her face looked tired, and there were dark circles under her eyes. To Laura, the woman looked as if she'd aged ten years since the last time she'd seen her.

"Where's Enesco?" Burke said, his voice hard.

Karl came out of his own office, which was adjacent. "I

wish we knew," he said amicably. "He hasn't reported to work today and, what's worse, he's got our van."

"He'll be back soon," Nicole said wearily. "He does this every once in a while. I've warned him, but he just doesn't seem to understand."

"So why haven't you fired him?" Laura asked, more to see their reaction than because she really expected the truth.

"He and I come from West Medias," Nicole said. "I've spent most of my life here in the States, but I still have family over there. I know how hard it is for people when they first come to the U.S., particularly if they're not fluent in English, and I felt sorry for him."

Burke stared at her, suddenly understanding why he hadn't been able to turn up much on Nicole.

"How long have you known Michael Enesco?" he pressed.

"Not long. He came here looking for work a few weeks ago. We needed a driver, so I helped him get his chauffeur's license and then gave him a job."

"We're both very disappointed in him," Karl said. "We've given him every possible chance to straighten out."

Burke placed his card in front of Nicole. "The moment you hear from him, call me. And don't be surprised when the police come around."

"Has something happened?" Karl asked quickly.

"He tried to run us down last time we saw him," Burke answered evenly.

Nicole paled visibly, but Karl's expression remained guarded. "Are you sure it was him?"

"Yes," he answered. "And he was driving a blue van."

"Ours is blue," Karl conceded.

"It'll be a positive ID on the vehicle if it turns up with its windshield broken and a couple of bullet holes in the back panels. It'll also have damage on the passenger side. He sideswiped my vehicle.''

"If any of that turns out to be true, *I'll* call the police," Karl said. "I've had it with this guy."

Nicole still hadn't said a word. Laura looked at her and, for a moment, thought the woman was about to be sick.

Laura considered Nicole's reaction as they headed back out to Burke's car. "I wonder if she feels responsible for Enesco's actions. If she was the one who hired him…" She slipped into the passenger's seat. The door had been dented in, but it still worked, and the window hadn't been broken.

"The way they're acting, I suspect Enesco may have something on Nicole, or maybe even on both of them. If he's blackmailing them, they would have to put up with whatever he dished out." Burke headed toward the agency to change vehicles. "Once we get to Gray Wolf, I'm going to find out if our bookkeeper has finished auditing the files I got from Foster. Then I want to go talk to the man who is translating your foreign editions."

He couldn't win fighting blind and he knew it. This time—one way or another—he'd get the answers he needed.

LAURA WATCHED BURKE as he faced the camera and spoke to the altered voice known only as Handler. Burke was self-confident and reserved, relating what had happened to them last night in detail, though he had already given a brief report hours ago. He stated his findings in a cool voice, totally in control of himself, and showing no trace of emotion.

If she hadn't known him as well as she did, she might have believed that this was the real Burke—someone impervious to anything life threw at him. But she could see past that now because she knew the man he kept hidden.

the one who'd known pain so deep that he'd learned how to build barriers to shield himself.

In that respect, they were the same, and that's why they understood each other so well. But there was one major difference that would ultimately tear them apart. He thrived on danger—and she needed security.

When the case was closed and he finally left, she wouldn't try to stop him. It was wrong to hold on to what could never be. But there was no way around the heartbreak that lay ahead.

"Our accountants have finished auditing the senior center's accounts," Handler said. "Foster has given us some very useful information. I also managed to pull some strings and get some additional data. You'll find everything in that packet on top of the file cabinet."

Burke opened it and began to study the contents.

"Right at the top, you'll find a compilation of computer records our hacker managed to tap into," Handler said. "They reveal something you might find helpful. As recently as last week, withdrawals for vaguely labeled expenditures like 'supplies' or 'maintenance' continued draining the center's resources, each above and beyond the budgeted expenses in those categories. The increasing frequency of the withdrawals was what caught our attention, and the fact that almost all were cash withdrawals made and signed for by Nicole Maurer."

Somehow Laura wasn't surprised, and she saw from Burke's expression that he wasn't, either.

"Of course, this only furnishes you with a lead. We have nothing you can take to the police, despite the suggestion of embezzlement, because of the methods we used to get those records," Handler said. "So what's your next step?"

"This case is complex. Things are happening on a variety of levels. Right now, I'd like to focus on Laura's connection to the center's staff especially regarding Enesco.

And we still need to find out how Douglas Begay, our client, fits into all this. As soon as I switch cars, I'm going to go talk to the translator concerning the foreign editions of Laura's novels. Those books may shed additional light on what's been happening.''

"All right," Handler replied after a pause. "The professor should be at home now. He took the day off to complete the job."

Burke called to Wolf and, as they headed out to his replacement vehicle, a heavy SUV, both man and dog stayed ahead of Laura. "From now on, we can't take anything for granted. When we leave a building, I'll go first. You stay close, but behind me."

"So far they've come after both of us," she reminded him. "You're not any safer than I am."

"Yes, but it's my job to protect you, and I intend to do that to the best of my ability. It's what I've been trained for, remember?"

"If there's something in one of my books, what do you think it'll be? I suppose a microdot could be planted inside, but wouldn't there be other, more effective ways to smuggle out something like that?"

"Yeah, you bet. Besides, Handler would have looked for something of that nature and spotted it right away. If there's anything to be found, I think it'll be subtler. I would expect Doug's handiwork to be something along the lines of a phrase that doesn't seem to belong there, but is really a coded message."

"You still haven't heard from him, have you?"

Burke shook his head. "But Doug can take care of himself. He's as smart as they come."

Laura heard the trace of uncertainty beneath his words and fought the impulse to reach for Burke's hand. Right now he needed to believe that his friend was fine. Offering him comfort would only remind him of the precarious position Doug was in, and undermine him.

They drove in silence to the professor's home, both lost in their own private thoughts. The drive was a pleasant one, and Wolf was obviously enjoying the extra room in the vehicle, which allowed him to lie down in the carpeted storage area behind the rear seat.

The professor's home was located in a quiet rural area east of Farmington where livestock clearly outnumbered people. It was late afternoon, probably close to feeding time, and horses rushed to the white-painted, welded-pipe fence as they entered a long, gravel driveway.

"I've always wanted a place like this," Burke admitted quietly.

"With horses?"

"The land, more than the horses, especially in the river valley, where you could have a well. You're not living on top of your neighbors here. But then again, this is the sort of place that needs a family to fill it, and I don't think that's in the cards for me."

"Why not?"

"My lifestyle, mostly." Burke paused thoughtfully. "But, you know, maybe I should stop ruling things out. I'm a different man today than I was when I started working for Gray Wolf Investigations. Back then, I was never comfortable with the idea of settling down in any one place. That's why I've always rented and never bought a home. But for the first time in my life, I'd really like a place of my own to call home." He glanced at Wolf. "Maybe I'll even get a pet dog."

"A toy poodle," Laura suggested with a straight face.

He burst out laughing. "Sure. Three days after they sprinkle salt where hell froze over."

Before long they were shown inside the professor's home, a large, northern New Mexico style house with a steeply pitched, corrugated metal roof and blue wooden trim. Inside, comfortable-looking sofas and chairs graced the living room, and Navajo rugs accented the hardwood floors. Two large black-and-white cats wandered lazily around the room, and Wolf eyed them with interest, licking his chops from time to time.

"Don't even think it, furball," Burke said, his voice low.

Professor Milton DeWitt, a slender middle-aged man who had lost most of his hair, seemed all nervous energy as he checked out Burke's credentials.

Looking down at Wolf, and seeing the animal stare back intently, he suddenly stopped moving. "He won't bother the cats...or anything else he's not supposed to, will he?"

"You have nothing to worry about, Professor. He's exceptionally well trained," Burke assured him.

With a satisfied nod, Professor DeWitt led them quickly to his office, a large but cozy room with dark wood paneling, bookshelves and a massive desk. In the center of the desktop was a small but powerful computer and oversize scanner. "I was about to call your agency," Dewitt said, sitting down in front of the machine. A foreign edition that Burke had taken from Laura stood propped up in a plastic holder beside the monitor.

"This is quite amazing," Dewitt muttered, studying a few sentences, then typing out a translation on screen.

Laura looked over the professor's shoulder at the monitor, read what was on the screen, then mouthed to Burke, "I didn't write this."

The professor continued working for several more minutes. Burke didn't interrupt him at first, but finally ran out of patience. "What have you got for us?" he asked at last.

The professor jumped and looked around. "Oh, I'm sorry. I forgot you were there. But you see, this is such a remarkable discovery."

"What is?" Burke said, his voice hard.

"The first two hundred pages held no surprises. But then, hidden in the middle, I found the personal journal of a West Median political prisoner believed to have died years ago. But these writings prove he's still very much alive, because they allude to certain dates and events subsequent to his alleged death."

"So you're saying that the book contains evidence that an important dissident is still alive?" Burke asked.

"Yes, but it's more than that. The journal is of incredible importance, because of the information it contains about the prison system there and the existence of a holding facility no one in the West knew about—one where people 'disappear,' never to be heard of again. I doubt even the CIA knows for certain that this prison exists. If these pages are taken to the proper international authorities, an incredible amount of pressure could be brought upon the West Median government to free this man and others who are there with him."

"How can you be so certain that it's genuine?"

"I verified some of the facts, such as the whereabouts of people mentioned in the journal and the timing of certain events. Also, this man published papers prior to his incarceration, and the writing style, certain phrases and even misspellings match. Of course, the method used to get this out of West Media also should support the claim that it's legitimate. To smuggle writings of this nature out of a prison like that one, then out of the country in this particular manner, means that lives were risked all the way down the line."

"Someone sure wants it back, too," Laura added, thinking of Michael Enesco and all he'd apparently done to try and locate it.

Burke thought about it awhile before speaking again. "Professor, I'm going to have Gray Wolf send someone to escort you to a safer place, where you can translate the rest of the journal without having to worry about anyone interfering with your work.''

''I'm safe enough here. No one knows I have it.''

''There's always the slim possibility that someone followed us today. Though I doubt it, something this important demands we take precautions.''

''All right. But what about my family?''

''We'll arrange security for them, too.''

After Burke had made all the arrangements, forcing Handler to pull Gray Wolf operatives off ongoing cases, he checked out the property, then joined Laura on the patio ''We'll stay here until more help arrives. But that shouldn' be long,'' he said.

''Something just occurred to me,'' she murmured ''From the tactics they used when they broke into my home, I don't think Enesco and his people know what form the journal took when it was smuggled out. If they'd know that, they would have stolen those foreign editions the firs time they broke in. They obviously didn't have time to read the books or skim them far enough to find that section.''

''Good point.''

''That gives us at least a marginal advantage.''

''But as long as they see *you* as the link, your life wil continue to be in danger,'' Burke said, and grew somber ''We're up against highly trained agents who are prepared to win at any cost.''

''Which brings me to my next point. The journal's the key—that's what they want. We shouldn't allow it to remain with the professor even if there are people guarding him. Let him scan copies into his computer, but the original—the book itself—should be placed in a safe deposit box or somewhere like that,'' Laura said.

''I agree,'' he said with a nod. ''But the bank won't be

open till tomorrow. For tonight, we'll need to make other arrangements.''

Following their suggestions, the professor scanned the remaining pages of the book onto his computer. Afterward, he and his family were taken to an agency safe house along with the supplies he needed to complete the translation.

As soon as the professor and the others were on their way, Burke headed out with Wolf and Laura, the book safe inside his jacket pocket.

''We need to find a secure place for the journal tonight—somewhere no one can get it,'' Burke said.

''Any ideas?''

''I'm going to turn it over to another Gray Wolf operative I trust—as soon as possible. But you and I are going to have to make some decisions. From this point on, Laura, there are no safe options.''

She nodded silently. So much had changed. She'd lost Elena, and now Burke's life was in jeopardy, as well as her own. Fear left a bitter taste in her mouth.

''Check your seat belt and make sure it's fastened tightly,'' he said, glancing in the rearview mirror. ''There's a blue van behind us again. I caught a glimpse of it as it passed a streetlight. He's staying back, but he's there.''

''Does it have a cracked windshield?''

He smiled. ''No, but that's not a surprise. He wouldn't have let it stay that way for long. It's a dead giveaway.'' Burke took another look in the side mirror, trying to make it out more clearly.

''Look out!'' Laura shouted as a pickup suddenly veered into their lane, coming at them head-on.

Burke saw Enesco behind the wheel. The man wasn't suicidal. Burke was almost sure he wouldn't deliberately cause a crash, but he also knew he couldn't risk it. Burke hit the brakes hard and yanked on the steering wheel, whipping the car around so the driver's side took the brunt of the impact.

Chapter Seventeen

The truck struck them, but it was only a glancing blow.

Glass shattered and metal screeched, but Burke's air bag deployed and his seat belt held. By the time the heavy SUV came to a stop in the middle of the road, he was already planning a good defense. The engine had died, and he quickly turned off the headlights.

Enesco had planned it well, but now it was Burke's turn. He glanced over at Laura and saw the terror on her face, but she didn't appear to be hurt. Wolf had been tossed against the padded sides of the storage compartment, but he was already trying to climb into the back seat.

The door on Burke's side wouldn't open, so he'd have to find another way out. "Get down on the floor, Laura, and stay in the vehicle! Down, Wolf!"

She unbuckled her seat belt and scrunched down, as Burke scrambled into the back seat. He opened the rear door on Laura's side and slipped out, shutting the door behind him. Drawing his pistol, he looked over the hood in the direction of the pickup.

There were no houses in the immediate vicinity, but a solitary lamppost beside the intersection gave some illumination. The van that had been following them was now stopped sideways in the road fifty feet away, beside the damaged pickup. The driver's door was open.

As Burke tried to figure out their next move, an armed man wearing a ski mask appeared between the van and the pickup, his pistol aimed at them. Burke fired, but the bullet struck the hood of the truck and the man ducked back out of sight, unharmed. Enesco suddenly rose up farther behind the shooter and fired. The bullet whined over Burke's head.

He returned fire and, while Enesco sought cover, tossed his cell phone to Laura through her open window. "Call 911. Just tell them there are shots being fired, give them our location, then hang up. And stay down."

Enesco made an attempt to run from the pickup to the juniper woods at Burke's left, but Burke had anticipated the move, and drove him back to cover with two quick shots.

As the sound of sirens became noticeable in the distance, Enesco opened fire, pinning Burke down as the other man climbed into the van. Then the man in the van opened up, and Burke had to duck down as a bullet grazed the hood of the SUV. Soon, both the van and the pickup were screeching away.

Burke rose up and got into the rear seat fast. Any other time he would have given chase, but right now he had other priorities.

Not wanting to waste time, Laura moved quickly into the driver's seat. The engine started on her first try. "Do you want me to go after them?"

"No. Drive in the direction we were heading before the collision, and go slow. Put the lights back on if they'll work."

She turned the vehicle around, and both headlights came on. There was a hard scraping sound coming from beneath the floorboards, but for now, it was merely an inconvenience. Slowly she crossed to the proper lane and continued down the empty street.

Finding his phone, Burke called Handler. "The police

are on their way here, so I'm clearing out for now. I'll explain later what's going on, but I can't afford to spend hours right now with the law, trying to clear ourselves. I'd like the agency to contact the feds while I ditch the agency's SUV and get other transportation.''

''I'll take care of that. Stay sharp,'' Handler replied.

As Burke hung up the phone, he glanced at Laura and saw her hands on the wheel. She was shaking.

''We're okay. It's over,'' he said gently, reaching for her hand.

She pulled it away instantly. ''The way you turned the car around...you could have been killed...because of me,'' she said, her voice trembling.

''No, not because of you,'' he replied evenly. ''What happened would have been the result of my own actions—something I chose freely.''

She shook her head.

''Laura, listen to me. I care about you and I won't let anyone hurt you. But I'm fighting not only for us, but for what's right. It's what I do. Do you understand?''

She nodded. ''Yes, I'm just part of a case,'' she said, her voice strained.

Spotting a gas station ahead, Burke asked Laura to pull in.

She did so, then switched off the ignition and looked at Burke anxiously. ''Now what?''

In response, he dragged her to him, branding her mouth with a hungry and possessive kiss that took everything from her, and at the same time gave back. After long, pleasure-filled moments, he allowed her to take the lead, wanting her to feel everything he felt and more.

When he finally drew back, they were both trembling. ''Now do you understand how I feel about you?''

''Tell me,'' she whispered, her head buried beneath his chin.

"Why do women always value words more than actions?" he muttered, exasperated. Tilting her head up, he met her gaze and held it. "I love you, Laura."

When he kissed her again, her mouth parted eagerly. He felt her needs and longings as clearly as he did his own. A wave of pure emotion filled him. He loved her. It was as simple—and as complicated—as that.

"I won't make you any promises I can't keep," he said, his voice gruff. "You mean too much to me for that. I know that I'll never be able to offer you the kind of security your heart needs. But I can give you love—the kind that won't fade away when times get tough. The kind that stays the course."

Laura started to answer, but he placed a finger over her lips. "No, don't say anything. Just think about it, Laura. That's all I ask. I can't change who I am, but no one will ever love you or cherish you more."

Burke could see the emotions on Laura's face—her fears colliding against her yearnings, tearing her apart. He thought of kissing her again—hard—until she could think only of the feelings they shared. But this wasn't the time for love. Theirs was a game of survival. He'd have to stay focused or they'd never make it through this in one piece.

Burke made another phone call, and within twenty minutes, an SUV of the same make and model normally used by the agency pulled up. The driver was a man Burke suspected was Wind. He was wearing sunglasses and a baseball cap. The brim placed his face in shadow.

"And you are…" Burke asked crisply as he walked across the parking lot to meet him.

"Wind," the man replied.

Burke breathed a sigh of relief, recognizing Ben Wanderer's voice. "I need you to take this," Burke said, turning over the journal to him. "Keep it safe—at all costs."

Wind nodded and placed it in his jacket pocket.

"Springer has applied for a job in Albuquerque. He's been over there since this morning. Shall I continue to watch Al Baca?"

"No. Your job as of right now is to safeguard this book." Burke was about to say more when his cell phone rang.

"I've got good news," Handler said. "Our client, Mr. Begay, has contacted us. Please come to the office."

Burke felt an incredible wave of relief. There had been very few victories to celebrate in this case, but finding out for sure that Doug was alive was definitely one.

"He's in one piece?" Burke asked in a taut voice.

"Yes. I was told to assure you of that."

Leaving Wind to take care of the journal, Burke ran back to the borrowed car, and he, Laura and Wolf drove across town as quickly as possible.

They arrived at the Gray Wolf office a short time later, and Handler instructed Burke to press the speaker button on the phone.

"Hey, buddy." Doug's voice came clearly over the wire.

"You had me worried," Burke growled. "Are you in the country?"

"I'm safe and in friendly territory," Douglas hedged. "And you'll be glad to hear that I can finally tell you what's going on."

"About time," he snapped.

"Two months ago, I was approached by dissidents and asked to help them get a journal written by Vladimir Rogov out of the country. The authorities were closing in on them and three people had already died. As you know, I'm part of Freedom International, so I agreed. The journal had been written on scraps of paper that were slipped to Rogov in secret, then smuggled out. To insure the success of the operation, everything that left the prison went out in sections. The portion that became part of Laura's book was only one of several. But all the couriers except one were captured by the secret police, and only the journal segment you now have in your possession made it out.''

''And that's why the agents we've been fighting want it back so badly,'' Laura said.

''Exactly. The information you now have could bring down the current government by exposing gross human rights violations and naming names. Hopefully, it'll lead to reforms that will restore basic freedoms.''

''But why did you choose *my* book?'' Laura asked. ''Was it just chance?''

''Not exactly. It was more like fate. After I learned of the journal, I ended up having to leave West Medias to attend a book fair in London. I couldn't take the pages with me, because by then I was being watched. So I kept to the familiar routines expected of me. The book fair was filled with U.S. publishers who were selling foreign rights. That's when I started getting the idea to smuggle the pages out in one specially printed book.''

''But why mine?'' she insisted.

''Your publisher is affiliated with us and had a booth close to ours. Your books were prominently displayed, so I picked one up and read your bio. When I realized you lived in the same town as my buddy Burke, the plan just unfolded.''

''But why didn't you simply send the book to Burke?'' she asked.

''Sending it to anyone but you, the author, would have instantly alerted people who had begun to monitor and censor my e-mails and personal mail. It had to go out as routine business for the publishing firm I worked for, and, most important of all, in a way that wouldn't raise suspicion. I knew you'd been sent copies earlier of West Median editions of your books. We do that all the time as a courtesy to the authors, so it was the perfect cover. And, in case someone checked, two of the three books I sent you were accurate translations. Of the other one, the first two hundred pages and last hundred were straight from your book. Only the middle was replaced.''

''Good plan, buddy. That explains why Enesco didn't find it. So what went wrong?'' Burke asked.

''There was an informant in our office. He caught on to the fact that I'd received a section of the journal—but he couldn't figure out what I'd done with it. I was able to ship the book out past the authorities, along with other West Median editions that went to American authors.''

''And then they came after you?'' Burke asked.

''Yeah. I knew that eventually, by checking up on my past and my contacts, they'd be able to deduce that Laura was the recipient. What I was hoping they wouldn't figure out, at least right away, was the exact form the journal took when we smuggled it out. That would buy you guys—and me—some time to finish the operation. But I knew you two wouldn't be able to fight a danger you weren't aware of, so I contacted you. I told you as much as I could, then went underground. I was being monitored, so I couldn't say any more than I did.''

''Well, you did a good job. The journal's safe,'' Burke said.

''But now you're not,'' Doug answered. ''As long as you have the book, you're still a prime target.''

''I hope you're not advocating that we hand the journal over to you and just walk away,'' Laura said angrily. ''The people who came after me are responsible for the death of someone I loved. I can't just pretend it never happened.''

''But once we have the journal, the danger to you diminishes considerably.''

''Unless, of course, these agents decide to retaliate against us,'' Laura objected. ''But even if that doesn't happen, they can't be allowed to come to this country and

terrorize people here. They started this, but now we have
to finish it. To not fight people like these tips the scales in
favor of those who knowingly do what's wrong, because
they think they're above our laws. To me, that's not an
acceptable option.''

No one said anything. Finally Douglas spoke. ''I can't
argue with your motives. I know they're mine and Burke's
as well. But you realize that by trying to catch those involved, you'll be exposing yourself to even more danger?''

Handler spoke at last. ''Mr. Begay, though I realize your
goal's been met, there are other issues here that also demand attention. I'm expecting two FBI agents here shortly.
Laws have been broken and people have died. Miss Santos
is right. This has to be handled here and now.''

''I'm glad the FBI are coming,'' Laura said. ''Burke will
need their protection.''

Burke choked. ''I can handle myself.''

''You've protected me, but no one's protecting you. You
could get killed as easily as I.''

''Not quite,'' Burke said. ''I shoot back.''

''There are also two important issues we need to factor
in,'' Handler said. ''The good news is that once the journal
is made public in a convincing way, Vladimir Rogov's life
will no longer be in jeopardy. The fact that he's alive and
imprisoned—which the evidence from the journal will es-
tablish to the world—will throw public opinion in his favor
and virtually guarantee his freedom. But there's a down-
side, too.''

''What is it?'' Laura asked.

''Unless the agents who are after the journal are arrested,
they're going to be in a position to try and destroy the
credibility of what Mr. Begay sent to you. The second they
find out what form the journal took when it was smuggled
out, they can produce a variety of credible fakes, all with
different information, and have people all over the United

States take copies to different newspapers. They'd convince the world that the one we have is simply one of many smuggled to the U.S., and all part of a disinformation plot pulled by dissidents. The whole thing would be made to look like an anti-regime propaganda stunt."

"There's no way we're letting this slide, Doug," Burke said. "The agents operating here on our soil also pose a threat to other West Medians living in the U.S., and constitute a security risk for our government."

"You're right," Doug agreed. "There's also another problem. If they discredit the journal, the West Median secret police could quietly do away with Rogov, and only a few people would ever know the truth. You'll have to round these agents up before they can do any more damage."

"The ball's in our court now," Handler said. "We'll handle it."

"If we want to catch these agents, we're going to have to force them to come after us—but on our terms." Burke glanced at Laura. "You shouldn't stick around for this. We'll find another woman who fits your general description and keep you out of it."

"I'm not going anywhere. And, for the record, you don't have time to go shopping for a double of me. They know what I look like—exactly. If you play a trick they can catch on to so easily, they'll begin to suspect that the journal is already in the hands of the authorities, and they'll start their countermeasures before you take your next breath. We have to play this out fast, here and now."

Burke expelled his breath in a rush. "All right. It's time to set a plan in motion." He paused, glancing at the speaker phone. "Doug, from this point on, it becomes an agency operation and strictly confidential."

"Understood. But keep that journal safe."

"That's been taken care of." After Doug said goodbye,

Burke filled Handler in on the accident and his meeting with Wind.

"And Wolf? Is he all right?"

"He seems fine, though he got tossed around a bit in the collision."

"Can you identify the other driver, the one in the van?" Handler asked.

"Enesco was driving the pickup. But no, I don't know who was in the van," Burke answered. He looked at Laura questioningly.

"I saw Enesco briefly as well, but I never saw the other man's face," Laura admitted.

A moment later, a knock sounded at the door. Burke looked through the special monitor and asked the arrivals to identify themselves. "There are two men outside holding up FBI badges," he told Handler.

"That will be FBI agents John Wylie and Albert Miller. Let them in," he said. A buzzer sounded, and the door unlatched.

The two agents, clad in lightweight suits, one gray and one dark blue, stepped into the office and, after brief introductions, were offered chairs. The men were both well over six feet tall, and looked guarded and cold, a combination that fit seasoned agents who'd dealt with the seamy side of human nature, Laura guessed.

As she glanced at Burke, she saw the beginnings of that same telltale expression on his face. Burke loved the work he did, but she could see that it exacted a high toll on those who pursued it.

Yet Burke also possessed an inner strength that wasn't apparent in the others. His Navajo beliefs and his sense of mission—all part of what he called "walking in beauty"— would give him an edge most didn't have.

John Wylie appeared to be the senior agent, both in age

and rank. He leaned back and regarded her and Burke thoughtfully.

"We were briefed about your situation. As I'm sure you've discovered, you're up against a world of trouble."

"I've asked the Bureau for backup, and your superiors have granted it to us. That's why you're here," Handler said.

Looking somewhat uncomfortable, Wylie glanced at the speaker that carried Handler's altered voice through the room. Burke saw the questions in his eyes but, because he didn't ask them, assumed that once again Handler had managed to pull some strings.

"The journal, is it in a safe place?" Wylie asked.

"It is," Burke answered.

"It would be safer with us," Albert Miller said, his tone almost defiant.

Burke shook his head. "To bring it out now, even to hand it over to you two, would entail a risk we shouldn't take. People have died to get that journal excerpt to us."

"Tell me more about the suspects," Wylie said to Burke.

"Michael Enesco, the senior center's driver, is the only one I'm sure is directly involved. But Enesco has had help, so there's at least one other player," Burke answered.

"Handler reported that the woman, Nicole Maurer, is somehow involved with Enesco and his illegal activities," Wylie said. "Clarify that connection for me."

"We haven't established that conclusively," Burke said. "Our theory is that Nicole's being blackmailed into providing a cover for Enesco."

"That wouldn't be unusual. Often, immigrants are blackmailed into doing things they never would otherwise, when the safety of those they left behind in their country is threatened."

"We need to bring Enesco and whoever his accomplice

is out into the open," Laura said. "And I have an idea of how we can do that."

"We're listening," Wylie said.

"I want to call Nicole Maurer and tell her that I've recently received a leather-bound book written in what I've learned might be Rumanian, and that I'd like her to take a look at it and tell me what it is. I'll explain that although my books get translated all the time, the copies I get usually have regular cover art, so I'm curious to find out what this is." She paused and looked at the men. "I think that should get her going, don't you think? And it's something we could easily fake."

"Bad idea," Handler said. "I know you're hoping to follow the trail of the fake and identify the players that way, but the second they realize you've conned them, they'll come after you. They'll know you played them— and that you know about the real journal. More importantly, they'll know you haven't turned it over to the authorities or they would have heard about it. They'll either assume it's a trick to identify them—remember, they know you've been searching for the man who tried to kidnap your godmother—or that you're angling for a big payoff."

"It doesn't matter what they think. The important thing is that they'll know I still have it and they'll come after me. What happens after that is up to the FBI and this agency."

Burke saw the response in the agents' eyes. Courage was always respected by people who all too often put their own lives on the line.

"Okay," Wylie said. "You two will be our bait. Go back to Miss Santos's place and carry out your normal routines while we work out the rest of the details. Be sure to wait for word from us before you make that phone call and set things in motion."

Laura walked out of the agency with Burke ahead of her

and Wolf beside her. She wasn't afraid for herself, but it terrified her to know that Burke would be in the line of fire along with her.

"We'll be ready when they come, Laura," he said, almost as if in response to her unspoken thoughts.

"I hope so, because there's no turning back now."

Chapter Eighteen

By the time they reached her house, Agent Wylie had telephoned Burke, and now Laura understood the other half of the plan. The agents, and support personnel gathered from the local police, would remain out of sight, watching the house. She would be guarded day and night, and whenever she left the premises. The moment Enesco made his move they'd be there.

"Are you sure you're ready to set this plan in motion?" Burke asked, letting Wolf out first to keep watch, then opening the car door for Laura. Handler had arranged for the vehicle to be returned to the gas station owner later.

"I'm scared, I won't deny it. But I won't back down," she said as they went inside the house. "Let's just do what needs to be done," she added, and, somehow, her voice stayed even.

BURKE WATCHED HER GO to her room, her head held high, after asking for a few minutes alone. He needed her in his life. But not at any cost. Maybe the highest proof of his love would lie in letting her go. He thought about the work he did. The danger was there, even when he was coordinating the other operatives, because he was usually working on a case himself at the same time. That was why he strapped on a gun every morning.

Cops' wives put up with a constant state of fear, an
many learned how to handle it. But it was different wit
Laura. She'd already had too many losses in her life. Ye
the thought of living without her left him feeling hollow
inside.

Later. There would be time then to sort all this out i
his mind. Right now he had to watch out for her—and fc
himself.

When she came out of her room several moments late
she looked composed. She went to the phone, turned an
nodded to him.

"I'm ready."

Burke called Agent Wylie, then gave Laura a thumbs
up. The conversation would be monitored and they'd hav
officers to protect her. But setting the trap would be he
job. She was at the center of the operation.

Bracing herself, Laura made the call. "Hello, Nicole
This is Laura Santos. I need a favor from you."

"What can I do for you?" the woman asked in a guarde
voice.

"I received something in the mail a few days ago. I
appears to be a leather-bound document of some sort—lik
a book, really, but not very long. I can't tell what it i
because it's not in English. I did some checking and I thin
the text is written in Rumanian. Then I remembered tha
you said you'd come from West Medias, and I was won
dering if you could help me by looking through it and tell
ing me if it's a translation of one of my books. I get foreig
editions all the time, but they're always in book form, th
same as those sold to readers in other countries."

There was a long pause at the other end. "Sounds inter
esting. When can I see it?"

"Well, it's late right now, and I'm going to bed soor
Why don't we meet tomorrow?"

"I don't mind the time. I could come over to see you tonight and save you a trip."

"No, let's wait till morning. I'm really beat, and I'm going to bed early. But thanks for the offer. I'll call you first thing tomorrow and we'll set up a time then," she said. "If for some reason you can't make it, I'll check with the local branch college and see if one of their language teachers can read it for me." She hung up before Nicole could respond. "How was that?" she asked, looking up at Burke.

"Fine, and that touch about the language teacher will put even more pressure on them to act fast, before you go to someone else. But now you're going over to my place. The call was made from here, something she'll be able to verify with caller ID, and she's been led to believe that the journal's here. Let them make the next move. A team of officers will be waiting and watching."

The two-way radio clipped to his belt crackled, and Burke pressed the commmunication button.

"Someone just drove up in a green pickup," Wylie said. "It's an adult male, dark hair and medium build. He's walking up to the house."

"You think Nicole sent him? But how could he have reacted so quickly?" Burke asked, noting that Wolf was already standing by the door, alert.

"I don't think this is connected. Just sit tight. We're on top of it," Wylie responded.

Letting Burke know in advance that he was about to enter the house, Wylie, who'd been hiding in the garden, used the back door and slipped into the kitchen. "I'll cover you from here," he said, removing his handgun from the holster, then ducking back out of sight as the doorbell rang.

Burke answered it while Laura hung back, Wolf now sitting in front of her.

"I came to see Laura," a man's voice boomed. It was an order, not a request.

Laura recognized the voice immediately. She went toward the door, but before she could get there two men came rushing up from behind Al Baca and shoved him inside. They held his arms by his sides.

"Let's see some ID, please," Miller, who was one of the men, ordered, easing his grip.

"What?" Al, wild-eyed and confused, looked at Laura then at Burke and the others. Wylie, who'd been in the kitchen, came out, pistol in hand.

"Your identification please, sir," Miller repeated, watching Al's expression carefully.

"It's all right. He's kind of a relative of mine," Laura said, then looked at Al. "What are you doing here?"

"I stopped by...to tell you I've decided not to file a lawsuit contesting the will," he blurted. "If you've hired all this security to protect you from me, you're just wasting your money now. Call them off."

"Okay, you've delivered your message, Baca," Burke said. "Now I suggest you leave."

"Maybe we should talk some more," Miller said, grasping Al's arm again. "Sir, I'm afraid we'll need to interview you downtown."

"Why? I haven't broken any laws."

"If that's true, you don't have anything to worry about. We just need to clear up a few things."

As Miller led him away, Wylie, who'd come up beside Laura, spoke. "We'll have some deputies take him to the station. Then we'll arrange to hold him for twenty-four hours, just to make sure he doesn't blab what he saw here tonight."

"Do you think Enesco will make his move before then?"

"Oh, yeah. There's little doubt in my mind about that, especially after you suggested you might go to the college for a translation. Nice touch. Enesco has been making some bold moves lately, and I expect that to continue. He must be working on a tight deadline from his superiors. So let's cover our bases. Right now, Ms. Santos, I need you to go out the back and head to Silentman's house. We'll stay here and close in on them when they make their move.''

Burke led her quickly out of the house. She unlocked her back gate and entered his backyard through a similar gate.

Wolf, ready for action, stayed a few steps ahead most of the way, his ears pricked up and alert.

Once they got inside, Burke breathed a little easier. ''Stay away from the windows and doors,'' he told her, checking once more to make sure the curtains were closed.

''Neither one of us will get any sleep tonight,'' she observed, feeling the tension of the operation setting in.

''I'll have to stay on guard, but there's no reason you can't try to take a nap.''

''How will you stay alert if you can't get any sleep tonight?''

''I'll catch an hour here and there while the others are keeping watch outside.''

Weapon in hand, Burke stayed near the window that faced her home.

Sensing that he didn't want any distractions, she took a book from his bookcase, then went to the room she'd used before. She tried to sit down, but then got up and began to pace.

The tension in the air was as palpable as the cold desert wind blowing outside. Wolf had followed her, but even the dog couldn't relax. He'd lie down, then get up and wander around the room before doing so again.

Trying to force herself to relax, Laura stretched out on the bed with Burke's book, a thriller, but she couldn't keep her mind on anything except what was happening outside.

Hours passed slowly. She turned off the lights, but sleep wouldn't come. At long last she heard Burke come down the hall, on a break, and head to his room. She knew he needed a chance to be alone and relax, so wouldn't let herself go talk to him.

Thirty minutes later, unable to stand the total silence in the house anymore and too nervous to stay still, she went to find him. If he was sleeping, she wouldn't bother him, but if not, maybe he could use some company, too.

The door to his room was open, so she went right in. Burke stood by his bed naked, a damp towel on the floor.

"I thought you were asleep," he said, looking up. "Did the pipes make too much noise when I took a shower? I needed something to help me stay alert."

Even naked, he was supremely confident. His body was lean and strong—a play of textures ranging from rough to smooth. He grew aroused as she looked at him, but this time he didn't ask her to turn around, as he had a lifetime ago when she'd first caught him coming from the shower. She didn't offer to, either.

"We've come a long way, you and I," he said softly.

She nodded, her mouth too dry to speak. The urge to step into his arms was nearly overpowering.

"You shouldn't stay here," he murmured, his deep voice reverberating with unspoken needs. "I can't touch you—not tonight—no matter how much I want to. It's more important that I get back on duty and do my best to protect you."

"One kiss," she said breathlessly. Their time together was running out, and she desperately wanted one more memory.

Laura stepped into his arms, feeling his hard body against her, and reached up to kiss him.

She'd meant it to be gentle, but the fire inside both of them was too hot. His mouth took complete possession of hers, ravishing her, loving her. Then with a groan, he let her go.

"Tonight you need me to protect you, Laura. And that's exactly what I'm going to do. No one will ever harm you while you're under my care. You may choose to walk away from me one day, but when that time comes, the road before you will be free of danger."

She wanted to say something, but could barely breathe.

"Go now. I have to get dressed."

Though she wasn't sure how her legs actually managed to hold her up, she walked out and closed the door.

Alone in her room again, Laura found her body trembling with desire. But what she felt was so much more than that. She loved Burke Silentman more than life itself. And his words, his sense of duty, the depth of his feelings for her, had touched her heart, bypassing her fears and all the barriers she'd placed between them. Burke was a part of her soul. Yet with that knowledge came an almost overpowering sense of vulnerability.

Burke came into her room a short time later, dressed, with his handgun at his belt. "We'll be facing a great deal of danger in the next few hours. I don't know what'll happen and, because of that, I need you to know how much you mean to me." Placing his palm against her cheek, he gazed steadily into her eyes. "I want to give you something no Navajo ever yields to another easily. My secret name—what gives me power and makes me who I am—is *Hashké*. It means fierce warrior. By revealing it to you, I willingly place myself under your power." He leaned over and kissed her gently. "This warrior will protect you—tonight and always."

Before she could gather her thoughts and respond, he walked out.

The importance of what had just happened stunned her. She felt more connected to him now than ever before.

Laura walked out of her room and found him standing

by the mountain lion fetish. He was sprinkling something over it.

Although she hadn't made a sound, he must have felt her presence because he turned around. "I'm feeding corn pollen to the fetish to keep its medicine strong. In turn, it'll strengthen me." He took the fetish from the bowl and placed it inside a leather pouch, then fastened it to his belt. "Now I'll watch and wait until they come."

He walked into the darkened den and took his position beside the window again.

Deeply touched by everything that had happened between them, she gave him the privacy he needed to concentrate on his job, and she went into the kitchen and fixed herself some tea. Hopefully it would help her get through what promised to be an endless night.

IT SEEMED TO LAURA that she'd only just drifted off to sleep when she was suddenly startled awake. At first she wasn't sure if she'd dreamed the explosion, but the glass of water she'd placed on the nightstand was still vibrating.

Fear shot through her, and without thinking, she ran to the window. It was dawn outside, and she could see flames shooting out of the roof of her house.

With a strangled cry, she ran through the living room, past Burke. He tried to grab her, but she rushed outside, into the lightening day, before he could stop her.

"Laura, no! Wait!" Burke yelled, rushing after her.

She glanced back, but didn't stop. "My things! My work! I've got to save what I can!"

She was halfway down the sidewalk to her home when Burke caught up to her and pulled her beneath an evergreen tree. "*Think,* Laura! This must be a diversion. And by leaving the house, you've done precisely what they wanted. You're out in the open, and they know exactly where you are. I've left Wolf back at my place to make sure the house

stays secure, but we have to get back inside right now."
He stopped speaking the second he heard a fire truck coming up the street.

"Wow. They sure got here fast," Laura said, staring at the flames on her roof. They didn't seem so bad as before, but she didn't know if that was good or not.

"Yeah, *way* too fast," Burke said, taking her hand and running with her back to the house. Seeing Agent Miller standing behind a tree in Laura's front yard, Burke yelled, "Don't trust the firemen. They could be ringers."

They rushed to Burke's house and, as Laura dashed inside, Burke remained in the doorway, making sure they hadn't been followed. Laura walked to the center of the kitchen, then stopped. Wolf was lying on his side on the living room floor directly ahead of her. He wasn't moving.

As she turned to warn Burke, she saw him stop in midstride and pull out what appeared to be a dart imbedded in his neck.

"Laura…" Before he could say another word, he collapsed to the floor.

With a strangled cry, Laura went toward him, but before she could reach him, someone grabbed her from behind and held a damp cloth over her mouth and nose.

She fought hard, but her strength ebbed quickly, and soon an all-encompassing blackness descended over her.

SHE WOKE UP TO PAIN, blinding pain. It filled her head and throbbed through her body, making her feel disjointed and disoriented.

"You'll be okay soon," Laura heard a woman's trembling voice say from someplace close by.

Laura tried to open her eyes and then realized that they *were* open. The room was encased in almost total darkness except for a little bit of light leaking under a door. The floor felt cold and hard, like concrete. Slowly her eyes adjusted to the gloom.

"Where are we?" Laura asked, biting back the wave of panic that filled her as she realized that her hands and feet were securely tied.

"I have no idea whatsoever," the woman answered. "But I'm glad I'm not alone here anymore."

Laura struggled against the ropes that bound her, but they didn't give. Feeling a wall behind her, she tried to use that for support as she wriggled to a sitting position.

"It's been a nightmare. I can hear sounds of something scuttling across the floor, but I can't see anything."

"Probably lizards, or maybe it's a cat," Laura answered, trying not to think too creatively right now.

"No, not a cat. But yeah, maybe a lizard. I hope it's just a lizard."

The voice sounded familiar. "Nicole?" Laura asked.

"Yeah?"

Laura swallowed back her fear. Was Nicole a prisoner, like her, or just a plant? She'd have to be careful. "How long have you been here?"

"Since after I spoke to you last night."

"What happened?"

"Michael Enesco happened," Nicole said, then began to cry softly.

This was no game. Every instinct Laura possessed assured her of that now. "Where's Karl?" Fear pried into Laura. If Karl was dead, Burke might soon follow. The last time she'd seen him... Terror slammed into her, but she forced herself to ignore the string of what-ifs that suddenly filled her mind. She couldn't afford to panic now. She had to think clearly.

"Karl's with Michael."

"*With* him? You mean helping him? Why? I thought you said Michael's the one who brought you here."

"Michael's been blackmailing us. At first we went along with what he wanted because we were afraid. But then Karl and I had enough and we refused to cooperate. When Michael realized that he wouldn't be able to control us anymore, he kidnapped me. Karl will do whatever he asks now because he knows as well as I do that Michael will kill me if he doesn't.''

The conviction in Nicole's voice made a shiver run up Laura's spine. ''What's your involvement with Michael, Nicole?''

''You mean am I having an affair with him?''

''No. I know you're not. When you look at him... What I see isn't affection at all.''

''Diplomatically put,'' she answered. ''All I feel for that man is loathing. When he came to us and told us he was from my old country, Karl hired him in good faith. Michael said he needed a little money for his family back home, claiming that they were in desperate need of food. I still have family there, and I know how far American dollars go.''

''So what happened?''

''Not knowing Michael was actually a spy, we didn't watch him very closely when he was working at the senior center. He stole our passwords and got into the bank accounts, stealing money a little at a time. He forged my signature and made it look like I'd been embezzling, and trying to cover for it with phoney expenditures. Then he told us what he'd done. He said he'd see to it that I either went to jail or was deported. He also knew the names of my relatives in West Medias, and said they'd suffer unless Karl and I did exactly what he told us to do. Karl has been forced to help him, even tried to kidnap Elena Baca.''

Laura realized then that Burke and she had been right. Nicole's revelation held no surprises, only confirmation. ''You must have been terrified.''

"Yes, especially about being deported, and bringing harm to my family. I'm not a citizen yet."

"And now we're both here," Laura said, still struggling against the ropes that bound her.

"He won't kill us until he's got the journal. When he brought you in, he bragged, calling us his bargaining chips."

"He'll never get the journal, Nicole," Laura assured her "But now we've got to do something to help ourselves. Brace yourself. I'm going to start screaming."

"Don't waste your breath. When Michael dumped me here, he told me I could scream all I wanted. From that, I figured we're in the middle of nowhere. But I still gave it a shot. I yelled until I was hoarse, but no one came."

"When he brought you here, and me, did you see anything that might tell us where we are?"

"No. He drove me here in the trunk of his car, tied up and blindfolded. I worked the blindfold off once he left, but, as you can imagine, it wasn't much of an improvement. And when he threw you in, all I got was a glimpse of some trees before he shut the door again."

"Well, let me give screaming another try. Feel free to join me."

They made a formidable noise for the next several minutes, but as Nicole had warned, no one came. Winded, with her throat starting to hurt, Laura finally fell silent. They needed another plan.

"I'm going to see if I can find something sharp around me so I can cut through these ropes."

As she searched, Laura thoughts drifted back to Burke and silent tears began spilling down her cheeks. If fate had chosen to steal him from her, she'd never forgive herself for not taking advantage of the time they'd been given together. Fear had held her back when she should have let love guide her. If life gave her a second chance, she'd never make the same mistake again.

Holding to that, Laura forced herself to concentrate only on the job before her.

Chapter Nineteen

Burke woke up slowly. A paramedic with a stethoscope was checking his heart. "Damn, I feel as if I've been clobbered by a mule," he muttered, sitting up. "What happened? How did they get past our stakeout team?"

"They posed as utility men who read the gas and electric meters. Agent Wylie spotted the pair and went to warn them off, but they got him before he could draw his weapon. Then they came here and hit the dog, then you, with tranquilizer darts," Miller said.

"Wolf?" As Burke tried to stand up, a wave of nausea engulfed him. He swallowed back the bad taste in his mouth and held on to the counter for a moment. His head felt as if it was about to explode.

"We'll all be okay," Wylie said. "But the dose each of us took was hefty. My guess is that they stole the drugs and dart guns from a vet. The police said that one of the local clinics reported a break-in two nights ago."

Burke focused on John Wylie's face, trying to get his vision to clear up. The man had some scratches on his forehead, probably from the fall when he passed out, and looked sympathetic.

As he glanced around, Burke also saw several officers in sheriff and police department uniforms, and some plain-clothes detectives. "Since you're all here, I assume you caught them, and Laura's safe?"

Wylie and Miller exchanged glances.

"She *is* safe, right?" Burke demanded.

"I don't think they'll harm her. My feeling is that they took her for leverage to use against you," Wylie answered.

Burke forced himself to stand up. "How the hell did that happen? You guys were supposed to be keeping her house and this one under surveillance."

"We were, but all hell broke loose. The roof was burning, you and Laura ran outside and the fire department arrived," Miller said.

"Nobody knew I'd been taken out already," Wylie added, "or that you and the dog had been neutralized when you went back inside. Only three or four minutes went by before our people came to check, but by then, the utility truck and Laura were gone."

"Then the firemen were real?"

"Yeah, but trying to verify that only added to the confusion."

"And the fire? How did it happen?" Burke asked.

"Enesco or the other guy lobbed a crude fire bomb onto Laura's roof from the utility access easement behind the house," Miller said. "We were expecting an intruder, and had a man out back, but they were a step ahead. The utility truck was real—stolen obviously—and nothing about it was out of the ordinary," Miller said.

"But the diversion, as well planned as it was, wouldn't have worked if you and Laura had stayed put," Wylie added in a hard voice. "What the heck happened?"

Burke cursed. "The explosion woke her up, and as I was looking through the window, checking things out, she ran past me. I couldn't stop her in time."

"And when they saw you both running out of here, they

slipped into your house, took out the dog and waited for you to return," Miller concluded.

"I'm getting her back," Burke said, checking his weapon, then placing it back in its holster.

"You're not going anywhere half-cocked. Sit tight. We don't even know where to start searching at this point," Wylie said.

"I do. The senior center. The people who run that place are at the heart of everything that's happened." He was about to say more when his cell phone rang. Burke took it from his pocket, flipping it open with one hand.

"You know who this is, right?" The man's voice came through clearly.

The accent was gone, but the voice belonged to Enesco. Burke knew it in his gut. "Yeah, Enesco, or whatever your name really is. Lost the accent, have you?"

The man's laugh was cold. "Time for a trade. You get your woman, and I get the journal. But if you don't come alone, I'll mail her back to you in pieces. Remember that image, if you think you'll be able to slip something past me. You and I have been around the block too many times to underestimate each other now."

"Where do we meet?" Burke asked, his voice glacial and deadly.

"About a quarter mile upstream on the Animas River where it meets the San Juan. Go to the north shore, where there's a small backwater stream running parallel to the main body of water."

"When?"

"Thirty minutes. Come alone," he said, then hung up.

Wylie shook his head after Burke filled him in on everything except the exact location. "You're not going anywhere by yourself with that journal. It's a setup. You know that as well as I do. And the second you hand over the journal, you and Miss Santos are dead."

"We don't have a lot of choices here. Enesco's a trained agent. If you guys tail me, he'll know. The most you can do is wire me, and even that's tricky."

"And you're prepared to give him the journal?" Wylie asked.

"No, I can't do that. It's not mine to give," Burke said. "But the agency can give me something I can pass off."

"In time?"

"Yeah. In about two minutes I can get some pages of the original text faxed here. Then I can bind them in a small three-ring leather notebook I have in my office," he said, remembering that the professor had scanned the journal into his computer. "It won't be the complete journal, but enough to fake them out."

Wylie nodded, taking him at his word. "You alert whoever you need to while we work on this."

Burke walked into the living room and flipped open his cell phone. "Wind, I need you to bring me a car and leave it around the corner from my house. But be careful. The area is crawling with feds and it's imperative you don't get caught."

"Consider it done. What's the plan?"

"I've got to give the FBI the slip, which may be difficult. But I've got an idea," he said, and filled him in quickly. "Just have Handler call the professor, and get that car over here."

"On my way. Give me ten minutes."

Burke remained on the phone, keeping his voice low, stalling for time, while Wind used another line to call Handler, then came back to finish his conversation with Burke. Finally, when Wind announced he was in position, Burke hung up.

Hearing the fax machine running in the den, Burke retrieved the pages, then shrank them, using his copier.

Lastly, he placed them in the small leather-bound notebook. He was ready.

Slipping it into his jacket pocket, Burke walked over to the doorway leading to the kitchen. Several officers, including Miller and Wylie, were standing around the table, discussing strategy.

"He's getting antsy," Burke said, gesturing to the dog pacing in the living room. "I'm going to take him outside and work him for a minute or two. He's a powerful dog, and when he gets wound up like this, he's a little on the unstable side. You don't know if he's just going to raise his leg, or take a chunk out of somebody's thigh."

Wylie gave the dog a worried glance. "Then get going, but don't go far."

Burke opened the door, then gave Wolf an almost imperceptible hand signal. The dog rushed out the front door, heading straight down the street. Burke cursed.

"I've got to go after him," he yelled back at Wylie. "There must be a female dog in season around here."

"You need help?"

"Nah. The way he's acting he's likely to bite someone, but he'll respond to a command if I get close enough." He gestured to the table. "Throw me that leash."

Wylie did as he asked, then halfheartedly added, "Let me know if you need help. You've only got thirty minutes, remember."

Burke headed out the door. It had been easier than he'd expected. Wolf had done exactly as he'd been taught: he'd gone about fifty yards in a straight line, then stopped.

Burke ran toward him, leaving the house and the agents behind. As he reached the corner, he saw a young Navajo cowboy in boots and faded jeans, with blue tinted sunglasses and a brown Stetson. The cowboy was leaning against a four-door, mid-size sedan parked beside the curb.

He resembled no one Burke had ever seen, but the car was one of the models the agency favored.

"Code name?"

"Wind. This is your car." He nodded. "The keys are in the ignition. Now I'm outta here on foot—unless you want backup."

"I do, but not in the way you expect." Burke put the dog in the back seat, quickly briefing Wind on his plan. "Tell Handler what I've told you," he said. "Now I need you to head back to the house and stall the FBI. Tell them that I'm trying to get the dog out of your yard—whatever. Just buy me some time."

"I won't be able to keep them for long once they catch on," he warned.

"Wrangle five minutes for me. After that you can square it with them."

"Yeah—FBI agents are bound to be real reasonable." He smiled, then held up a hand. "Don't worry, I'll handle it. Do they know exactly where you're going?"

Burke shook his head, then gave Wind the specific location. "You can bring them. But take the long way."

"Okay. Knowing where you are will give me an edge. They'll need me," Wind said.

Burke slipped behind the wheel. "I better get going."

"If I recall, the area where you're headed has a lot of underbrush and young trees. That little backwater is pretty shallow, but there are lots of branches and logs beneath the surface. Are you sure you want to go in there alone? You're not going to have a clear line of fire except across the water."

"Neither will they," he answered. Then, putting the car into gear, he drove off.

Burke didn't envy Wind's next task. The FBI wouldn't take kindly to the ruse. But with luck, he'd have a good head start. He knew Wind would hold them off as long as he could.

While driving, Burke tried to come up with a plan of action. The place where Enesco had told him to go wasn't far southwest of where he was now—fifteen minutes at most, providing he could find the right road. But convincing him he had the complete journal might be tricky. Burke reached into his jacket pocket, feeling the small, leather-bound notebook. One way or another, he'd have to pull it off. It was his only shot.

LAURA LOOKED AROUND, now that her eyes had adjusted, trying to make out shapes and objects in the dark room where she and Nicole were being held prisoner. As near as she could tell, it was a small workshop or garage constructed of unpainted cinder blocks, with an aluminum roof. There was an inexpensive fluorescent light fixture hanging from a wooden rafter, but it didn't appear to have any bulbs, and there was a wide wooden workbench that ran all along the opposite wall.

There weren't any windows, and the door was metal with a metal frame, so breaking out was unlikely. She scooted across the bare concrete floor, searching for a nail, a tool or a jagged spot on one of the wooden pallets stacked against one wall. What she needed was a way to slice through the ropes that bound her hands. Once she was free, she'd try to pick the lock or loosen a hinge on the door.

As she reached the pallets she felt a sliver of glass that had somehow became wedged against one of the wooden crosspieces. "I've got a piece of glass that probably came from a broken light tube, maybe stuck here when the rest of the glass was swept up. It isn't much, but if I'm careful I think I can use it to cut through the rope, one strand at a time."

"Can I help? Maybe I can roll toward you."

"No. You wouldn't be able to tell if you're cutting me or the rope. Besides, there's no telling what else is on this floor. You could end up rolling into a black widow spider's web. Stay put for now," Laura said.

As she tried to cut through the thick ropes, the glass sliver dug into her flesh, cutting her as well. She tried to ignore the pain, but it was difficult. To make matters worse, the blood trickling down her fingers was making her grip slippery.

Determined to get free, she continued sliding the edge of the glass against the rope fibers with her thumb and forefinger. "I'm almost there," she said, after what had seemed forever.

"If we both get free, then what? Even if we can somehow get the door open, we don't know where to go."

"We'll figure it all out one step at a time, Laura murmured. "First, we have to get free." The individual strands of rope felt looser now and, as she tugged against them, the final threads broke and the rope fell away from her wrists. "Got it!" She untied the rope at her feet, then stood and moved toward the gray shape she knew was Nicole. After so long in the low light, it was easier to see now. "Come on. We need to try and get out before Enesco returns."

She was struggling clumsily to undo the knots holding Nicole's hands when the door was suddenly thrown open and bright daylight came streaming into the small workshop.

Squinting, she looked at the dark silhouette in the doorway, but before she could jump up and run, the man grabbed her by the arm and threw her against the far wall. She landed hard, hitting her side against the workbench and her knee on the floor.

"Just where did you think you were going? I'm not through with you yet," Enesco snarled.

He shoved her against the stack of pallets, and she slammed her head painfully against the rough lumber before staggering to her feet.

"Down on your knees, with your hands behind your back. Don't make me have to knock you to the floor," he snarled.

"Where's Karl? What have you done with him?" Nicole yelled out from behind Laura.

"He got uncooperative just when I needed him the most. But if *you* cooperate, you may get the chance to see him again alive," Enesco snorted.

"Michael, please don't leave me here alone again," Nicole begged.

Enesco ignored her as he pushed Laura to her knees, retied her hands behind her back, then slipped a noose around her ankles, tightening it with a yank.

"I can't walk with a rope around my feet," Laura protested.

"You'll get by," he said, then grabbed the rope holding her hands behind her back and pushed her toward the door. She had to shuffle her feet quickly to keep from falling, but managed to get outside without tipping over, pushed along by Michael's hold on the rope at her wrists.

In those precious fifteen or twenty seconds it took to reach the car, she looked around, trying to memorize everything. She was somewhere in the valley, and the distinctive bluffs on the north side of the river were visible above an old orchard to her left. She got the impression of an old white farmhouse behind her, with faded green trim. The open ground to her right was uneven, as if plowed in rows, and yellow stalks of last year's corn crop told her the workshop was beside an old field. A fence stood beyond the car, and past that was a grove of cottonwood trees and what looked like the transmission tower of a cell phone network. She could see the number 131 on the antenna.

Laura promised herself that she'd remember every detail. Sooner or later, she'd get away, and once she did, she'd be the only chance Nicole had to be rescued.

"We're going to meet your boyfriend," Enesco said. "And after that, if things go as planned, I'll let you go."

"The assurances of a liar don't mean much," she said.

Enesco laughed. "Hope is the only thing you've got, lady, so you better hold on to it."

"You're wrong. I have something else—something you want—the journal."

"Not for long. You and I are about to pick it up from your boyfriend."

He brought out a dark pillowcase, and Laura saw that he was going to cover her head.

She knew in her heart that Burke would never meet a kidnapper's demands. He'd also know, as she did, that Enesco wouldn't let either of them live long after he had the journal. They had only one option now—to fight. With luck, they'd do that better than Enesco ever dreamed they could.

BURKE DROVE INTO the *bosque,* a Southwestern term for the cottonwood forest, along the floodplain of the Animas River. He parked the car, then, after taping a long throwing knife to the small of his back, proceeded with Wolf into an area filled with brush, salt cedar and cottonwoods.

With Wolf at heel, Burke picked his way along the north bank of the river until the small backwater appeared.

Entering a thicket of slender willows in a crouch, he gave Wolf the "out" command, sending him farther into the undergrowth on his right. The dog would parallel his own movements.

Burke continued on slowly, until a voice came from across the stream on the small peninsula between that narrow channel and the much wider river beyond.

"Stop. You've come far enough. Now walk out to the center of the channel, holding the journal over your head above the water. Watch where you're stepping so you don't trip on something, fall and ruin it. Once you get close enough, throw the journal over to our side."

"First I want to see Laura and make sure you haven't harmed her."

Only a minute went by, but it was the longest minute of his life. Finally two forms appeared in the thick brush on the far side of the little channel. He saw Laura first. She had her hands behind her back, and was being pushed forward roughly by Michael, who had a pistol in his hand. He alternately aimed the muzzle at Laura, then back at Burke.

"Are you okay?" Burke asked, stepping toward the water.

She nodded. "Yes. But Enesco still has something coming to him."

"You're right about that." Burke smiled grimly, stepping into the icy water slowly. He'd caught Laura's message. There was just Enesco with her. Wolf and he could handle it.

Out of the corner of his eye, he could see Wolf's muzzle in the water halfway around the bend, upstream. The dog was crossing over to outflank Laura's captor, just as he'd hoped.

"The journal. Show it to me now!" Michael yelled, aiming the gun at Laura's head.

Burke reached into his pocket, pulled out his notebook with his left hand, then waved it in the air. "Here it is. Satisfied?"

"Don't let it fall in the water, you idiot—not if you value her life," Michael cried.

Burke felt his way across the slow channel, the cold water coming up to his knees, but apparently no deeper as he neared the center of the twenty-foot-wide stream.

"Stop right there and throw the journal to me," Enesco finally ordered.

Burke was about eight feet from dry ground and close enough to see that Laura's hands were tied. If she fell into deep water, she couldn't swim.

"Here it comes." Burke brought his left hand back slowly, noting the low, black shape moving toward the man from behind. He tried to give Wolf a few more seconds to get in place before throwing the notebook.

"Throw it, you idiot!" Michael ordered. He cursed in a language Burke didn't recognize, but the meaning was clear from the inflection.

Burke did more than that. He almost put it into orbit. As the notebook sailed over the man's head, Enesco made the mistake of jumping for it.

At that precise moment, Laura pushed away from him. With a clear target, Wolf rushed out of the brush and attacked. Enesco, taken completely by surprise, fell backward, then rolled, fighting to free himself from the dog's jaws. For a second he managed to break free, getting to his knees and swinging his pistol toward the dog.

Burke reached for the knife taped to his back, and threw it with all the skill he'd learned in the Special Forces. The blade caught Enesco in the center of his chest. The kidnapper dropped the handgun, then slipped down onto his side, writhing in pain.

As Burke hurried out of the water, Laura jumped into his arms. He held her protectively, tears stinging his eyes. "I've been through hell worrying about you," he murmured.

"I kept hoping you'd be okay," she said.

Burke shifted his gaze to Wolf and the man on the ground before him. Wolf's jaws were open, and he was ready to pounce.

"Keep him off me," Michael whispered.

"I will, but take my advice. Don't move. He's hoping you'll give him a chance to tear your arm off."

Burke gave the dog the command to guard. Wolf remained in front of the man, growling, saliva dripping from his mouth.

Burke brought a pocketknife out of his jacket and freed Laura's hands. "Here," he said, handing her his cell phone. "Call 911, and have dispatch relay to the FBI team that we're going to need paramedics. If Michael dies, or refuses to talk, we may never find the Maurers. I've got a feeling Enesco has them stashed somewhere as insurance."

"I was held with Nicole," Laura said. "He took us both to the same place. He covered my face before we left, but I think I can take the police to where she is."

Leaving Wolf to guard Laura, Burke attended to Enesco, who was barely conscious now and losing blood rapidly. "I can't remove the knife or you'll bleed to death in minutes," he said. "But help will be here shortly, probably in five minutes or so."

When Laura handed him back the phone, Burke noticed the blood on her fingers. "What the hell did he do to you?"

"I did it to myself," she said, and explained how she'd cut the ropes earlier.

Before he could say anything, Burke heard the sound of men's voices from the other side of the narrow channel. As he turned his head, he saw Wind at point, leading the FBI team to them, along with Karl Maurer, who was handcuffed. "About time you all got here," Burke said. "What about the paramedics? Are they on their way?"

"They're here now, unloading their gear. Knowing you, I made the call ahead of time," Wind replied.

The federal agents reluctantly waded the icy channel in their street shoes, and once across, Agent Wylie signaled the paramedics to join them. Wind had already disappeared, which didn't surprise Burke at all.

"Where's my wife? Enesco kidnapped her, and when I wouldn't help him anymore, he locked me in the trunk of his car." Maurer moved toward Enesco angrily, but Agent Miller grabbed his shoulder.

Hearing Wolf's throaty warning growl, Burke turned his head quickly. Karl certainly wasn't going to get close to Laura. "Wolf, come!" Burke ordered.

The dog looked at Maurer, teeth still bared, then reluctantly went to Burke's side.

"If I were you, Karl, I wouldn't give Agent Miller a hard time," Burke said. "Wolf is just looking for an excuse to attack. He really seems to want a piece of you."

"I'll cooperate. I'll tell you whatever I can, and testify against Enesco. Just find my wife," Maurer said.

"We will," Laura assured him.

Talking to Burke and Wylie, Laura described the workshop where they'd been kept and details of the grounds surrounding it.

"You're sure about the number on that antenna?" Wylie asked.

"Positive."

"I'll use that to zero in on the location then." Wylie made a call, then supervised as two deputies took Maurer away. Enesco was lifted onto a stretcher and carried across the channel, accompanied by Miller. An ambulance waited a short distance away, on one of the levees.

"Coming here alone was a damn fool thing to do," Wylie said to Burke, shaking his head. Then he reluctantly stepped into the water again, heading after the others.

Alone with Burke, Laura wrapped her arms around him and rested her head against his chest. "You risked everything for me today," she said, tears streaming down her cheeks.

He buried his face in her hair. "Laura, don't you understand? You *are* my life." He took her mouth roughly in a kiss. He'd fallen hard for her. And if she never understood anything else he ever said or felt, he wanted her to understand that.

When he finally eased back, he saw the dazed look on her face and smiled.

"Guys, let's go," Wylie called out to them from across the channel, where he'd been speaking to a county sheriff's deputy. "I've got a possible address on the place where Mrs. Maurer is being held, and I need Laura to help us out."

Epilogue

After Nicole was freed, frightened but unhurt, she was taken into custody. Burke and Laura went to the station and made their statements.

"We're all set here," Wylie said at last. "You'll have to make some court appearances, but this case is now closed."

The words filled Laura with relief and sadness. At the very least, Burke would be moving out now. Once other cases took up his time, she wasn't sure what would happen to them. The thought that they would drift slowly apart made her chest tighten.

They said goodbye to the agents and officers, then headed to her home. The day she'd dreaded was finally upon her.

"Handler said that the journal has been picked up by a representative of Freedom International, and copies are being distributed to various governments as well as the world press. They expect Rogov to be released soon," Burke told her.

"I'm glad. My godmother would have been proud."

"And I've heard from an officer at the station that the criminals that have been preying on the seniors have been arrested. They followed a elderly man home, but he saw the tail and called the police on his cell phone. They were caught in the act,'' Burke added.

Laura smiled. ''Looks like some serious justice is taking place today.''

They arrived at her house a short time later. As they went inside, Laura looked around, checking out the fire damage. Except for the odor of smoke, there really wasn't any visible sign of it.

''Fire retardant shingles really saved the day, I guess,'' she said.

''And the fact that it served Enesco's purpose to call the fire department before throwing the fire bomb,'' Burke added.

''I'll have a roofer out here tomorrow for an estimate, but it shouldn't take them long to get things squared away. When you come to visit next time, you can see how it went.''

Suspecting he had a ton of reports to file and a million things to do now that the case was at an end, but unwilling to say goodbye to him just yet, Laura began talking fast—too fast to even think of what she was saying. Horrified, she realized she was babbling, but she couldn't stop. ''I'll miss having Wolf around. Maybe I'll get a dog,'' she said, and continued on that thread without scarcely a breath.

Hearing his name, Wolf sat up. Cocking his head to one side, he looked at her as if she'd suddenly gone crazy.

''The furball *does* get under your skin,'' Burke said, managing, at last, to get a word in edgewise.

''It's too bad he's got a full-time job. I'd take him myself,'' Laura said. ''Maybe I'll write about what happened. What do you think?'' She didn't wait for an answer. ''You could help me brainstorm.''

''Laura—''

Oh, God, he was trying to say something, but she couldn't shut up.

Suddenly Wolf barked once, then shot down the hall.

"What in the heck..." Burke followed, Laura right behind him.

They found the dog sprawled across Laura's bed as if he didn't have a care in the world.

"Hey, get off there!" Burke ordered.

Wolf yawned, but stayed where he was.

"Wolf, off!" Burke said, his voice sharper this time.

Wolf gave him a panting grin, then shifted to his side and laid his head on Laura's pillow.

"Furball, you're trying my patience." Burke went to get the dog but Wolf wriggled away and stayed where he was.

"Don't be so rough with him," Laura said, coming to help. "Come on, Wolf. Be a good boy." She tried tugging gently on his collar, but the dog remained on his side, sliding his muzzle under a pillow to hide his eyes.

Muttering an oath, Burke sat on the bed and tried to slip his arms beneath the dog, preparing to lift him off.

"Wait, let me help," Laura said as Wolf twisted away. "Don't let him fall off and hurt himself."

She leaned over, reaching for the dog's upper half, but suddenly Wolf bounded to his feet and wiggled free like a greased pig.

Laura, knocked off balance, fell sideways, crashing into the nightstand. But before she could topple backward, Burke reached out and pulled her toward him onto the bed.

Not giving her a chance to gather her wits, he wrapped his arms around her tightly and lay back, dragging her on top of him.

"Laura," he murmured. Their eyes met and suddenly nothing else seemed important. In one fluid motion, he rolled over, pinning her beneath him, and pressed his mouth to hers. His kiss deepened until it became a mating of two desperate souls.

"We have to talk," Burke said, releasing her mouth for a moment.

"I've been talking," she said, reaching up to kiss him again.

"Incessantly. Now you have to *listen*. I love you, Laura. Tell me what it'll take to keep us together."

"Come home to me every night and love me. If I have that, I can live with the rest."

"But I thought—"

"You think too much. And why do men always want to *talk* so much?" she teased, reminding him of something he'd said to her once. "Women like action. Show me what you've got."

"Sweetheart, you don't have to ask me twice." He kissed her deeply, drinking in her passionate sighs.

"Hashké!"

"...is yours forever."

PHOENIX
BROTHERHOOD

Men who fight for justice in the shadows...
and discover love amidst the ashes.

HARLEQUIN®
INTRIGUE®
presents

RAFE SINCLAIR'S REVENGE
November 2002

the newest addition to the thrilling Men of Mystery series by bestselling author

GAYLE WILSON

Former CIA operative Rafe Sinclair had no intention of ever going back to the agency...until a madman goes after his former partner-and-lover, Elizabeth Richards, and Rafe find himself on a life-and-death mission to protect Elizabeth...whatever the cost!

Available at your favorite retail outlet.

HARLEQUIN®
Makes any time special®

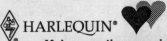

If you enjoyed what you just read,
then we've got an offer you can't resist!

Take 2 bestselling
love stories FREE!

Plus get a FREE surprise gift!

Clip this page and mail it to Harlequin Reader Service®

IN U.S.A.
3010 Walden Ave.
P.O. Box 1867
Buffalo, N.Y. 14240-1867

IN CANADA
P.O. Box 609
Fort Erie, Ontario
L2A 5X3

YES! Please send me 2 free Harlequin Intrigue® novels and my free surprise gift. After receiving them, if I don't wish to receive anymore, I can return the shipping statement marked cancel. If I don't cancel, I will receive 4 brand-new novels each month, before they're available in stores! In the U.S.A., bill me at the bargain price of $3.99 plus 25¢ shipping and handling per book and applicable sales tax, if any*. In Canada, bill me at the bargain price of $4.74 plus 25¢ shipping and handling per book and applicable taxes**. That's the complete price and a savings of at least 10% off the cover prices—what a great deal! I understand that accepting the 2 free books and gift places me under no obligation ever to buy any books. I can always return a shipment and cancel at any time. Even if I never buy another book from Harlequin, the 2 free books and gift are mine to keep forever.

181 HDN DNUA
381 HDN DNUC

Name	(PLEASE PRINT)	
Address	Apt.#	
City	State/Prov.	Zip/Postal Code

* Terms and prices subject to change without notice. Sales tax applicable in N.Y.
** Canadian residents will be charged applicable provincial taxes and GST.
   All orders subject to approval. Offer limited to one per household and not valid to current Harlequin Intrigue® subscribers.
   ® are registered trademarks of Harlequin Enterprises Limited.

INT02

Princes...Princesses...
London Castles...New York Mansions...
To live the life of a royal!

In 2002, Harlequin Books lets you escape to a
world of royalty with these royally themed titles:

Temptation:
January 2002—*A Prince of a Guy* (#861)
February 2002—*A Noble Pursuit* (#865)

American Romance:
The Carradignes: American Royalty (Editorially linked series)
March 2002—*The Improperly Pregnant Princess* (#913)
April 2002—*The Unlawfully Wedded Princess* (#917)
May 2002—*The Simply Scandalous Princess* (#921)
November 2002—*The Inconveniently Engaged Prince* (#945)

Intrigue:
The Carradignes: A Royal Mystery (Editorially linked series)
June 2002—*The Duke's Covert Mission* (#666)

Chicago Confidential
September 2002—*Prince Under Cover* (#678)

The Crown Affair
October 2002—*Royal Target* (#682)
November 2002—*Royal Ransom* (#686)
December 2002—*Royal Pursuit* (#690)

Harlequin Romance:
June 2002—*His Majesty's Marriage* (#3703)
July 2002—*The Prince's Proposal* (#3709)

Harlequin Presents:
August 2002—*Society Weddings* (#2268)
September 2002—*The Prince's Pleasure* (#2274)

Duets:
September 2002—*Once Upon a Tiara/Henry Ever After* (#83)
October 2002—*Natalia's Story/Andrea's Story* (#85)

Celebrate a year of royalty with Harlequin Books!

Available at your favorite retail outlet.

HARLEQUIN®
Makes any time special®

Visit us at www.eHarlequin.com

HSROY02

$ Saving Money $ Has Never Been This Easy!

Just fill out and send in this form from any October, November and December 2002 books and we will send you a coupon booklet worth a total savings of $20.00 off future purchases of Harlequin and Silhouette books in 2003.

Yes! It's that easy!

I accept your incredible offer!
Please send me a coupon booklet:

Name (PLEASE PRINT)

Address   Apt. #

City   State/Prov.   Zip/Postal Code

In a typical month, how many
Harlequin and Silhouette novels do you read?

❏ 0-2   ❏ 3+

097KJKDNC7   097KJKDNDP

Please send this form to:
  In the U.S.: Harlequin Books, P.O. Box 9071, Buffalo, NY 14269-9071
  In Canada: Harlequin Books, P.O. Box 609, Fort Erie, Ontario L2A 5X3

Allow 4-6 weeks for delivery. Limit one coupon booklet per household. Must be postmarked no later than January 15, 2003.

PHQ402

The holidays have descended on

COOPER'S CORNER

providing a touch of seasonal magic!

Coming in November 2002...
MY CHRISTMAS COWBOY
by Kate Hoffmann

Check-in: Bah humbug! That's what single mom
Grace Penrose felt about Christmas this year. All her plans
for the Cooper's Corner Christmas Festival are going wrong—
and now she finds out she has an unexpected houseguest!

Checkout: But sexy cowboy Tucker McCabe is no ordinary
houseguest, and Grace feels her spirits start to lift. Suddenly
she has the craziest urge to stand under the mistletoe...forever!

HARLEQUIN®
Makes any time special ®

Visit us at www.cooperscorner.com

CC-CNM4

HARLEQUIN®
INTRIGUE®

A royal family in peril...
A kingdom in jeopardy...
And only love can save them!

THE CROWN
AFFAIR

Continues in November 2002 with

ROYAL RANSOM
BY SUSAN KEARNEY

In the second exciting installment in
THE CROWN AFFAIR trilogy, Princess Tashya's baby
brothers have been kidnapped. With no time to lose,
Her Royal Highness sets out to save the young princes,
whether her family—or the dangerously seductive
CIA agent hired to protect her—liked it or not!

Coming in December 2002:
ROYAL PURSUIT

Look for these exciting new stories
wherever Harlequin books are sold!

HARLEQUIN®
Makes any time special ®